Please return on or before the latest date above.
You can renew online at *www.kent.gov.uk/libs*
or by telephone 08458 247 200

LOVING AND LOSING

LOVING AND LOSING

Pamela Oldfield

Severn House Large Print
London & New York

This first large print edition published 2009
in Great Britain and the USA by
SEVERN HOUSE PUBLISHERS LTD of
9-15 High Street, Sutton, Surrey, SM1 1DF.
First world regular print edition published 2007 by
Severn House Publishers Ltd., London and New York.

British Library Cataloguing in Publication Data

Oldfield, Pamela
  Loving and losing. - Large print ed.
  1. Influenza Epidemic, 1918-1919 - Fiction 2. Large type
  books
  I. Title
  823.9'14[F]

  ISBN-13: 978-0-7278-7760-4

Printed and bound in Great Britain by
MPG Books Ltd, Bodmin, Cornwall

One

Eve Randall walked slowly through the old London churchyard, one hand clutching her long skirt in an attempt to avoid muddying the hem, the other clasping a small spray of late roses. Years of soot from the surrounding chimneys had darkened the stonework of the church and the gravestones, but the grass and ancient trees made the place an oasis of peace, somehow remote from the roar of the traffic which encircled it. Autumn had set in with a vengeance and a rough wind blew dead leaves across the gravestones and the sun appeared only rarely between gathering clouds.

Eve was tall and slim and moved with a natural grace. Today, however, her head was bent, a frown darkened her face and she noticed little of what was happening around her. That morning a letter had come from her husband in America, which had given her cause for concern and she was silently planning her reply.

'Morning, Mrs Randall!'

Eve glanced up at the familiar voice and immediately smiled, pushing her anxious thoughts to one side. 'Ellen! I haven't seen you for a long time. How are you?'

Ellen Beatty, small and round with straggly fair hair, grinned. 'You'll never guess.' Much younger than Eve, Ellen was the wife of Jon Beatty who worked for the Randalls as a gardener and handyman.

Eve maintained her smile with difficulty as she suddenly realized what was coming.

'Not another baby!' she exclaimed and then added hastily, 'How wonderful!'

Life was so unfair, she agonized silently. This woman produced children like rabbits from a hat yet Eve, married for six years, had no children. Separated from him by family circumstances and four years of war, Eve was stranded in England while her scientist husband worked in America. A baby was impossible and the years were passing her by. She was twenty-eight and becoming anxious.

Ellen grinned. 'I been away so you wouldn't have seen me. Born three weeks ago. Little boy! Sunny little duck, he is. We been to stay with me old auntie down in Todleigh, near Exeter. She's the only family we've got now. I have all me babies down there with her.'

'Doesn't your husband mind being on his own?'

'Lord no! See, Jon can't bear the palaver of me producing little ones. I take them all with me and they love it. It's like a holiday. Mind you, it almost wore her out, poor old soul, but she's always pleased to see us, having no children of her own on account of never marrying. Jon's that pleased. Like a cat with two tails, he is! Always wanted a boy and it was girls, girls, girls. Jon reckoned I done it on purpose to annoy him!' She giggled again.

Eve nodded, recalling the names of the Beatty children. Kate, Amy, Lucy – and now a boy.

'We named him Sam, after Jon's brother that died young. Samuel, that was. Died of the typhoid at eighteen.' She glanced at the roses. 'They for your pa's grave?'

Eve nodded. 'They were his favourites. Today's his birthday – or would have been.'

'How's your ma?'

'Fine. Still knitting for the troops! It gives her something to do and she feels she's help-ing the war effort.'

Ellen sighed. 'They say it might be over by Christmas, fingers crossed – but they said that four years ago!'

'If it is she'll go back to doing the jigsaw

puzzles and crosswords. She spends a lot of time in bed but I try to persuade her to get up when she feels up to it. The doctor says she'll get bedsores if she stays there all day and there's not really anything wrong with her. Just weakness – and a desire to be pampered!'

'We could all do with a bit of pampering. How's your hubby doing, all those miles away? I dunno how you can bear it. I like to have Jon within shouting distance.' She laughed.

'He's well, thank you. He plans to join me here as soon as the war ends. Let's hope it's sooner rather than later. I'm hoping we'll—' She stopped abruptly. This young woman would never understand her need to start a family. It was better not to share that particular problem. Eve had a horror of being pitied.

Ellen appeared not to notice her unfinished sentence. 'I'd hate me and Jon to be separated for more than a week or so. If I was you, I'd have stayed over there with your hubby.'

'I dearly wish I had but I came to England to be with my mother. Her bad rheumatism meant she needed my help to get about. She also suffers with her chest.'

'Must be lonely for you without him.'

'We didn't know we'd be apart for so long.

Harvey meant to follow when his contract ended three months later but then they offered him a wonderful new job researching in a very modern laboratory. Then the war came and it was considered dangerous to travel by sea...' She shrugged.

Ignoring her explanation, Ellen went blithely on. 'Mind you, at least you know he's going to come back to you. There's many a lad not coming home at all, thanks to the blooming war! If it wasn't for Jon's crooked foot he'd as like have been killed by now in them horrible trenches – like the Sturmer's lad, Donald, and that odd Matt Brewin and poor old Mr Carter as used to run the Pig and Whistle. He never should have volunteered at his age. Daft, I called it. Jon reckoned he wanted to get away from that nagging wife of his!' She rolled her eyes.

Eve smiled. 'Still, the end is in sight. A few more months, maybe, if our prayers are answered, but as you say, too late for some poor souls.'

'It hits the womenfolk hard,' Ellen said, her face clouding over. 'Ma never got over losing our Billy. Silly devil, he was. Enlisted without telling us, pretending he was eighteen cos he was tall for his age. Lots of young men lied and the army didn't care.'

Eve shook her head. 'You could understand at the beginning when the lads thought it

9

would be an adventure but later ... You have to blame the propaganda, I suppose.'

'He'd only been over there two months, our Billy, before he got his bullet in the neck. Ypres, that's where it was. October the eleventh. They said he never felt a thing. Killed instantly, they said. It killed Ma. She never got over it. Doc reckoned she died of a broken heart.'

Eve remembered Jon telling her that his mother-in-law had collapsed and died and they couldn't find a cause. For a moment they were both silent, thinking of all the young men who had rushed so heedlessly into battle.

'My friend's hubby's still in one piece,' Ellen continued. 'Nellie's hubby, that is. Had a letter the day before yesterday. Not a scratch on him! She swears she's keeping him alive.' She tapped the side of her nose. 'Got a special good luck thing, she has. Now, what does she call it? Oh, yes! A good luck *ritual*.'

'A charm? Is that it?' Eve marvelled silently at people's gullibility. A ritual! Still, was it any less potent than the prayers in which people put their trust?

'Yes. That sort of thing. Every night she lights a candle for him and sets it on a small table with his photograph on it and a pair of his shoes he used to wear and every morning she thanks God for watching over him and keeping him safe. Reckons that God would be too embarrassed to let him die! Calls it the power of suggestion.' She tapped her head. 'Sort of thought waves. Sort of hypnotism. I don't know. I don't go in for that superstitious stuff. Mind you, Nellie's always been a bit fey, that one.'

Eve said, 'There's a lot we don't know about the human mind.'

Ellen shrugged. 'Well, I'll leave you to it. Kate's keeping an eye on the little ones and they play her up something cruel!' She pointed over her shoulder. 'If you want Jon, he's over there.'

Eve bit back her surprise that eight-year-old Kate had been left in charge of three younger children. Not your business, Eve, she reminded herself quickly. What do I know about bringing up children? Ellen has so much experience and seems a very good mother. If I prove as good as she is I shall be content. Harvey would make a wonderful father. She smiled at this vision of their future happiness.

Two minutes later she was settling the roses into the copper vase, before throwing the previous week's flowers on to the appropriate pile. She stood by her father's grave and hurried through the prayers she always uttered for his eternal peace. Another ritual?

11

Too late now for the candle and the shoes. She had never been close to her father who had been a remote figure throughout her childhood. Edgar Collett had been a successful auctioneer and travelled regularly across a wide area, often staying overnight in a variety of superior lodging houses which catered for businessmen of his standing. He had never approved of her marriage to an American, even though Harvey Randall was a highly qualified scientist who was moving into the field of medical research, so the father and daughter had remained largely estranged for the past eight years.

The roses Eve had brought were on behalf of her mother, Dorothy, who, crippled by rheumatism, was cared for by her daughter. For a long moment Eve stared down at the wording on the tombstone and wondered about her father. Had he made her mother happy? She didn't think so. Had he made *anybody* happy? Had he been happy himself? Comparing her father with Harvey, she smiled with contentment. Harvey Randall was slightly shorter than she was with a sturdy frame, a cheerful disposition and a mop of unruly curls that made him look younger than his forty-one years. He had a brilliant mind and loved his work and Eve had never resented the time he had to spend away from her because she knew the work was valuable.

Having dealt with the flowers, Eve follow-ed the direction Ellen had indicated, and picked her way through the long grass towards a young man who was digging a new grave. Jon was first and foremost a grave digger but the work was sporadic and he filled the gaps by working as a gardener and odd-job man.

'Good morning, Jon.' Eve smiled. 'I've a little job for you when you have time.'

He glanced up, thankful for the excuse to stop and mop his face with a red spotted handkerchief. 'Morning, missus. Little job, eh? You know me. I'll be along first chance I get.' He waved a proprietary hand at the partly finished grave. 'Old Colonel Suther-land, up at the big house. Snuffed it three days ago. Pneumonia. That's what the housekeeper reckons. Nasty, that. Coughing his lungs up, she tells me. Couldn't hardly breathe he was so choked up.' He shook his head. 'We gotta go some time but that's a horrible way to go! Mind you he was knock-ing on eighty. He'd had a better innings than most of us get. And he'd been right through the Boer War without so much as a scratch.' He ran his hands through his thick fair hair. 'So what's this job, then?'

'The side gate, Jon. The top hinge is coming loose. I expect they are both a little rotten. When it's windy it rattles and makes a screeching noise that goes right through my head. I'm hoping you can take the gate off and fix two new hinges.'

'No trouble, missus. Maybe the day after tomorrow.'

'Thank you.' She turned to go then turned abruptly back. 'Dear me! I was forgetting. Congratulations are in order, I hear. A son called Sam. I'm so pleased for you.' She fished in her purse and found a shilling. 'Buy something for him with this and give him my love.'

With a nod she hurried away but the smile quickly faded from her face. As soon as she reached home, she decided, she would pour herself a glass of sherry and re-read Harvey's disturbing letter.

Jon, leaning on his spade, watched her until she was out of sight. He wouldn't swap his Ellen for anyone else in the world, he reflected, but if he *had* to swap her – if he had no choice – he'd like someone like Eve Randall. She was his ideal woman. He admired her smooth dark hair and those dark brown eyes – she looked almost foreign. Could be Spanish. They were dark but her skin was so pale. No, she couldn't be Spanish. Any way, she *wasn't* Spanish because one day, when he was repainting her front door, he'd asked her

daily woman and she'd said Eve Randall was
a Londoner, born and bred. So that was
that. Not a cockney, because she wasn't born
within the sound of Bow bells but Shardeloes Road in Brockley was near enough.

With a sigh he turned back to the grave he
was digging. Another two hours would see it
finished and he'd report back to the vicar
and take himself off home. Ellen had promised him a nice bacon roll with some onion
sauce and he was looking forward to that. It
was one of his favourites, although he did
like a nice mutton pie with the crust a bit
burnt round the edges. Ellen was a real
wonder when it came to food. The war had
been on for four years but they had never
gone hungry despite food shortages and
rationing. They might live in a town but she
could always scrounge a bit of meat from
somewhere.

He continued digging, ignoring the drops
of sweat that fell from his face, and thought
about his children. Three bonny little maids.
Kate, eight years old, was already a little
bossy boots. Amy, five, was a biddable child,
and four-year-old Lucy had a fiery temper
and a scream of rage that could be heard a
mile away! And now a boy. A slow smile lit
his face. Good old Ellen! She'd made him
wait but she'd come good in the end.

Poor Eve Randall had no children, he

15

remembered. What was her hubby thinking of to leave her childless? Yes, the poor soul must be lonely in that house with only her bed-ridden mother for company. Serve her husband right if she found herself another man – though she never would. He shook his head at the mere idea of such a thing. She was not that kind of woman. He was sure of that. He straightened up for a moment to ease his back and sweat trickled into his eyes so he took out his handkerchief and mopped his face again. Not much longer, he comforted himself. The bacon roll beckoned.

Eve settled herself on the sofa and, armed with a large sherry, began to re-read her husband's letter which was dated September 10th.

My dearest Eve,
I begin to think that I shall never get back to England! Always, when I think the way is clear, and I begin to think I might risk the crossing, something happens to delay me further. This time it is 'orders from above' but rather unexpected. It seems that a particularly virulent form of influenza has broken out at two or three army camps but there is a news embargo in place so I regret I cannot be more specific.

Eve smiled faintly. Harvey's letters were always a little formal. It was partly his nature and partly his scientific training. Even his love letters had been serious in tone. She read on.

A large number of soldiers have succumbed to the disease and, more seriously, more have died than might have been expected...

Eve frowned. Influenza? What was so special about influenza? It came and went most years and was much less dangerous than other diseases she could name – diphtheria, polio, whooping cough or consumption.

At this time, with the war hopefully coming to an end, the authorities do not want any information of this kind leaking out to give comfort to our enemies. We are hopeful that these outbreaks can be contained. I, and several of my colleagues, have been sent to B—— (I cannot be more specific) to see what we can do, if anything, to prevent it spreading and to help treat and hopefully save some of the stricken soldiers.

My secret worry, which I have kept to

myself, is that many of our troops are being sent to Europe to reinforce the French and British battalions. They may carry the flu with them! The unfortunate wretches in the trenches have enough to cope with without an outbreak of this very aggressive flu to make their situation even more miserable.

On a more cheerful note, there is talk here of a possible armistice to be declared later in the year, so pray, my love, for this to be the case. As soon as peace is declared I shall take a berth on the next ship making the Atlantic crossing and we will be together again. You will never know how much I have missed you. Please believe me, dearest Eve, that I will never leave you again under any circumstances. We shall start our family and, rest assured, you will be the best mother in the world. So no more worries on that score, my love.

May God be with you.

Your adoring husband,

Harvey

'Later in the year,' Eve whispered, hardly daring to hope. When could that be? Not later than the end of December, of that she was certain, and it was already the end of September. She sipped her sherry, grateful for the warmth it instilled. Closing her eyes, she tried to imagine greeting her husband at the railway station. He would be leaning out of the carriage window, searching the crowded platform and his face would light up at the sight of her. She would run along the platform and as he stepped down from the train she would rush into his arms. She would take him home happy and no longer sleep alone. She allowed herself forbidden thoughts – of course it was not too late to have a child, or two or even three! She was not yet thirty. Upstairs the nursery waited silently. It was months since she had ventured in, unable to bear the sense of loss.

'You're such a coward, Eve,' she muttered and, entirely unbidden, Ellen's words came into her head. *'Think positive thoughts.'*

Perhaps we *do* have the power to make things happen, she thought, and imagined the empty nursery upstairs. Could wishing bring them a child? It was a romantic, entirely superstitious, notion, she knew, but in her present state of mind she was prepared to try anything. Harvey would soon be home. Maybe she could prepare herself mentally and emotionally. There was no harm in trying. There was no one to see her. No one to call her a gullible fool.

Before she could change her mind, Eve drank the rest of the sherry and stood up.

She would do it. She would go upstairs and into the nursery. Once there she would close her eyes and imagine the months passing and their first child asleep in the crib. Believing it might make it so. She might even burn a candle! Setting down the empty glass, she found a candlestick, a candle and a box of matches and made her way up the stairs. With her hand on the door knob she hesitated, but then turned it and walked into the room.

Blinking back tears, she looked round the empty nursery, at the crib with its flimsy frills, the nursing chair, the low table and the rocking horse that had once been her own. The window sill was piled with toys awaiting an owner – among them an elderly teddy bear that had once belonged to Harvey and a beloved rag doll that had been given to Eve on her seventh birthday. There were pretty curtains at the window, looped back with ribbons and a chest of drawers already full of baby clothes.

'No!' she said aloud in answer to the unspoken question. She would not, *could not*, look at the clothes. That would be a step too far. She closed her eyes and tried to concentrate, willing herself to imagine the future she so desperately wanted for herself and Harvey.

Opening her eyes, she lit the candle and

watched the small wavering flame. 'Please let us have a family,' she prayed.

She felt rather foolish but the deed was done. After a moment she walked softly from the room and closed the door behind her. On the landing, a grandfather clock chimed. It was time to take a cup of tea and a biscuit to her mother. Eve drew a deep breath. She was pleased with herself. She had been into the nursery without weeping – and if the war ended, Harvey might be home before Christmas.

Things are looking better, she assured herself and went down to the kitchen with a lighter heart.

Inside the nursery, the small flame flickered suddenly, wavered and went out.

Three thousand miles away, in Camp Devens, Harvey Randall was making his way through the main ward of the camp hospital with terror in his heart. He was seeing for himself just how brutal this new influenza could be and was overwhelmed by a feeling of utter helplessness. Since his arrival with his colleagues, the flu had continued to spread with frightening rapidity, felling the young victims with astonishing speed so that the hospital facilities had already proved inadequate and further beds had been ordered. Their research had so far provided no

21

clues as to the cause of this particular strain of the disease and they were no nearer discovering an antidote or even a successful treatment.

'My God!' he muttered, gazing round the vast ward filled with the sick, the very sick and the dying. 'What is this flu and where the hell has it come from?'

The nurses did their best to maintain the normal levels of hygiene but it was impossible to deal with so many patients. The soldiers lay on stained mattresses on metal framed beds, untended for long periods. Orders had been sent for extra bedding and towels, but some were still in transit. The smell was atrocious and it was all Harvey could do not to gag. It was a mixture of sweat, blood, unwashed bodies, antiseptics – and fear. On all sides men lay groaning, their faces slick with sweat, their throats parched, limbs aching while their heads throbbed painfully with the high temperature – all part of the initial stages of the disease. Some men, propped on an elbow, coughed ceaselessly, trying to rid their lungs of the fluid accumulating there. These were the unlucky ones, Harvey thought, shaking his head despairingly. Their original flu symptoms had developed into a second stage which could prove fatal and frequently did. This was a form of pneumonia he had never seen before. Congested lungs failed to provide enough oxygen and there was a horrifying side effect to this condition. Cyanosis appeared – a sinister darkening of the skin.

Harvey shivered, not with revulsion for the suffering men but from fear. Only the newly arrived researchers understood just how far they were from finding a cure. The army was preparing to send their young troops to fight in Europe but many would develop the dreaded disease during the journey and might well be dead before they could reach the troop ships, let alone set foot on foreign soil to be shot at by the enemy.

The stricken hospital staff went about their work with quiet fortitude and a stoic refusal to give way to despair but they were not immune to the infection either and many of them fell ill. Calls went out for people to replace them. Harvey took in the pitiful scene with a deep sense of panic.

A voice beside him said, 'Ever seen anything like this, Harvey?'

It was James Ferber, a senior army pathologist who had been seconded from New York where he frequently lectured on his subject and wrote the occasional treatise on up-to-date procedures. He had the unenviable job of examining the dead but he was a skilled pathologist and took pride in his job.

With a quick glance to make sure nobody

was within earshot, he lowered his voice. 'We can't keep up with it. The bodies are coming in quicker than we can deal with them. I'm half dead on my feet from exhaustion. We all are, in the morgue. I hope to God that Washington knows about this. Somebody has to take charge or it will get totally out of control.'

James Ferber was a slight man, average height, blue eyes beneath smooth brown hair. He was quick-witted and normally smiled a lot but for many days past he had found nothing to lift his spirits.

Harvey nodded but still said nothing. What could he say? It was a nightmare and there was no comfort to be had from words. As the ward sister approached from the far end of the ward, he noticed that somehow she moved with her usual briskness and what appeared to be confidence still radiated from her. She had a cheery word for each patient as she passed but, as she drew nearer, a closer look revealed that her face was lined with misery and her eyes were dark from lack of sleep.

Glancing at the two men, she said dully, 'This is a total disaster!' As she walked on, Harvey and James stared after her until distracted by a sudden commotion further down the ward which sent them hurrying to see what was wrong.

A young man was sitting upright in his bed, his face bright with fever, his hair snow white. He pointed a trembling finger at the soldier in the next bed. 'You're lying, Pete!' he said thickly through parched lips. 'Tell me it's a lie!'

Harvey said soothingly, 'Just lie down, fella. You need to stay calm.' He put a firm hand on his shoulder, pushed him gently down and drew the sheet up to his chin.

The young man repeated, 'You're lying, Pete!' Two large tears trickled down his face.

Ferber turned to the second man. 'What does he mean?'

Pete blinked reddened eyes. 'His hair's turned white. It was brown before. I just said ... He doesn't ... believe me.' He began to cough and then to gasp for breath.

Harvey looked at the white-haired man. 'Don't worry about it. It's the high temperature,' he said. 'So you're a blond! It suits you – and women love it!' He patted his shoulder and turned back to Ferber who was shaking his head. Disconsolately they moved on, talking in lowered voices.

'I'm told they've ordered another hundred coffins,' Ferber said. 'I'm on my way to speak with the General. A hundred won't be enough. Not nearly enough – unless there's a miracle on the horizon! There are thousands of men in this camp and once they fall ill they'll have a one-in-four chance of dying.'

'My God!' exclaimed Harvey.

'I must get back to the morgue. We started at five thirty this morning and we'll go on until nearly ten. It's a punishing schedule and three of my staff have gone down with it. As for me ... I'm beginning to feel like a zombie!'

On that resigned note he left Harvey alone in the middle of a sea of beds with a growing realization that his own chances of survival must be similarly bleak and he decided to write a last letter to Eve which he would leave with a request that it be forwarded if he died. For the present he would be careful what he wrote to her since there was no point in frightening her. He regretted his last letter but there was no way he could put that right. If the flu spread to other countries she would soon understand the scale of the disaster.

Slowly he walked along the rows, occasionally pausing to read the clipboard report on the end of a bed. Here a young redheaded man, still in the first stage of the disease, mumbled in delirium. Harvey frowned. Either he would recover or the infection would spread to his throat and lungs and turn into pneumonia. If the latter happened his chances of survival were extremely low.

He chose another report at random.

'Sergeant O'Leary,' he said. A large man was propped up against his pillow, breathing stertorously, his eyes open but unfocussed. Already his sheet was splattered with the blood he had coughed up and his skin was darkening – the strange blueish-brown which Harvey had come to dread. The man failed to answer to his name. Presumably he was too far gone – or too ill to care. There was no need to study the report, Harvey thought tiredly. This man would be dead within twenty-four hours.

They desperately needed an effective flu vaccine but this was a new and deadly strain and so far they had not been able to identify it. The first stage of the disease was a viral infection but the second stage was bacterial. Until they could isolate and identify this new strain, the scientists were helpless.

Two

Three days later Jon turned up as promised to mend the hinges on the gate. With him came eight-year-old Kate, a small, fierce-looking child with tangled dark hair which was tied with a limp blue ribbon. It was the first time Eve had met any of the children and her first sight of the girl was not encouraging. Kate's small eyes were dark brown – almost black – and there was something vaguely feral about them. Her nose was thin and her chin jutted stubbornly. Only a mother could think her pretty, thought Eve, and at once regretted the unkind judgement.

'Begging your pardon, missus,' Jon said, 'and I hope you don't mind but Ellen's feeling poorly and this one's a handful. I thought she'd be better with just three of them.'

'I don't mind,' Eve said. She smiled at the girl but received a deep scowl in return.

'Want to go home!' Kate declared.

Jon glared at her. 'Well, you can't. You can come round the side of the house and watch me – and behave yourself unless you want a wallop!'

Kate tossed her head and Jon cuffed her lightly round the ear.

'That's for nothing. Now be careful,' he told her.

Unsure what to say, Eve wondered whether she could find something interesting for the girl to do so that Jon could concentrate on repairing the gate.

'Would you like to help me in the garden, Kate? Then your father can get on with...'

'I want to go home!'

'We could pick some flowers.'

'Don't want to!'

'Would you like a biscuit?'

Kate's eyes gleamed. 'Yes.'

'Manners!' said Jon, reaching out to give her another cuff but this time she was too quick and ducked out of reach.

The girl reminded Eve of a rebellious sprite. She was wondering if she dared to take her into the kitchen.

Jon said, 'Say please!'

'Don't want to. I want to go home.'

Eve smiled at him. 'You go ahead, Jon. Kate and I will find something to do – after we've had the biscuits.'

Jon took his chance and left the two of them together. They regarded each other warily.

Impulsively, Eve said, 'Why do you want to go home, Kate?'

'Cos of Sam!' Pleased at the chance to air her grievance, Kate elaborated. 'Cos Sam loves me best.' Thinking about her baby brother, her dark eyes lit up and for a brief moment Eve saw a new, more attractive side to her. 'Amy always wants to hold him but he loves me best. He wants me to hold him all the time.' Her face fell. 'I bet Amy's holding him. She's only five. She's too young. She'll drop him. I told Ma but she wouldn't listen. I should hold him. I'm the oldest. It's not fair.'

Her mouth set in an aggrieved line and Eve finally understood. The girl was becoming possessive of the long-awaited baby brother and was jealous of her sister, Amy, and wanted the baby all to herself. 'Let's find those biscuits,' she suggested and led the way into the kitchen.

Eve opened a tin of home-made almond biscuits and put three on a plate. 'These are for you, Kate.'

The girl snatched one up and stuffed it into her mouth without a word.

Suddenly inspired, Eve found a pad of paper and a pencil and set them in front of Kate. 'Perhaps you could draw a picture of Sam. You could take it home to show to him. You could give it to him as a little present.'

A second biscuit followed the first. 'Don't want to,' Kate mumbled through a spattering of crumbs. 'Want to go home.'

Eve shrugged and turned away. She began to busy herself with the washing up in the hope that, receiving no attention, her young visitor would decide to use the pencil and paper. She was very quiet.

Mrs Banks, the daily woman, would be in soon and Monday was wash day. Eve liked to get the breakfast things put away so that the kitchen was free for the soaking, washing and rinsing. The mangle waited outside in the backyard. Eve had intended to write to Harvey again but she felt unable to do so with Kate in the house. She would certainly get in the daily woman's way so Eve thought she might take her into the park.

When she finished, she turned to suggest this but the girl had gone – and so had the rest of the biscuits. The biscuit tin was empty and the paper and pencil were untouched.

'Little minx!' She went outside, expecting her to be with her father but Jon hadn't seen her.

He shook his head. 'Run off home, no doubt,' he said. 'I brought her the long way round but she'll find her way back. Ellen won't be too pleased and Kate's going to get a wallop when I get hold of her. She's nothing but trouble, that one! Always been

31

difficult but getting worse. Same at school. Got the cane the other day. Came home laughing about it.'

Eve bit back her suspicion that jealousy was the cause of Kate's bad behaviour. It was probably better not to interfere, she thought. Jon was not asking for her opinion. Kate's not my daughter, she told herself. Let Jon deal with her.

She went back into the house in time to open the front door to Mrs Banks. Soon the fire under the copper was lit and water was heating above it. Mrs Banks piled in the sheets and put the wooden lid in place. Eve left her to it, went into the parlour and closed the door. Relieved to be alone, she sat down at the writing desk and, with a sigh of pleasure, dipped her pen into the ink. Writing to Harvey always seemed to bring them closer together.

After writing her letter, Eve set off for the post office. As she walked she thought about Jon's eldest daughter, trying to see life from the child's point of view. Why she bothered, she couldn't say, but for some reason the girl intrigued her. Defiant, bold – and a thief! Poor little thing. From being the first and only child she had later had to deal with the arrival of Amy. Having mothered her baby sister, she had then been faced with Lucy's arrival but her role as Mother's precious helper continued. How she must have enjoyed the position – until everything changed. Baby Sam was born but by now Amy, five years old, vied with Kate to look after him. Kate had to share the responsibilities with her younger sister and wasn't finding it easy.

Eve thought about the empty biscuit tin and wondered if stealing was tolerated in the Beatty household or whether Kate's behaviour was growing worse. Eve had decided against telling Jon. It might have been an impulse and nothing more.

Eve bought some stamps at the post office and then stopped by the butcher's shop. Her mother ate very little and Eve had lost interest in cooking but today she was determined to make a special effort. She knew she had lost weight – her face was thinner and her skirts felt loose around the waist. Harvey might be home within weeks and he would notice the change in her. He claimed to dislike skinny women so Eve was going to try to replace some of the weight she had lost.

'Good morning, Mrs Randall. Bit of a stranger, aren't you?' The butcher smiled to soften the criticism and set down the meat cleaver. Eric Thwaite was a giant of a man with a ruddy complexion and had recently taken over the business from his father. Deftly he arranged a few lamb chops on a clean tray and added a few sprigs of parsley. Although meat was rationed, he tried to keep up appearances.

'Now, how can I tempt you?' he asked.

He kept such phrases for his female customers and Eve smiled obligingly. He was a cheerful soul with a smile and a wink for each customer. In his youth he had helped his father in the family business, working on Saturday mornings and after school. Now he was married and a father himself.

At that moment another woman entered the shop. Small and brisk, she wore a faded felt hat pulled down over her hair. Eve knew her by sight and smiled politely at the retired school teacher. The butcher greeted her cheerfully with a mock salute.

'Good morning, Miss Harding. Heard from that nephew of yours, have you? I heard he was coming home.'

It was a common question and had been so for the past four years of war. Everyone, it seemed, had someone involved in the fighting – soldiers, airmen, sailors – and many had already lost relatives. Eve was considered fortunate that her husband was in America, far away from the front line, and she was well aware that the distinction set her apart from other women.

'He'll be back in England before long,' Miss Harding told them. To Eve she said, 'I was telling Mr Thwaite last week – my nephew got hit in the knee. Shrapnel from a mortar shell at Passchendaele. Lucky it wasn't higher, I told him. You might have lost an eye! Poor Lewis. They've told him he'll never walk without a serious limp but at least he's no longer in the firing line. You've done your bit for King and country, I told him. We keep in touch as well as we can. He's my brother's only child and we've always been very close.'

Eve smiled and turned back to the butcher. 'The chops look nice,' she told him. 'Before you put them in the window I'd like two, please.'

He shook his head. 'One only, I'm afraid, otherwise they won't go round. Your mother might enjoy it, being a bit of an invalid. But I can let you have a rabbit as well if you'd like it. Make a nice pie, that would, with a bit of onion.'

'Rabbit?' She raised her eyebrows.

He tapped the side of his nose and grinned. 'I've got my sources.'

Eve was about to refuse because she wasn't fond of rabbit but she hesitated. Impulsively she decided she would take it round to the Beatty family. They had five mouths to feed, not counting the baby. 'Thank you, I'd like that.'

He produced a grey furry body from

beneath the counter and wrapped it in a sheet of newspaper, tucking a single chop in with it as he did so.

The door bell jangled again and a boy came in with a shopping list in his hand. He looked nervously at Miss Harding, who said, 'Helping your mother, are you, Stevie? Good boy.'

'Yes, miss.'

She frowned. 'Shouldn't you be at school?'

'Me ma's took bad with her leg. Grandpa says I'm to stay home and look after her.'

'Ah, yes. Ulcer, is it?'

The boy shrugged.

Before they could say any more, the telegram boy from the post office opened the shop door and handed an envelope to the nearest customer which was Miss Harding. She handed it to the butcher and Eve was immediately aware of a sudden chill in the air. Nobody spoke but they all regarded the telegram with apprehension. With trembling fingers, Eric Thwaite slit open the envelope.

'Oh Jesus!' he gasped as soon as he had unfolded it. He read a line or two aloud and they caught the familiar, formal words – *'It is my painful duty to inform you...'* Then the colour drained from his face. He cried out – a great bellow of a cry – 'Mary! Oh God, Mary!'

His wife Mary, a small slight woman, came

36

running into the shop from the living quarters behind him and the customers froze as their worst suspicions were confirmed.

Before Mary could reach for the telegram it fell from the butcher's hand on to the counter and he groped blindly for the meat cleaver. With an agonized cry he raised it and brought the blade down so heavily on the telegram that the cleaver dug itself deep into the wooden counter, roughly severing the small sheet of paper. As Eve began to stammer some awkward words of comfort, Mary snatched up the two halves of the telegram, pieced them together and gave a small choking sound.

The butcher stared round the shop with wild eyes that Eve saw were full of unimaginable pain.

'Get out! All of you!' he cried and then suddenly staggered back against the wall. His eyes were closed as he slid heavily to the floor. Miss Harding took young Stevie's arm and steered him quickly from the shop.

Eve hesitated and caught the eye of the butcher's wife. 'Can I help you with him?'

'No. Just leave us,' she whispered. She knelt clumsily beside her husband and tried to put her arms round him. Glancing back at Eve, she said, 'He'll come round. We'll be all right.'

In spite of her brave words she looked

dazed and Eve longed to say or do something to help them but felt helpless in the face of such overwhelming grief. Turning, with tears in her eyes, she left the shop and walked quickly in the direction of home, oblivious of the fact that she hadn't paid for her purchases. She imagined what was happening in the shop – the grief-stricken couple trying to support each other through the first day of their ruined lives.

Halfway home, at once shaken and depressed, she decided that she could not face Mrs Banks and the noise and smell of wash day. She turned abruptly. She would take the rabbit to the Beattys, she decided. Seeing them might take her mind off the tragedy she had just witnessed.

Brushing her tears away, she made an effort to think positively and was soon knocking at the door of Number 20, Leopold Street. It was no worse and no better than most London streets, she thought – a terraced row of sound but unimaginative houses with minute front gardens where a few sooty pansies or drooping hollyhocks bloomed unnoticed. Some of the houses had a neglected air but she noticed that the step of number twenty had been recently scrubbed and the windows were clean. She felt ashamed of her reaction. Why, just because the Beattys were poor, did she assume they were also feckless? Ellen Beatty was obviously a good housewife.

There was no answer so she rang the bell again and waited, already half regretting the purpose of her errand.

'What d'you want?' The voice came from low down on the door and Eve saw two eyes regarding her nervously through the slit in the letterbox.

'I'm Mrs Randall,' she said, bending low. 'I want to speak to Mrs Beatty. Is your mother...?'

'She's asleep. I'm not to let anyone in.'

It wasn't Kate so it must be one of the younger girls, Eve thought. 'I have something for her,' she began but at that moment she became aware of a regular squeaking sound that was approaching along the pavement. It was Kate proudly pushing a very battered pram. She caught sight of Eve and her eyes widened.

She said quickly, 'I never took them! I never took nuffink!'

'You mean the biscuits? That doesn't matter, Kate. I've brought something for your mother. A rabbit. She could make a pie or a stew.'

At last the front door opened and a small fair-haired child appeared. She came out to help her sister lift the pram inside.

Kate, immediately possessive, cried, 'Leave

off, Amy. I can do it!' and a short sharp struggle ensued. The pram was jolted so violently that Eve cried out in alarm and tried to steady it, afraid that baby Sam would topple out headfirst on to the pavement. Above them a window opened and Ellen looked down.

'What the hell's all that noise?' she demanded. 'How am I supposed to get me bit of rest?'

Nobody answered her and she slammed the window down. Moments later the pram was safely inside the narrow hall, Sam was crying and Amy was despatched to look upstairs for the baby's dummy. Kate was blaming her sister for waking Ellen and the latter was regarding her visitor with some irritation. From behind her mother four-year-old Lucy, a thumb in her mouth, peered inquisitively at Eve.

'I brought you something from the butcher,' Eve said. 'It's quite fresh. I thought you might...'

Ellen, tousled from sleep, received the gift with a poor grace. 'Ta!' She opened the paper and stared without enthusiasm at the contents.

'Rabbit? Ugh! I shall have to skin it. Still, beggars can't be choosers.'

Kate wrinkled her nose. 'I hate rabbit!'

'You do not hate rabbit. You've never had

it, so how can you hate it? You'll eat what you're given and no whining! And say ta to Mrs Randall.'

Stubbornly Kate's small mouth closed but Ellen chose not to notice.

Amy reappeared and the dummy was thrust into the baby's mouth. Eve felt the need to say something nice about the infant and leant over the pram. Pretending not to notice the vile smell, she studied Sam. He was very small and bald and the oversized bonnet had slipped sideways across his forehead giving him a rakish appearance. His mouth was open and his small hands were clenched into tiny fists.

'He's wonderful,' said Eve.

Ellen snorted. 'You should 'ave heard him at four this morning! It was enough to wake the whole street – but he's a good little 'un on the whole.' She smiled down at him and there was an awkward silence.

'Well, that's good,' Eve said.

Ellen handed the rabbit to Kate who disappeared into what Eve assumed was the scullery. 'What do I owe you?' she asked Eve.

'Oh, no! It's a gift. I must be off.'

No one tried to dissuade her and she made her escape. As she walked home she was in two minds about the Beattys. Did she envy them or pity them? Perhaps a bit of both, she thought, and suddenly going home to supervise wash day didn't seem quite so bad an idea. She was almost back before she realized that she had given away her chop as well as the rabbit.

Over a cup of tea, while the washing blew on the line outside, Eve told Mrs Banks about the death of the butcher's son.

Mrs Banks shook her head and tutted regretfully. 'The worst of it must be having no one to bury,' she said. 'You have to think of them in a foreign land, maybe with no headstone and no one to take a few flowers! That must be the worst of it – apart from losing someone you love, of course.' She sipped her tea thoughtfully. 'Ruddy Germans! That blooming Kaiser! It's all his fault. What I wouldn't like to do to him!'

Eve sighed. 'I feel I should have stayed to help them but I didn't know what to do. I do hope he's all right. A shock like that's enough to give him a heart attack.'

'I had a bit of a shock myself yesterday,' Mrs Banks admitted. 'My Annie's decided to go up north and work with her cousin in a munitions factory. Maude, that's her cousin, she reckons it's a bit of a lark. You know how these young people are. I told Annie it'll be hard work, but she's determined to do something now that she's turned eighteen. If it's not munitions she says she'd do nursing but she's not too good with blood.' She paused, gulped some air and continued. 'When she was nine she fell off a swing and bit her lip. As soon as she saw the blood on her hankie she rolled up her eyes and was off in a dead faint!'

Eve said, 'It might not be for long. They say the war's grinding to a close – and not before time! She should be safe from any bombing up there now. The Zeppelins seem to have eased off, thank heavens.' She finished her tea and stood up. 'You'll be off in a minute or two so I'll go up and spend some time with Mother. Your money's on the dresser – and thanks, as usual. The washing will dry in no time in this breeze.'

Dorothy Collett was only fifty-two but, after a prolonged bout of congestion of the lungs, she had been reluctant to return to her previously active life and chose to see herself as an invalid. Nothing the doctor said could dissuade her from this idea and as time passed Eve had partly given up the struggle. After her father's death, when her mother first came to live with her, she found it difficult to share a kitchen and as her mother spent more and more time in bed, Eve was secretly pleased to have time to herself. When Harvey came home, she realized, they would value their privacy even more.

'I know my weakness better than you do,

dear,' Dorothy had told her daughter on more than one occasion. 'I'm a good judge of what I can and cannot manage and I have no intention to put a strain on my failing resources.'

Now, as Eve entered her bedroom, Dorothy held up her knitting with a smile.

'I'm tired of socks for sailors,' she explained. 'All that navy blue was a strain on my eyes. This is a glove for a soldier. It's supposed to be in stocking stitch but I think that's rather boring so I'm doing it in moss stitch.' Eve stepped closer to admire it and Dorothy chattered on. 'I'm sure one of our brave boys will appreciate that a little more style and imagination has gone into the gloves. And of course khaki wool is a nice change and more restful for my eyes.'

She was wearing a knitted bed-jacket that Eve had bought for her, and her dark hair, now laced with grey, had been neatly drawn back into a chignon. As always, Eve was touched by how pretty she still was and how well she maintained her appearance.

'I'll parcel up the socks, if you like, and take them to the post office,' Eve said. She was wondering whether to tell her mother about the butcher's son although bad news rarely seemed to affect her. It was as though Dorothy was cocooned by the bedroom walls and protected from the shocks.

Briefly Eve recounted what had happened earlier. Dorothy carried on with her knitting without a word, but when Eve finished she glanced up. 'I'll write to them tonight,' she said. 'A well-written card is a great comfort at such times and I do have a neat hand. When your father died I was touched by people's sympathy and even now I sometimes re-read them. Such cards and letters are to be kept and cherished.'

'But you don't even *know* the Thwaites, Mother.'

'So much the better! I shall write as one of thousands of anonymous but grateful men and women who acknowledge the supreme sacrifice that their son has made on our behalf.'

'Of course, Mother. When you put it like that...' Eve suddenly saw her opportunity. 'Why don't you finish that row and then let me help you downstairs? It's easier for you to write at my desk than to manage on a tray, sitting up in bed.'

To her relief her mother agreed and twenty minutes later Dorothy was sitting at the writing desk, composing her letter of condolence to the Thwaites. As she watched her, Eve felt a pang of guilt that she herself hadn't thought of writing a letter. Tomorrow she would take some flowers round and offer to help them in any way she could.

Three

The weeks passed in a daze for the exhausted staff at Camp Devens. James Ferber, a gauze mask across the lower part of his face, followed the Sister through the rows of beds with a heavy heart. Ten minutes earlier he had heard the news he dreaded – one of the scientists in the research laboratory had gone down with the disease and he suspected it might be Harvey Randall. Common sense told him to stay away from the wards but over the past few weeks he and Harvey had become more than colleagues. A friendship had developed from their shared work among the unfortunate victims of the disease and the need to save as many lives as they could. Not that James could save the men he saw in the morgue but he nursed a secret hope that during his examinations he might stumble on a clue that would be of value to the researchers.

The numbers of sick and dying men in the camp had rocketed from hundreds to thousands. Elsewhere the flu had spread to the civilian population where it was proving equally aggressive. There were reports, too, from the troop ships which described the number of deaths on board from influenza and hinted at the hundreds of men stumbling from the ships on to foreign shores in the early stages of the disease.

The Sister came to a halt beside one of the beds and said loudly, 'There's someone to see you, Mr Randall.' She plucked the clipboard from the end of the bed and read it with a frown.

James leaned over and patted Harvey's arm. 'It's me, James Ferber. You don't look too hot. I wish I could help you. We ... We're doing all we can for you so you just hang in there. You hear me? You can...'

Receiving no response, James's voice trailed away. Eventually Harvey opened bloodshot eyes and stared at him in obvious confusion. Already James could see the darkening skin tone spreading from the ears – the fateful precursor to death.

He swallowed hard. 'It's me – James Ferber. You remember me. I'm one of the pathologists. This is a bloody awful thing to happen – pardon my French, Sister – but it is. We need this guy.' He gripped Harvey's hand, it was hot and sweaty, and he noted how gaunt his friend's face had become. 'You can beat this thing, Harvey. You must!'

Harvey groaned and tried to speak but was

wracked by a fit of coughing which produced a small amount of red-flecked fluid. The Sister grabbed a towel from beside the pillow and wiped it away. She caught the pathologist's eye and shook her head. The gesture told James that there was no way the patient could survive and any lingering hope he may have had was instantly dashed.

'I'll leave you to it,' said the Sister, 'but don't linger unless you want to be next.'

James leaned over the sick man. 'I've got your letter safe. If anything happens to you, I'll see your wife gets it.'

With a lump in his throat, he patted his friend's arm again, and mouthed a silent, 'Goodbye.' He turned quickly and walked back the way he had come with misery taking hold of him. Harvey Randall was one of the best but he was dying and nothing could save him.

At the end of the ward, following instructions, James pulled off his white coat and threw it into a bin, then washed his hands and face thoroughly before fetching a clean coat from the cupboard and putting it on. In his heart he knew these routine precautions were useless but it was important for morale that everyone was seen to be adhering to the rules. He set off through the echoing corridors, fearful that even at that very moment, the disease could be taking hold of him, working its dreadful way through the tissues of his body, preparing to lay him low like poor Harvey Randall. As he neared the morgue, he made a big effort to throw off the notion. He had work to do and must keep his mind sharp.

Outside the morgue half a dozen bodies were stacked on the floor against one wall, awaiting attention from the exhausted pathologists. Inside the morgue every examination table was occupied and three more bodies rested on impromptu tables, consisting of wooden planks propped on bricks at either end.

The ugly scenes depressed him and the knowledge that they could see no end to the spread of the disease frightened him more than he would admit. The Sister was right, he thought. He should never have taken such an unnecessary risk. Suppose he also died. He would leave a wife and young child to fend for themselves. Was that what the future held for them? Once again, a cold fear clutched at his heart.

One of his colleagues glanced up from the corpse he was examining, and saw James's stricken face. 'Any chance for Randall?' he asked, aware that the two men were friends.

'Not a hope in hell!' he answered bitterly. 'It would take a miracle and they're damned thin on the ground right now!'

'Poor devil! How long's he got?'

James Ferber drew in a long breath. 'Not more than twenty-four hours, I'd say.'

'He was married, wasn't he?'

'He's written to her and I said I'd forward it. She's in England with her mother.' He drew a long breath. 'I wanted to spend a few minutes with him so he didn't feel abandoned but the Sister didn't approve of me being there. She was right. I know it was stupid but ... I had to show up just for a minute or two.'

'Let's hope you don't regret it. We need you.'

James took the place of a colleague who was due to take half an hour's rest and as he took up his position two young volunteers hoisted a fresh corpse on to the table. As he began the familiar work, James considered the situation with a mixture of alarm and depression. The influenza was spreading faster than anyone could ever have imagined. The bodies were arriving from the wards faster than they could be autopsied. The senior staff had advertised for more pathologists but it seemed they were all needed elsewhere.

The young man on the slab before him had once been somebody's son, he thought, but now he was little more than a statistic. A young woman arrived beside him carrying a pile of winding sheets in which to wrap the cadavers after the death certificates had been issued. He recognized her as one of the young volunteer workers.

'Are we *all* going to die?' she whispered through her mask, her blue eyes wide with horror.

James forced what he hoped was a reassuring smile. 'Certainly not! Remember your prayers!' Even as he said it, he knew how trite it sounded.

'Prayers?' Her lips trembled. 'Prayers didn't save my mother.' Tears sprang into her eyes but before he could reply she threw down the sheets and ran back the way she had come.

A shudder ran through him. Whatever people said or did, they were all thinking the same thing – that the influenza was unstoppable and it was only a matter of time. He vowed that when he finally fell into bed that night he would summon enough energy to write to his own wife before it was too late. Louise now lived in New York with their son Toby, sharing her widowed mother's home, while they all waited for the war to end. The photograph of her, with two-year-old Toby on her lap, stood on the small table next to his bed and their faces were the last thing he saw before turning out the light. If anything happened to him, he knew it would break her heart.

A couple of weeks later, on October the twenty-second, Eve was surprised to find the retired school teacher on her doorstep.

'Miss Harding?' *What on earth could she want?* she wondered. 'Will you come in?'

'Thank you, I will. I've come to ask a big favour.'

She stepped inside and followed Eve along the passage and into the parlour. For a moment she glanced round appraisingly then sat down in the chair Eve indicated. She placed her feet neatly together and clasped her hands in her lap. She looked nervous, thought Eve curiously.

'Mrs Randall, I told you my nephew, Lewis, was expected home, didn't I, when we met at the butcher's some weeks ago? Well, he's arriving in London on Thursday and I want to be there to meet him.'

'Will his parents not be there?'

'No. They live in Devon and my brother is housebound with a very weak heart. It is too far for my sister-in-law to travel. They've asked me to do it. Lewis has a crutch, of course, because of his knee, so he'll find it difficult to get around. I've told my brother that I'd meet him off the train. Just so he can see a familiar face.' Miss Harding glanced down at her clasped hands then up again. 'The truth is, Mrs Randall, I'm not a very seasoned traveller and I do find the railways rather intimidating. I know you are well-travelled – you've lived in America – so I wondered if you would consider coming to the station with me to meet him. Could your mother manage on her own for a few hours?'

Surprised, Eve hesitated a moment. Meeting a wounded soldier from the train was the last thing she had expected. It was true she had travelled further than many people but always with Harvey to smooth the way. Miss Harding would be relying on her to organize the trip and she felt a rush of anxiety at the prospect. Whenever she had travelled with her husband, the journey had always gone according to plan but undoubtedly Harvey's planning skills were better than her own.

Noting her hesitation Miss Harding's face fell. 'Oh, dear! I shouldn't have put you in this position. It's such a responsibility. My dear, forget that I asked. It was hardly fair of me.'

Eve had a picture of the elderly woman struggling alone to meet her wounded nephew and realized that she must agree – and with a good grace. 'Not at all,' she said quickly. 'I think ... Yes, certainly I will. Why ever not?' Stop stammering, she told herself, and she smiled at Miss Harding.

'Two heads are better than one, aren't they?'

'Oh, thank you so much!' gasped Miss Harding, her anxious frown fading.

'I'd be pleased to go with you to London. It will be a bit of an adventure and I think we would make good travelling companions.'

The frown was replaced with a smile. 'Oh, that is such a relief! I'm in your debt for life, Mrs Randall. I shall naturally pay all your expenses. It will be rather an adventure, you're right, but so worthwhile. Poor Lewis will be so thrilled to see us.' Her smile widened. 'We might all have a cup of tea and a biscuit in the station tea shop! My brother has sent me some money for our expenses.'

Now that she had committed herself, Eve began to see that it would be an interesting day and something to tell Harvey about in her next letter. 'I shall look forward to it,' she said and began to mean it. If a young man had risked his life in a dreadful war the least she could do was help to welcome him home. The thought pleased her.

'It won't be an ordinary train,' Miss Harding warned her. 'It will be reserved for servicemen who are being repatriated. Troop trains – I think that's what they call them. Some are coming home on leave but most will be wounded men, some walking, others on stretchers, but there will be medical orderlies with them and a few nurses, of course. Lewis said they'd be a motley crew, some straight from the front line. But I shall recognize him. If I don't, he'll recognize me.' She laughed suddenly. 'Four years of war may change a young man but elderly aunts stay the same!'

To celebrate the coming expedition, Eve poured them each a small sherry, and they sat for nearly an hour making plans and inevitably talking about peace which now seemed a distinct possibility.

Thursday morning arrived and the two women travelled by taxi to the station and made their way very comfortably, and without any problems, to Charing Cross. Once there however, they were faced with a vast bustling forecourt, full of travellers all rushing in different directions. Many of them were closely followed by station porters pushing barrows piled with luggage. It seemed that hundreds of people were trying to leave London while an equal number were arriving. The noise was deafening – loud voices mingled with the sound of the engines, and the rattle of carriage wheels and slamming doors drowned out the shouts of the porters.

Miss Harding clutched Eve's arm, desperate that she and Eve should not become accidentally separated by the crush of people who surrounded them. Slowly they found their way to one of the barriers and asked a harassed ticket collector which platform the boat train from France would arrive. He shouted an answer and jerked a thumb and Eve and her companion turned right and set off once more. They had purchased platform tickets so that they could watch for Lewis as he descended from the train.

It was obvious they had found the right place. Crowds were already waiting on the platform but none of them had any luggage. Uniformed nurses stood around in groups, chatting, and men in white coats were also in attendance. There was a row of wheelchairs on the platform alongside a stack of stretchers. A sprinkling of immaculate military uniforms revealed the fact that senior army personnel were present. Presumably, thought Eve, to oversee the proceedings. It would be left to lower ranks to check lists of names, arrange for the onward journeys of seriously injured men to the designated hospitals, and to generally supervise the entire operation which should, at all costs, be seen to go smoothly. This was the nearest these returning troops would get to the heroes' welcome they had been promised when they enlisted in a rush of patriotism four years ago. Here and there among the waiting families, Eve spotted an occasional reporter, notebook at the ready.

Miss Harding watched breathlessly, impressed by the scene. 'It's wonderful, isn't it?' she said. 'It makes you proud to be British.'

A distant whistle from an approaching train caused a ripple of excitement throughout the waiting crowds and when it clanked and shuddered into place alongside the platform in a fierce rush of steam and shrieking brakes, there was a roar of welcome. Hats were tossed into the air, brollys were waved and screams of excitement filled the air and Eve began to feel something of the excitement of the moment.

Every window of the train was filled with dishevelled men with beaming smiles and Eve watched them with a lump in her throat. Behind the smiles the troop's faces hinted at the hideous experiences they had somehow survived. They were mostly thin and pale with a few days' stubble and haunted eyes. Their uniforms were crumpled and stained, their hair straggled from beneath their helmets, forage caps or bandages.

Miss Harding cried, 'He'll be walking with a crutch, remember!'

She stepped forward eagerly as the train doors swung open and the waiting crowd surged closer. Nurses hurried up and down the platform, lists in hands, calling out names and, when they found the owner, ticking them off on their papers and herding them into bewildered groups. The men straggled along in their worn boots and muddy gaiters, dragging kitbags and rifles. They looked weary but dazed with relief. After all they had gone through, they had made it home.

A smartly dressed woman wearing a fox fur raised a heavily ringed hand and called, 'Tommy, darling! Over here!'

An elderly man cried, 'There he is! Teddy! ... Oh, no! It's not him!'

Two young girls were being pushed by their mother towards a weary soldier with a sergeant's stripes on his sleeve. 'That's your daddy! Give him a big kiss!' but they approached him warily as he crouched down to sweep them into his arms.

A large woman pushed roughly past Eve, nearly sending her flying. 'I see him! It *is* him! Oh, Monty! It's Mother!'

Relatives ran distractedly along the platforms, using elbows to force their way through the throng. A group of soldiers stood patiently, waiting to be claimed – like lost puppies, thought Eve, close to tears. Five sailors, arm in arm, made their way towards the ticket barrier, laughing hysterically as though determined to celebrate their return to Blighty.

A solitary airman stared round him in

search of someone until a young woman ran, sobbing, into his arms. Eve, watching them cling together, felt very alone. Was she ever going to greet Harvey like that? she wondered. These men were returning from Europe but Harvey had to cross the Atlantic before they could be reunited. It seemed to her at that moment that the gulf between them was too great ever to be overcome and she swallowed hard, fighting down the growing notion that for her, at least, the war would not end happily.

'Stop it, Eve!' she whispered to herself. 'Stop whingeing! You're luckier than thousands of women. Much luckier than poor Mr Thwaite and his wife.'

Thinking of them made her feel guilty. She had avoided the butcher's shop lately, afraid to meet up with him again, knowing she would stammer out some words of consolation which would mean nothing to the butcher.

Miss Harding, her eyes narrowed in concentration, was watching three men with crutches being helped along by nurses. No doubt she was hoping that one of them was her nephew, Lewis.

'No! He's not one of them,' she told Eve. 'It's so confusing. Could we have missed him, do you think?'

'Maybe, but he won't go far, will he? He's

expecting to be met.'

Miss Harding put a hand to her heart. 'You don't think he's missed the train, do you? Or had an accident of some kind. He couldn't have fallen overboard, could he?'

'I doubt it. I think they'd be well supervised. It's more likely he's missed us. Passed us in the crowd. Look, there are still men coming from the train.' She pointed to several who were being carried on stretchers and others who were being supported by various members of the medical staff. In spite of her encouraging words, Eve was beginning to wonder if there *was* something wrong. 'Shall I ask someone? Or maybe you should do it because you know more details than I do – about his full name and regiment, I mean. One of the officers should be able to tell us something.'

As though on cue, an army officer was approaching and Eve took the initiative and put up a hand to attract his attention. Frowning he paused, a look of irritation on his face. His uniform was immaculate, his leather belt and boots highly polished and there was a small row of medals on his chest. Eve guessed that he was probably a major.

She began, 'We're looking for...'

'Don't ask me!' he snapped. 'It's not my job to know all the answers!'

'He has a leg injury and his name is...'

'I tell you I don't know anything!' He was searching the far end of the platform and suddenly waved imperiously at someone. 'Chaos! Ruddy chaos!' he shouted, slapping furiously at his leg with his cane and glaring at Eve. 'Couldn't organize a pillow fight!'

Eve felt dislike for him. Refusing to be ignored she said firmly, 'Private Lewis Harding. He may have been taken sick. Do you think he might be on a stretcher?'

'Anything's possible. If you hurry you might find him up the other end.' He pointed further up the platform. 'Now, you must excuse me.'

He strode away leaving Eve feeling slightly crushed. Miss Harding, however, was already hurrying towards the rows of stretchers on the platform just inside the ticket barrier. Eve hurried to catch up with her, and when she finally reached her she was questioning to a young nurse.

Miss Harding began to make her way along the rows where several other civilians were doing the same thing – looking for their loved ones. She stopped at each one but Eve saw with a jolt of surprise, that she was holding a handkerchief to her face.

'What's happening?' Eve asked the nurse.

The nurse was young with smooth fair hair and a worried expression. 'We think it's influenza,' she told Eve in a low voice, glancing nervously at a nearby doctor to make sure he couldn't hear her. 'Some of the men were already ill when they boarded the ship but others were taken ill on the boat coming over. They have to go into isolation until we know for sure. There's been—' She stopped abruptly as a young man appeared beside them with a camera.

'Good morning, beautiful!' He flashed the nurse a cheeky smile and said, 'I'm from the *London Standard*. What's wrong with these men?' Without giving the nurse time to answer, he took a photograph of them and the flash going off alerted a nearby doctor to his presence.

'No photographs!' he snapped. 'And no interviews. Remember what you were told, Nurse Harrington!'

'Yes, doctor.' She coloured guiltily.

Undeterred the reporter shook his head. 'They look pretty sick to me, these men.'

The doctor closed in on him angrily. 'What do you expect after a rough sea crossing? They were weak to start with. They're dehydrated. They'll be fine. Now take your camera and get out of here.'

The nurse avoided Eve's gaze and moved quickly away.

At that moment Miss Harding called to her. 'Mrs Randall! I've found him!'

Eve hurried round to her, pulling a clean

handkerchief from her pocket and covering her mouth and nose with it.

Lewis Harding lay huddled on his stretcher with his eyes closed. A fine sweat was visible around his bristly beard and his eyes were closed. He was breathing heavily and his arms were clutched around his chest. There were dark stains on his faded uniform and a button was missing from his tunic. Eve stared down at him in shocked silence. Suppose this man was her brother, son or lover – how would she feel, seeing him like this?

'Are you sure it's Lewis?' she asked.

'It looks like him but with the beard...'

Eve turned to the nearest nurse. 'Is there a Lewis Harding on your list?'

The nurse consulted her clipboard. 'Yes. He collapsed just after boarding the train. We're waiting for a vehicle to take them to whichever hospital it is.' She pulled a bundle of small cards from her pocket and handed one to Eve. 'That's a telephone number. They'll give you more information but don't ring today. They're opening the line first thing tomorrow morning.' She moved away and the two women regarded each other doubtfully.

Eve said, 'I daresay she's right. There's nothing more we can do.'

Miss Harding knelt awkwardly beside her nephew and spoke clearly. 'This is Aunt

Edie, Lewis. I hope you can hear me although you seem to be asleep. Um...' She threw Eve a helpless glance then turned back to her nephew. 'I'm going to phone tomorrow – I've been given a special number – to find out where you are ... and maybe come and visit you. So don't worry about anything, Lewis. The doctors will look after you in the hospital. Goodbye for now, dear.' She tried to raise her nephew's head, cradling him awkwardly in her arms. She smoothed his hair and bent to kiss him. 'Oh, Lewis!'

Eve helped her to her feet and saw the tears glistening in her eyes.

Glancing at another young man who lay beside him, Eve saw something about him that sent a frisson of alarm through her – he was so very still. Acting on impulse, Eve stepped nearer and bent to study his face. He looked about eighteen with tousled dark hair which partly hid a scar running diagonally across his forehead, livid against his greyish skin. She had expected his eyes to be closed in sleep but instead they were wide and staring sightlessly. Eve, her throat constricted, recoiled with a gasp of horror. She called urgently to the nurse who hurried back.

'This man...' Eve stammered. 'I think ... He looks...'

Seeing her shocked expression the nurse

immediately knelt beside the young soldier. She put fingers to his bare throat in search of a pulse and then shook her head. Visibly shaken, she pulled the red blanket over his face, bowed her head for a few seconds as if in silent prayer, and then stood up.

'He's dead,' she whispered and ran to tell the Sister.

Eve put an arm round Miss Harding's shoulders. 'Don't think about it,' she said gently. 'Lewis will soon be in good hands, I'm sure, tucked up in a comfortable bed in the hospital. We've done all we can for today, Miss Harding. I know *I* need a cup of tea and I'm sure you do, too. Pop that card into your purse in case you lose it ... That's right.'

Miss Harding looked down at her nephew. She hesitated. 'I don't like to leave him here like this. What will I tell his parents? Suppose he gets worse?'

A woman wearing a blue cape, who looked like a matron, was passing and Miss Harding suddenly clutched at her sleeve. Pointing to Lewis, she said, 'This is my nephew. How can you tell that he's asleep? He might be in a coma!'

Trying to hide her impatience the woman said, 'One way or the other he will soon be in a hospital and receiving suitable treatment. Everything is under control. You must let things take their course.'

'But I'm his *aunt*! Couldn't I take him home and look after him myself?'

'Most certainly not!' The woman drew herself up. 'You must understand that your nephew is still in the army. He is still the responsibility of the military and they must deal with it. There really is no need to panic. I'm sure your nephew will soon be up and about. Go home and let us deal with it.' She moved briskly away.

Unconvinced, Miss Harding looked at Eve. 'What shall we do?'

'I think we'll have to take her advice. Now take my arm and we'll find somewhere to sit down and have a cup of tea. Lewis is in very good hands and he'll pull through. You'll see.'

She spoke confidently in an attempt to comfort her companion but in fact she had been seriously alarmed by the young man's appearance and dismayed to hear that he might be suffering from influenza.

Four

Saturday morning brought a clear sky but it was accompanied by a sharp wind and Eve, on the way to the churchyard, had wrapped a warm scarf round her neck to protect herself from the cold. After seeing to the roses on her father's grave she became aware of Jon's voice further over in the graveyard and made her way towards him. To her surprise she passed not one but two other men, both digging graves.

As she reached Jon, he saw her and straightened up. Ellen stood next to him, holding on to an obviously new hat which the wind was threatening to blow away.

'Hello, Mrs Randall!' she greeted Eve. 'What d'you think of my new hat? Birthday present from my nearest and dearest even though it was a month ago!'

'It's very smart!' Eve hid her surprise as she studied the brown straw hat decorated with matching feathers and yellow ribbons. It looked expensive.

Jon grinned. 'She looks a treat, doesn't she? I told her – every woman should have at least one beautiful hat before she dies!' He put a hand to his back to ease it and for a moment his grin faded as his face scrunched up with pain.

Ellen smiled proudly at him then turned to Eve. In a lowered voice she said, 'It's an ill wind! That's what they say, isn't it? All these people dying means more money for the grave diggers!' She raised her eyebrows humorously.

Jon nodded. 'Two funerals yesterday and another two today – one this morning and another at three. Eight altogether in the past seven days. Mr Hemmings, the church warden, said that was pneumonia; the Linleys's daughter ... and old Sydney from the paper shop. Dunno who else. The vicar's had to find two more grave diggers cos I couldn't cope with it.' He grimaced again and put a hand to his back. 'Can't get rid of this pain in my back.'

Ellen looked at Eve and the laughter had gone. In its place was a worried frown. 'He's been overdoing it. Wearing himself to a frazzle. Dig, dig, dig, from morning to night. If you don't tell the vicar, I will, I told him. Get some help.'

'We've got *two* more chaps digging away. How many more d'you want?' he protested.

Eve felt a shiver of apprehension. 'What is it? What's killing them?'

'Flu,' said Ellen promptly.

'It's influenza,' Jon agreed. 'There's a lot of it about.' He took out a handkerchief and wiped his neck and face.

'You're wearing yourself out, love.'

He shrugged. 'Got to earn the money while you can. Reckon the undertaker's doing all right as well as us, not to mention the doctors. They must be coining it in.' He turned back to his task and the two women regarded each other in silence for a few moments.

'Well, I'd get back home, Jon,' Ellen said. 'Can't leave Kate on her own for too long although I sometimes think she could look after the kids better than I do! So much patience, that girl. But bossy when she needs to be. Puts poor Amy in her place.'

Jon leant on his spade and put a hand to his head. He looked desperately weary, thought Eve. She wanted to suggest that he take the rest of the day off but realized it was none of her business. They obviously wanted the extra wages and would resent her interference.

She walked out of the churchyard with Ellen and told her briefly about meeting Miss Harding's nephew. 'He was obviously unwell,' she said, 'but the nurse tried to suggest it was the result of seasickness. They'd had a rough crossing, apparently.'

'She might have been telling the truth but you never know with medical people.' She glanced guiltily at Eve. 'Just now ... What I said about grave diggers and folks dying. I shouldn't have said it.' She glanced heavenward. 'Sorry, God.'

'I'm sure He'll forgive you.'

'Let's hope so! You know what they say – the wrath of God. That used to scare me when I was a kid. Like suddenly you might be struck by lightning or something if you pinched an apple from the greengrocer.' She shrugged. 'It's just that after scrimping and scraping for years, it's nice to have a few shillings to spend and not have to count every blooming penny!'

'I knew you were joking. And I understood. Jon's working hard and he deserves his money. What would we do without grave diggers?'

'I didn't want him to spend so much on the hat but he was so keen to treat me. The first nice present since we were wed.' Her smile returned. 'Kate and Amy got new shoes and Lucy got a little doll.'

'And Sam?'

'Nothing – but he's too young to appreciate anything. Well, love you and leave you. Remember me to your mother.'

'I will.' She watched Ellen as she disappeared round the bend in the road, proudly clutching her new hat, the feathers and ribbons fluttering cheerfully in the wind.

Eve and her mother were in the parlour when the knock came on the front door.

Dorothy glanced up from her knitting with interest. They had very few visitors and she always enjoyed company. 'I wonder who that is?'

Eve looked out of the window. 'It's Miss Harding! I expect she has news of her nephew.'

'Let's hope so, poor soul.'

One look at Miss Harding's face, however, and Eve knew the news was bad. Her new friend had been crying and she still clutched a handkerchief as if the tears were very recent.

'I had to come. I have to talk to someone and I thought you wouldn't mind.' Her voice shook slightly and Eve took hold of her free hand.

'Of course I don't mind. Please come in. My mother is sitting downstairs with me for an hour or so. She'll be pleased to see you.'

She led the way into the parlour and her mother smiled in welcome.

'Excuse me for not getting up,' she said. 'I'm a bit of an invalid, to tell the truth but ... O-oh!' Her smile wavered as Miss Harding got nearer and the reddened eyes warned her something was wrong. She glanced nervously at Eve who was guiding her visitor to a chair.

'Is it about Lewis?' she asked gently.

Miss Harding nodded. 'I rang the address the nurse gave me but I wasn't the next of kin so they wouldn't tell me anything. I got a telegram this morning from his parents to say ... saying that...' Her eyes filled with tears. 'Saying that he's gone. Dead. My poor lamb! I can't quite believe it. I'll never see him again – except in his coffin.'

'I'm so sorry,' said Eve.

Her mother said, 'After you had gone all that way to meet him. What a shame. But you did what you could for him.'

'But he's gone! Oh, Lewis!'

Tears streamed down her face and Eve handed her a clean handkerchief and murmured some words of consolation. Meaningless words which could do nothing to stem Miss Harding's grief. Not that she expected to. Eve believed that grief should be expressed. In her opinion it was normal and the body's way of starting the healing process. Being brave and tight-lipped was simply storing up problems for the future.

To her surprise her mother folded her knitting and stowed it away. 'Suppose I make us a pot of tea. It will give these old legs of mine some exercise. A warm sugary drink is very good for shock,' she said. 'You two need to talk.'

Eve watched in amazement as her mother rose from the chair and made her way unsteadily from the room. It was a long time since her mother had done anything but lie in bed or sit in a chair. It had taken Miss Harding's arrival to inspire some activity. Eve called, 'I'll bring the tray in, Mother, if you tell me when it's ready.'

Miss Harding wiped her eyes and took a deep breath. 'He died the same night,' she told Eve. 'They had just settled him in his hospital bed when he began to cough violently. It must have exhausted him. Moments later he was gone.'

Eve searched desperately for something comforting to say. 'How wonderful that you saw him on the station,' she said. 'You saw him and you were able to hold him and say goodbye.'

'But he didn't know, did he? He was unconscious.'

'Maybe but the doctors say that unconscious people can still hear although they can't respond. You kissed him and spoke to him and I'm sure he heard you.'

Her words appeared to have stemmed the flow of tears as Miss Harding considered this possibility.

'Do you think so? Oh, I do hope you're

right because then it means he heard a familiar voice before he died.' There was a spark of hope in her eyes. 'Because, of course, he didn't see his parents. How dreadful to come all the way home and die without seeing your family.'

Eve nodded, partly distracted by the sounds from the kitchen. Her mother hadn't made a pot of tea for at least three years and would be searching for everything. The unkind thought entered her mind that her mother had been exaggerating her weakness for a very long time.

'He heard your voice,' she told Miss Harding, 'and so he knew he was home in England. That must have been wonderful for him – and he died in a comfortable bed being properly cared for.' Unlike the poor soldier who died on the platform, she reflected.

Miss Harding was brightening slowly. 'At least he wasn't left for dead on the battlefield. I suppose we must be thankful for small mercies.'

At that moment Dorothy called and Eve hurried out to the kitchen. Her mother had found the tray and three cups and saucers and the kettle was boiling.

'Where's the sugar?' she asked. 'And the milk jug? Really, Eve, it's impossible to find anything in this kitchen.'

'Do you think so?' Eve counted to ten silently. 'The sugar's in that blue jar marked sugar and the milk jug is upside down on the draining board.'

'Oh, well, no wonder I couldn't find them.' She steadied herself with one hand on the table. 'I mustn't overtire myself, dear. I'll leave the rest to you. Do we have any biscuits?'

'We always have biscuits, Mother.' As Eve reached for the biscuit barrel, her mother left her to it and made her way back into the parlour.

When eventually Eve carried the tray in, she saw that Dorothy had resumed her knitting and was explaining why she had changed from sending socks to sailors in favour of providing gloves for soldiers.

Minutes later, sipping her tea gratefully, Miss Harding turned to Eve. 'Have you heard from that husband of yours?'

'Not for the last few weeks but his letters are often well spaced out. It depends if the ship gets through, although recently the German submarines have been less active. But I'm not complaining,' she added quickly. 'He's desperately busy and probably too tired to write.'

'Eve's husband is on very important work,' Dorothy said. 'He's helping to stamp out a nasty outbreak of influenza in America. He's a scientist and they are all doing vital work, contributing to the war effort.'

Eve thought she sounded very defensive.

'I'm sure he is,' Miss Harding said, sighing deeply as she accepted a second cup of tea. 'Another biscuit? Oh, yes, please. I suppose I must look after myself. It's all been such a shock.'

'Life must go on,' Dorothy agreed. 'Your nephew wouldn't want you to fall into a decline with grief. That can sometimes happen if you aren't aware of the danger.'

Eve said, 'I went into the butcher's recently and there was no sign of Mr Thwaite. His wife was serving and he had cut some chops and made the sausages before they opened the shop. "He can't bear the sympathy people offer," she told me. Poor soul – and his wife is also suffering, naturally, but he is still in deep shock. Hardly speaks. Doesn't eat. Refuses to go to church. The vicar called on them to express commiserations but I hear Mr Thwaite gave him short shrift, it seems.'

Dorothy sipped her tea. 'I wonder if he would like a pair of mittens. The butcher, I mean, not the vicar. His hands must get cold in that shop in the winter. No heating and customers coming in and out and letting the cold air in.'

'I think he'd be delighted,' Eve said.

Her mother smiled. 'I could make them striped – navy and khaki.' She glanced at Miss Harding again but the elderly school teacher was busy with her own thoughts, absorbed in her own sorrow.

Near the end of October there was a loud knock on the front door and Eve opened it to find Kate outside with Sam in his battered pram and Amy holding Lucy by the hand.

'Got any more of them biscuits?' Kate asked. 'Cos we'd like some if they're going spare.'

Lucy said, 'Bithkit!'

'Clever girl.' Amy looked at Eve. 'She can talk already. Ma says she's going to be clever when she grows up. She going to be the clever one.'

Kate's face darkened. 'No, she's not. It's Sam. He's going to be the clever one.'

'But he can't talk yet, so how d'you know?' Amy glared at Kate.

'Because I just do!' She turned her attention back to Eve. 'Have you got any biscuits?'

Eve hesitated. 'You shouldn't ask, Kate. It's not good manners.'

Amy said, 'See! I told you she wouldn't.'

Kate was looking desperate. It was obvious, thought Eve, that she had promised the children biscuits. It was a matter of pride for

Kate that the promised treat materialized. If not, Amy would gloat over her downfall. As she looked into Kate's intense eyes, she knew she would have to support her.

'I do have some biscuits,' she admitted. 'If you ask properly you can all have one.'

'She means "please".' Amy prompted.

'I know what she means!' snapped Kate. 'I don't need you to tell me, so shut up!' She turned to Eve. 'Please, miss.'

Amy stared past her curiously. 'Can we come in?'

'I don't think so,' said Eve, anticipating the chaos that might well ensue.

'Why not?' Kate gave her a fierce look.

'Er...' Eve searched her mind for a convincing excuse that would be better than a truthful answer. 'My mother's asleep in bed and you might wake her.'

The child's face fell. 'But we can still have some biscuits, can't we?'

Eve was wavering. Should she be encouraging them? They might start to call round every day! What was it her mother used to say? 'Give them an inch and they'll take a yard.'

The three pairs of eyes watched her beseechingly while the baby kicked so violently that his threadbare blanket slid off. Eve instinctively leaned forward, intent on recovering him, but Kate was there before her.

She snatched at the blanket and tucked him in then gave Eve a triumphant glance.

Eve said, 'Wait there and I'll fetch the biscuits.' She moved to close the door but at that moment Sam began to cry and both Kate and Amy bent over to fuss him. As they argued over who should plump up the baby's grubby pillow, a man cycling past said, 'Kids!' and winked at Eve.

She was mortified. He thought the unruly children were hers. 'You'd better all come inside,' she said hastily. 'Just for a few moments.'

Before the words were out of her mouth the children were all fighting to get through the front door and Eve had to flatten herself against the wall to prevent her feet from being run over by the pram. They all followed Kate into the kitchen and Eve closed the front door with the distinct feeling that she had made a mistake and should have left them outside. Too late! She wondered what Harvey would say if he could see them.

Once in the kitchen Eve gave each girl a biscuit and watched them gobble it down. 'So, where are you all off to?' she asked.

Kate shrugged. 'Ma said, "Get out and stay out! I need a rest." So we come round here. Can I have another one?'

'And me!' cried Amy.

Lucy said, 'Bithkit!' They all laughed.

'She's going to be clever,' Amy repeated.

Eve handed round the biscuits. 'Is your pa still busy?' she asked.

Amy shook her head. 'He's at home.'

Kate gave her a push. 'I'll tell it!' She turned to Eve. 'Pa's not feeling too good with his back and everything and because he got a dreadful fright yesterday evening and Ma says he's still shocked. He was helping another man with a coffin and they dropped it and it broke open and—'

Amy said, 'And the dead body fell out ... Ouch!' She glared at Kate who had pinched her arm.

'I'm telling her!' Kate said with a distinct note of desperation in her voice. 'Because I'm the oldest.' She turned back to Eve. 'So this old boy fell right out on to the grass and his wife fell down and Pa—'

'She fell down in a dead faint,' Amy interrupted.

'All right – in a dead faint – and then they had to carry the dead man and drop him in the grave because his coffin was all broke and...'

Lucy said, 'Bithkit!'

Kate ignored her. 'Pa says he was all old and his face was a funny colour...'

'And he smelled!' cried Amy. She met her sister's gaze and held her nose and suddenly both girls began to giggle.

Disconcerted, Eve said, 'Poor man. You shouldn't laugh.'

Kate straightened her face. 'Stop laughing,' she told Amy but immediately they were both giggling and then Lucy joined in.

Eve watched helplessly until, with an effort, Kate controlled her giggles and carried on with her story. 'His face was a funny brown colour, Pa said, and he was all cold and nasty but some of him was wrapped in a sheet and Pa says they threw the broken coffin in after him and when his wife woke up—'

Amy interrupted again. 'You forgot where they threw all the earth in and then...' She moved swiftly to avoid another pinch.

Kate tutted at yet another disruption. 'So they threw all the earth in and when the man's wife woke up they picked her up off the grass and said he was dead and buried properly and she'd missed it all.' She grinned impishly. 'Ma laughed like a drain!'

Eve didn't know whether to laugh or cry. The three girls were all staring at her. Waiting for a reaction. She said, 'Oh, dear! How dreadful!' Seeing their blank looks she added, 'I daresay it was rather funny.'

'There's only one biscuit left so shall I take it for Pa?' Kate asked.

'If you like.' Meekly Eve handed it to Kate who buried it carefully below the threadbare blanket in the pram. To her sisters she said, 'Right. You've had your biscuits. We're going. Say goodbye to the nice lady.'

'Goodbye!' they chorused obediently.

Amy grabbed the handle of the pram but Kate fought her off and the younger girl settled once more for Lucy.

The journey back to the front door was a little more decorous than their entrance had been and within minutes Eve was watching them make their way along the pavement, still bickering half-heartedly, without a single glance back.

As Eve closed the front door she was surprised to feel a vague sense of loss ... and the children had obviously forgotten her instantly. Illogically she felt rejected.

Then she heard her mother's bedside bell.

'What's going on down there?' Dorothy called and Eve made her way upstairs to tell her about their unexpected visitors. She retold the children's story, making light of it but when she reached the part about the body falling from its coffin her mother looked alarmed.

'What did he die of, this man?'

'I don't know. She didn't say.'

'It could have been influenza.'

'Oh...!' Eve's calm gave way to unease. If it had been influenza, could Jon have caught the disease from the corpse? Could he have passed it on? Eve clasped her hands nervously. She had stupidly invited all his children into the house! Her unease increased as she considered how vulnerable her mother would be if the influenza virus *had* been brought into the house. If anything happened to her, she would never forgive herself.

That night she lay awake until the early hours of the morning, wrestling with her conscience. If Jon had flu, she wondered, how on earth would Ellen cope with four children to care for – and suppose they caught it from their father. It was a frightning thought. Should she visit to see how they were faring? Maybe that was asking for trouble. She herself might catch the flu and then who would care for *her*? She thought about lying ill with no one to look after her mother.

The girls' description of the corpse who had fallen from his coffin worried her. The dark face was not a normal symptom of the flu but her husband had hinted at a more severe form of the disease.

There was a growing idea forming in her mind that she tried to ignore but it persisted. Just how far-reaching was this epidemic? She knew it was taking hold in America and that it was attacking the troops in Europe. Was it also prevalent among the enemy troops? And was it taking hold elsewhere in the world? What about Australia? Probably too far removed from it. New Zealand also. And South Africa? Eastern Europe, India...

The whole world? she thought to herself. But no. That was ridiculous, she reassured herself. That was a doom-laden scenario and she was being melodramatic. To distract herself from such dire thoughts she thought about Harvey but even this failed to comfort her because a letter from him was long overdue and he *was* in danger from the disease at Camp Devens. Possibly his own position was more dangerous than many a soldier on the battlefield.

'Please write to me, darling!' she whispered into the darkness. 'And come home soon and I will do my best to give you a child.'

He isn't dead, she told herself fiercely. He is *not* dead. I'll see him again. I will.

Eve sat in the kitchen with an unopened envelope clutched in her hand and waited for the dizziness to pass. The postmark and the unfamiliar handwriting warned her that the news was bad and she could not bear to open it. Seeing the words she dreaded would bring an end to her happiness and destroy everything she had lived for.

Open it, Eve! she told herself. You have to know. There's still hope.

But suppose it merely confirmed that her beloved Harvey was gone from her forever? Upstairs her mother's bell rang but Eve made no move to respond. Ring away, she thought dully, I cannot come to you. Indeed it felt that all her energy had been sucked from her and that climbing the stairs would be a physical impossibility.

'Eve? Are you there?'

No, thought Eve. I'm not here. The Eve you know is gone forever. Here there is only a shell. A lookalike. A woman who was once Eve Randall but is now a widow. She tried to imagine Harvey's last hours – no doubt in a hospital bed in an overcrowded ward, surrounded by other men, all as sick and as helpless as he was. The nurses would have done their best, she knew, and the doctors, too. They needed him to be alive doing his vital research. But somehow he had slipped away. He would have been thinking of her, she knew. He would have whispered her name...

She shivered. Her eyes were focussed on the envelope but all around her there was darkness she didn't understand, a darkness that seemed to cut her off from the life that went on around her.

'Eve? Where are you?' The bell rang again.

Eve remained silent. Her shivering deepened until she was shaking all over. Her heart seemed to have stopped beating. I'm going to die of shock, she thought, and prayed that she would.

From upstairs she heard the bedsprings as her mother left her bed and prepared to come to the top of the stairs and call her. Eve stared at the unopened envelope. If I don't read it, it needn't be true, she told herself again.

'Eve?' Footsteps on the stairs.

With her eyes closed, Eve waited as her mother came down the stairs and into the kitchen. Even then she didn't open her eyes. She knew she would see the shock in her mother's face as she saw the letter and understood its significance.

She heard her mother's sharp intake of breath.

'Oh, no! Eve! Oh God!'

Eve said 'Sit down, Mother, before you fall down.' She opened her eyes slowly. 'It's come. It's our turn. I thought he was safe but...' Her voice shook.

She watched as Dorothy lowered herself on to a chair.

'Open it, dear,' Dorothy said gently. 'You have to do it. This is the worst moment and you must get it all over and done with. Read the letter, Eve.'

Hardly knowing what she was doing, Eve obeyed her. Her fingers slid through the flimsy envelope and she unfolded the single sheet of paper. Silently she read the typed message but it meant little. She handed it to her mother.

After a moment Dorothy said, 'He was a good man, Eve.'

'How could he leave me?' she said desperately. 'How could he let this happen?'

Uninvited, Miss Harding's image rose before her and it was followed by the butcher and his wife. Only now did she understand what they had gone through. Can they survive? she wondered. Can I?

Wordlessly Dorothy filled the inevitable kettle and Eve heard her scooping three spoonfuls of tea into the teapot. Then Dorothy went into the parlour and closed the curtains. She went slowly upstairs and did the same in the front bedroom. Now all who passed the house would sigh and shake their heads. Another bereavement. Another broken heart.

It was a relief when her mother started to cry and Eve felt able to join her. No chance now of the family they had longed for. Harvey was gone and with it their chance of future happiness.

Once Eve had started to cry she couldn't stop. Her mother had sent her up to bed and had done her best to comfort her but eventually, seeing her daughter still prostrate with grief the following day, Dorothy sent for the doctor. He shook his head sadly, recommended rest and prescribed her a strong sleeping draught and watched until it took effect.

'That will see her through the next few hours,' he said to Dorothy, as Eve slept, 'and give her a chance to recover her senses. Grief is hard to deal with and it saps mind, body and soul together.'

Dorothy stared down at her daughter. 'She wanted a family,' she said softly. 'Harvey would have been a good father.'

'She might wed again. Give her time.'

'I think Harvey was her only love. It was a love match. She could never love anyone else.'

'We must hope you're wrong.'

Dorothy gave him a stern look. 'I think I know my own daughter, doctor!'

His look was equally stern. 'I shall pray you are mistaken, Mrs Collett. Life goes on.' He packed his bag and fastened the straps then helped her down the stairs but when they reached the hall he frowned. 'Will you be able to care for her? I could try and find a nurse but there is so much sickness.'

'Yes, doctor, I can manage.'

He seemed not to hear her, immersed once more in his own thoughts.

'This terrible flu! I've never seen anything like it in all my days as a medical man. They say Europe is also suffering and America ... Still, we do what we can.'

He promised to look in again when he could, but made no more promises. He had too many patients who needed him more than Eve.

Dorothy surprised herself over the next few days. She looked after her daughter, with the help of Mrs Banks, and in doing so found a new purpose in life. Struggling from her sick bed to rescue her daughter made her feel something of a heroine and she found her new life more stimulating than her old existence although she did not admit this to anyone. When she went to bed each night she fell into a well-deserved slumber and had no need of sleeping draughts. Each day was a new challenge which she relished and Mrs Banks's admiration and her daughter's gratitude buoyed her spirits and recharged her self-confidence.

'What would I do without you, Mother?' Eve asked, when on the fourth day she sat up, weak and drained, to face up to the rest of her shattered life.

'Nonsense, dear!' Dorothy cried, giving her a quick hug. 'It was nothing. What are mothers for, if they can't help in times of trouble.'

Dorothy watched her daughter cautiously. This was only the beginning and Eve had a long way to go before she could face the world without her husband. 'Mrs Banks will bring you up your hot-water jug and there's a new bar of Pears soap. I know how you like it. And you may use some of my lavender talcum. That will make you feel fresh and you can slide back into bed and I'll...'

'I shall come downstairs today,' said Eve. 'I have to. Please don't argue with me, Mother. I've done a lot of thinking. I'm no worse off than any other widowed woman and God knows there are plenty of those. Tomorrow I shall go out.' Her pale thin face was set in grimly determined lines – an expression Dorothy recalled from Eve's childhood.

'I can't bear to think ... That is, I have to find a way to forget.' Her voice shook. 'Not Harvey, of course, but the fact that he has gone. I have to *do* something!'

After a small protest Dorothy gave in. It was true. Millions of women throughout the world had lost husbands, brothers and sons in the war. Children had lost fathers. Now Eve had lost Harvey and nothing anyone could do would bring him back.

Eve said, 'First thing tomorrow I shall go round to the butcher's and see how they are – and I must visit Miss Harding.'

Dorothy did not argue. She knew she must

now stand to one side and watch as her daughter found a way to deal with the sorrow and began to build herself a new life. She reminded herself that Eve would be better to keep occupied and not dwell on her loss. Dorothy could see that the war might end soon and that life as they barely remembered it, might return for all those that survived. She wanted Eve to be ready for it.

Five

It was eleven at night that same evening, in a small room in Camp Devens. The white-walled room, adjacent to the morgue, was where the pathologists 'washed up' after their work before leaving for their quarters. James Ferber entered. He looked desperately tired, his eyes red-rimmed from lack of sleep and a deeply unsatisfying day at work.

He had been examining the dead less than two minutes ago – a mournful task. Normally he went through the familiar procedures without a second thought but, of late, the numbers of the dead and the manner of their passing bore down on him and depressed his spirits. So many young men, eager for life, were ending up on his examining table and there seemed no end to it. He tried to tell himself that at least they avoided death on a foreign field, shot down and left to die while their comrades rushed heedlessly past, each with his own fear in his eyes ... but the thought brought him little consolation.

He tossed his rubber gloves into the bin,

washed his hands carefully and dried them on a clean cloth which he then threw into the laundry bin. At the start of the epidemic he had considered bringing Louise and Toby near to the base so that he could go home at the end of each working day. He had wanted to retain his links with the family but his great fear was of infecting them. He therefore decided to stay on the base for the duration of the emergency. As soon as it ended, he promised, he would go home to them.

Earlier this evening he had joined a few other members of the team in the dining room for a mug of coffee but had been too tired to eat any of the stale cake or biscuits provided. The kitchen staff were under a tremendous strain, trying to provide invalid food for the patients as well as normal meals for the rest of the men. He was permanently hungry but was too tired to do anything about it.

Now, James's back ached from bending over his subjects and his brain reeled from the intense concentration required. All he wanted was to get back to the privacy of his room. He said goodnight to the few colleagues around him and made his way unsteadily back to his room. Letting himself in with his key, he closed the door behind him and let out a sigh of relief.

Leaning back against the closed door, he

stared round his room in a haze of exhaustion.

'What am I supposed to be doing?' he muttered.

The answer came to him and he slid on to the solitary chair and drew pen and paper from the drawer in the desk. More than anything he wanted to re-read his wife's last letter, stare at the photograph of her and two-year-old Toby and then go to sleep, but an unpleasant task nagged at his conscience, demanding to be done.

'Sorry, Louise!' he said aloud with a faint smile. At least he received regular letters from her. Harvey, poor devil, had had very few letters from England from his wife. James promised himself he would write to Louise tomorrow before he started the day's work – if he could wake early enough! It often felt, at the end of another nightmare day, that he might never wake again.

With a deep sigh he reached for the inkstand and, from beneath it, drew out the folded letter Harvey Randall had written to his wife, Eve.

'Sorry, Harvey!' he muttered to himself, even more guiltily. By now the notification of death would be on its way to his poor widow so by the time this letter reached her, she would know that her husband had succumbed to the disease. Maybe a letter from

Harvey would ease her grief a little. Whatever words his friend had found to write for
her were his last and Eve would doubtless
treasure them.

James thought about the influenza and
wondered if it had reached Europe. If so was
it anywhere near London? Was there any risk
of influenza where the Randalls lived? If so
Eve might have an idea how terrible the end
had been for the man she loved. He hoped
she had been spared that. With a deep sigh
he turned his thoughts to the wording of his
accompanying note and took a pad of note-
paper from the desk drawer.

Dear Mrs Randall,
   I am sure that by now you will have
heard the sad news of your husband's
untimely death. I am enclosing a letter
from him – the last one he wrote. As soon
as he knew he was sick he wrote this letter
and made me promise to forward it to you
if he should die. I hope it brings you great
comfort and helps you through the coming weeks and months.

It sounded so trite, he thought uneasily,
but how else did one write to the bereaved?
Was there a kinder way? He shrugged and
continued.

I shall always remember the friendship I shared with him, brief though it was. We talked whenever we had the chance about our loved ones and your name was always uppermost in his thoughts. I know how much he loved you. He carried your photograph with him and talked about the end of the war when you would be reunited.

Each in our own field, we worked to overcome the disease and shared the frustration that so far we have not achieved significant results...

He re-read it unhappily. Possibly it was too cold and clinical. He was a warm, passionate man and could write lovingly to his wife in a way that would inspire and comfort her but Eve Randall was a complete stranger. It was difficult to write to another man's wife. He hoped Eve would understand that he was doing the best he could.

Your husband was a brave, selfless man and worked relentlessly for his fellow men. Please rest assured that he was among friends when he died. The doctors and nurses did everything they could to save him and saw to it that he suffered very little...

What a lie, he thought. There was no way to die from this particular influenza without suffering. James rubbed his eyes wearily and straightened his back. Pushing aside the dread that one day he, too, might die, James forced himself to continue the letter that would accompany Harvey's final message.

I shall miss him and I grieve for your loss and wish I could do more. I send you my condolences and sincere best wishes for the future.
Yours regretfully,
James Ferber (Camp Devens)

Folding it, he pushed both letters into a larger envelope and found the address – 22 Shardeloes Road, Brockley, London, England. For a moment he stared at it, trying to imagine the postman walking up to Number 22, on a road of terraced houses with sooty walls and the distant roar of London's traffic. Harvey had once described his home and James had been struck by the difference in their backgrounds.

This address was London, the largest city in the world or so they said. He had seen photographs of London. Buckingham Palace and Marble Arch sprang to mind. He had always wanted to visit London but Louise was 'a home body' and the idea of travelling to Europe had always caused her great anxiety. After Toby was born she had flatly refused to even consider taking him abroad and James had reluctantly relinquished the idea.

He sealed the flap of the envelope before he decided to alter it in any way.

'Brockley, London, England,' he repeated and, with a sigh of relief, he propped the envelope on the desk. Setting aside pen and ink he pulled off his clothes and prepared belatedly for bed. He intended to say a prayer for his friend's soul but as soon as his head touched the pillow, he fell at once into an exhausted sleep.

The bells were ringing when Eve awoke which reminded her that it was Sunday.

'And November!' she marvelled. Soon it would be Christmas – not the first without Harvey but the first when she knew he was never coming home. From now on there would be many reminders of her loss – the first Christmas without him, the first Easter, his birthday which he could never celebrate again. She recalled the first birthday she had shared with him, on a rented houseboat on the Thames. Just the two of them. The sun had shone for the entire week and they had lazed on the river bank with a picnic or strolled in to the town for lunch at the Jolly

Bear. She'd prepared a meal for him on his actual birthday – cold chicken and ham from the nearby delicatessen, with cold potato salad. Afterwards she had lit a small candle and stuck it into an iced bun ... Would she ever be able to eat a similar meal again without missing Harvey?

Swallowing hard, she pushed the memories from her. Time to remember them when the country was once more at peace and the epidemic had worn itself out.

No feeling sorry for yourself, she urged herself. No self-pity, either. You have it no worse than anyone else. Think about others.

The brave words had a false ring to them, she knew, because she *did* feel sorry for herself but she would never confess it. She had put off leaving the house but today she would visit the butcher and his wife, then Miss Harding and lastly the Beattys. What would happen to Ellen and the children if Jon died?

She carried up Dorothy's breakfast.

'And not a moment too soon!' her mother told her. Eve sat down on a chair beside the bed watching her enjoy the toast and honey. 'I've rallied round, Eve dear, but it hasn't been easy. It's surprising what the body can do in an emergency.'

'You've been wonderful, Mother. Amazing. I would have been lost without you.' The words came from her heart. Her mother *had* amazed her and she was tremendously grateful. Now she was willing for Dorothy to retreat to her bed once more. She, Eve, would learn to live and accept her new life – whatever that was – without complaint. At some stage she would find out whether or not she would receive a widow's pension but it seemed unlikely. She and her mother might have to move to smaller accommodation and they might have to make certain economies – less food on the table, less coal in the grate, even renovating old clothes. But we can survive, Eve told herself, repeating the words like a mantra.

'We can do it! We can survive.' Without thinking she spoke aloud.

'What's that, dear?'

'I'm reminding myself that we can carry on. Whatever happens, we have our health.'

'And the will to go on. Don't forget will power, Eve. It's a powerful force.'

An hour later Eve entered the butcher's shop and found it empty apart from Mary Thwaite who smiled and wished her, 'Good morning.'

A young lad came in after Eve. He was busy pulling off his bicycle clips and ignored her entirely.

'Is that it, then, missus?' he asked the butcher's wife.

'You've delivered it all?' she asked.

'All except Number Three Hawthorn Road who was out so I left it on the back step in the box like you said. And I've put the bike in the shed round the back.' He handed over the clips and held out his hand. 'Can I 'ave me money?'

'You can.' Mary Thwaite fumbled in the till drawer, picking out coins. 'Were there any messages?'

He screwed up his face in an effort to remember. 'Don't think so.'

'That's not good enough.' She glared at him as he scratched his untidy hair. 'Were there or weren't there?'

'Er ... yes, there was one. Number Seven Shardeloes Road said the mutton was a bit on the tough side and her old man grumbled.'

Mary bridled. 'She would, silly great lump. Tough, indeed! Mutton needs slow cooking. She should learn to cook. Here, take your money and be on your way – and eight o'clock sharp tomorrow. Not five past.'

Both women watched him go.

Eve forced a bright smile.

Mary said, 'You're quite a stranger. I said to my husband, I do hope Mrs Randall has not gone down with this nasty flu. I haven't seen...' She paused, regarding Eve with narrowed eyes.

101

Eve's smile faltered under the scrutiny as she tried to remember what she planned to say about Harvey's death. The words escaped her. Instead she asked, 'How are you both?'

The woman shrugged. 'We keep going. What else can you do?'

Suddenly Eve's hand went straight to her heart and the fingers spread protectively. She had planned to come right out with the fact of Harvey's death but now the moment had come her heart began to beat rapidly and no sound would come from her parched throat. In the ensuing silence she saw realization dawn in the other woman's face.

'Oh, my dear!' Mary said. 'Not you too! Not your husband? I thought ... I mean, he wasn't a soldier.'

Eve shook her head. 'It was the influenza.'

'Influenza? In America, you mean?'

Eve nodded. She felt slightly dizzy. Don't faint, she told herself. This little woman didn't faint when her son died so why should you. When their telegram came she ran into the shop and ministered to her husband. Stand up straight, Eve Randall, and say something. Clutching the counter edge she stiffened her spine and forced words from her unwilling mouth. 'Harvey was a scientist. They were trying to find a cure.'

'And did they?'

'Not as far as I know ... when he last wrote.' She took a deep breath and knew that she was steadying.

Mary came round from behind the counter, took hold of her hands and pressed them to her chest. 'It gets a little easier,' she told Eve huskily. 'Day by day. I tell myself our lad loved us and he'd want us to recover. He wouldn't want us to go under, crying every time we thought about him. He'd want us to talk about all the lovely times we had together before this blinking war started.'

Eve nodded. 'And does it help, thinking that way?'

Mary released her hands. 'Sometimes. Sometimes not. Eric's finding it harder. He's full of hate for the Germans. I'm trying not to think about blame. The way I see it, some poor German mothers and fathers are going through the same as us and it's not their fault either.'

Eve sighed. 'I try not to think about Harvey but that seems wrong, too. It's hard to know what to do for the best.'

'I look at it this way. All these months our lads out there suffered in those horrible trenches and got shot at and everything. Well, now it's our turn. We shouldn't complain because they didn't complain, bless them. They made the best of a bad job and tried to keep cheerful.'

Eve could only nod, her eyes already filling with unshed tears.

Mary continued. 'Eric had such plans for the lad. Wanted to open another shop for him when he was older, maybe in Lewisham. He was always planning, was Eric. Losing our boy has knocked all the stuffing out of him, poor lamb. He's a big chap but he's a softie at heart and he thought the world of our lad.'

'I'm sorry.' Eve swallowed hard.

'You can't imagine the world without them, can you?' Tears glistened in Mary's eyes.

'I keep waiting for the postman, half expecting another letter from him but ... there never will be one, will there?'

Both women were silent. Eve longed to offer some kind of comfort but knew only too well that there was none. At last she said, 'No funeral for your lad either. That's very hard.'

There was another silence.

Mary said, 'But your man *will* have a burial and a headstone. Will you go to America one day?'

The idea had never occurred to Eve and she glanced up, startled.

'It's possible, I daresay, but not while my mother is still alive.'

From the rear of the shop a voice called,

'Mary!'

Mary called, 'Coming, dear!' She released Eve's hands and bustled back behind the counter. 'You shall have four sausages and blow the rationing. Two for you and two for your mother. She'll have had a bad shock, too, you see, and she'll be worrying about you. You must feed her as well as yourself.' She seized a sheet of newspaper and wrapped the sausages with practised movements of her thin wrists. Thrusting them into Eve's hands, she said, 'You heard about Jon Beatty, did you? That poor woman with all those children!'

'Jon Beatty?' Eve was jerked from her self-pity by the words. 'He's not ... Oh, no! Not Jon!'

'Dead. Yes.'

'I didn't know! I'm on my way round to see them.' She accepted the sausages, paid for them, and put them in her basket.

'They say it was those corpses they were burying. One fell from his coffin and...' She shrugged. 'Who knows. He might have caught the sickness from him.'

Eve thought about Miss Harding and asked after her.

'She's well as far as I know but she hasn't been in.'

They parted company and feeling vaguely stronger, Eve walked slowly towards Miss

Harding's house. Please God, she thought, don't let me find her a victim also. In her mind's eye she saw the elderly school teacher kneeling on the platform beside her sick nephew. She had kissed him. Was that enough to contaminate her?

She knocked on the door while her heart fluttered with anxiety. There was no answer so she tried again, louder. Perhaps she was lying in bed, already sick. Before Eve could decide what to do, the front door of the next house opened and a tousle-haired man blinked owlishly at her. 'She's not there. Gone to stay with her folks. Death in the family.'

He began to close the door.

'Wait, please! Who has died? Was it the nephew or someone else?'

'Nephew. She'll be back some time but don't ask me when.' This time he closed the door firmly before she could delay him further.

No doubt Miss Harding had gone to console the young soldier's parents, thought Eve. His death would have devastated the family. With a heavy heart Eve turned away, wondering if she had the stomach to visit the Beattys. She found herself walking in the direction of their house and was soon knocking on the door.

It was opened by Amy who stared at her

until recognition came. 'The biscuit lady,' she said.

Eve smiled. 'I'd like to speak to your mother. Is she in?'

Amy frowned in concentration. Then she said, 'I'm to say, "No we're not and please go away!"' The child's face was pale and there were traces of jam around her mouth. Relieved at having remembered her little speech she continued eagerly. 'We went to Pa's funeral in the rain and we all said a prayer about Jesus and then two men put his coffin in the big hole and Ma was crying. She said it would blooming rain and we said another prayer but the bell didn't toll and Ma says it's a wicked shame, us being Christians and all and Pa being a grave digger!' She blinked indignantly.

So Eve had missed Jon's funeral. 'I'm sorry I didn't come.' Illogically Eve felt she had let them down. 'Will you tell your mother it's Mrs Randall and I want to speak to her?'

'Kate says we don't need interfering busybodies around here.'

'I don't want to interfere, Amy, I just want to help.' A thought occurred to her. 'Where is Kate?'

'She's sick and so is Sam. Ma's got her work cut out and...'

As Amy argued, a window was pushed up overhead and Ellen's head and shoulders appeared. Her hair was matted, there were dark circles under her eyes, her face was bright with fever above the crumpled night-dress.

'I've nothing to say,' she shouted. 'We don't want nothing! Go...' She stopped and squinted down at Eve. 'Oh! It's you!'

'I heard about Jon. I didn't know. I'm so very sorry. I wondered if I could...'

Ellen shook her head. 'We don't need any help. We're all right. We just want to be left in peace.'

'But Amy says...'

'I tell you we're all right.' Her voice rose querulously. 'Just go away!'

'But maybe I could fetch something – from the chemist, perhaps. Or the doctor.'

Ellen began to cough but when she re-covered she insisted that they didn't need any doctors. There was a faint cry from with-in the room behind her and she disappeared briefly. When she returned she said, 'We can manage. Go away!' Then the window slid down with a bang that effectively ended the conversation.

Amy regarded Eve with waning interest.

Eve said, 'Do you have any money? Has the doctor been to see your ma and Sam and Kate? Are *you* well?'

Amy shook her head. 'Ma says if the doctor comes he'll take her away and stick her in the hospital and we'll be left alone and then we'll all die.' This depressing forecast did not appear to disturb her.

'Where's Lucy?'

'She's asleep.'

Eve thought quickly. 'Look, Amy, I'm going to buy some medicine for them and ... and some nice food. You'd like some biscuits, wouldn't you?'

Amy nodded.

'Then when I come back you must be a big girl and open the door for me. I won't try and come in but you must take the food and medicine to your ma. You understand? You must open the door to me. I'll knock three times. Knock, knock, knock! Like that.'

Amy looked confused but there was no time to worry about that. Pleased to have something positive to do, Eve hurried off to the chemist shop in the next road and bought a large bottle of tonic and some pills which the chemist recommended.

'They're very good,' he confided. 'Can't get enough of them. Bring you round a treat, they do.' He parcelled up the items, added them up on a scrap of paper and handed it to her. 'There you are. One shilling and one penny – but for you we'll call it a shilling!' He smiled cheerfully. As Eve opened her purse he rubbed his hands. 'Lot of it about,' he said. 'An epidemic, that's what this is. But what's the government doing to help us? That's what I want to know. Not a lot! That's the truth.' He shook his head but his smile remained.

'Thank you.'

'You take care now!'

Smug little man, thought Eve, but she had no time to develop her resentment. Instead she made her way to the small grocer's shop on the corner and bought eggs, milk, bread and a pound of mixed biscuits. This will do for a start, she told herself. It will teach the girl to trust me and to welcome my next visit.

Outside the grocer's shop, she stood, deliberating. She toyed with the idea of fetching the doctor but hesitated to interfere too far in the family's business. Suppose it was true and Ellen was taken to hospital. The children might be put into an orphanage to await her recovery. Could the authorities do that? Was the epidemic now considered a major emergency which gave them special powers? It seemed that while she was wrapped up in her own grief, the progress of the disease had speeded up and the community was obviously under severe stress. Suppose Ellen *didn't* recover...

'Think, Eve,' she muttered and wished she could consult her mother. 'I'll come back tomorrow,' she decided, 'and make a decision then. Maybe Ellen will be better by then and will allow me to help them.'

Putting her words into practice she made her way back to the Beattys's house and knocked three times on the door. There was no answer. After several attempts she was forced to assume that Ellen had forbidden Amy to co-operate. Perhaps she feared the authorities might force their way in.

She set the basket down on the step and shouted through the letter box. 'I'm back, Amy. There's only me out here. No doctors ... And there are some good things on the step, Amy. Medicine, food and biscuits.' She waited but nothing happened. 'I'm going now.'

Still nothing happened so she retreated about ten yards and watched the house. A curtain twitched in the downstairs front room and seconds later the door opened. The basket was drawn inside and the door slammed shut.

At least she had provided some form of help, she thought gratefully as she made her way back along the street. Tomorrow she might be able to talk her way inside.

Six

The following morning Mrs Banks arrived to do the washing and Eve sat upstairs with her mother, sharing their 'elevenses' of tea and biscuits and talking about the news. Eve had been reading the sheet of newspaper that had been wrapped around the sausages the previous day.

'There seems to be a swell of anger at the medical profession,' she told Dorothy. 'They are always so ready to boast about their achievements but now we really need them to conquer the influenza...' She shrugged helplessly. 'Where are they? Where are their solutions? Why haven't they produced a cure?'

Dorothy dipped a nice biscuit into her tea. 'You of all people should understand. You know how hard Harvey and his colleagues were working to discover the cause. If it wasn't that germ thing that Pfeiffer found years back when you were a toddler, then it must be another one – a stronger one. There was so much talk then, of a cure, and we all believed it. It was in all the papers.'

'This must be a new one. Maybe it's so small it can't be seen under the microscope.'

'Is there a germ that small?'

'Harvey always suspected there was. He said with time we'd improve the microscope and find all sorts of things.' She smiled wanly. 'He always dreamed of discovering something wonderful that would be of great benefit to mankind. I use to tease him about the Nobel Prize!' Her eyes darkened. 'Now his efforts have come to nothing, he couldn't even save himself.'

Dorothy swallowed the last of the biscuit and reached for a garibaldi. 'Your father used to love these,' she said. 'He was fond of biscuits.'

Forestalling her, Eve said, 'He liked almond biscuits best.'

There was a knock at the front door and they heard Mrs Banks hurry to open it.

'I wonder if that's Amy,' Eve said. 'Maybe her mother's relented and wants me to call in. I said I'd help if I could.'

'You be careful, Eve. You're still weak from shock and grief. You're in no state to go helping sick people – except from outside the house.'

Mrs Banks called up the stairs. 'It's Doctor Warby to enquire about Mrs Randall.'

'Thank you, Mrs Banks. I'll be right down.'

Eve found him on the doorstep looking grey with exhaustion but refusing to come in.

'My wife's ill,' he told her. 'I may not be able to call on you again for a few days. I dare not continue house calls in case I carry the infection. That's why I'm staying outside.'

'Is it the flu?'

He nodded. 'We don't know yet how far it will develop but poor Mabel has always had a weak chest so she is rather vulnerable.' He stared round him distractedly.

'Can I be of any help? I could fetch some shopping for you – or call on your patients to tell them you won't be calling round.'

'You're most kind but you have your own health to consider and your mother's, naturally. If I need you I'll get a message to you but I hope not to trouble anyone else. If you or your mother fall ill you *can* send for me because then I will not be bringing the infection as you already have it in the house.' He removed his hat and raked his hand through his thinning hair. 'Where will it end? They say it is even appearing in the Far East! Is the whole world sick?' He replaced his hat. 'Some of the schools have closed for fear of spreading the infection. Some theatres are closed. The churches are half empty. My advice is "keep away from crowded places",

Mrs Randall. No bus rides. Stay away from church congregations and say your prayers at home.' He sighed. 'I must go. You take care now.'

'God bless you, doctor. I shall pray for your wife.'

After he had gone she realized she should have asked him about the Beattys and what the authorities would do with the children if Ellen was taken into hospital or died. Too late. She would go round later and see how they were and take them more food. She decided she would make a jelly for Ellen and whip an egg into it for extra nourishment. A jelly would be light and easy to digest and would tempt her appetite if it were waning.

At this time, many miles away, James Ferber walked to the captain's office on leaden feet. He knew in his heart that his request would be refused yet he felt he must make it. He owed it to his wife to try and get home to her. Louise had never needed him as much as she did now and he had promised he would always put her needs first. That was his duty as a husband – but he also had his duty to the army. She would understand that but it wouldn't ease the situation.

Standing in front of the captain he waited for the words he dreaded. Captain Stockwell was a decent enough man, he thought.

Better than some. He was tall and thin, with an anxious manner and an accent that still spoke of his early life on a horse farm in Montana. He had worked his way up through the ranks with hard work and dedication. He was the first in his family to make a career in the military, if the rumours were true, and occasionally it showed.

'Compassionate leave, Ferber, at a time like this?' Captain Stockwell raised his eyebrows unhappily.

'Yes, sir. My wife is sick, sir. Very ill. I have just had a telegram from my mother-in-law. It's influenza.' He tried to keep his voice steady. 'We have a small son. I feel I should be with them.'

'Are they quite alone?'

James hesitated. Perhaps if he lied and pretended that Louise was alone ... His better nature triumphed over the temptation. 'No, sir. She is staying with her mother but she is asthmatic and will be finding the situation very alarming. She is widowed.' He didn't add that Louise's father had been a weak, selfish man. He had not wanted Louise to marry the son of one of his friends and had never really resigned himself to the disappointment when she'd insisted on marrying him.

The captain sighed. 'You must know it's impossible, Ferber.' He waved a hand to indicate the piles of forms and papers which covered his austere army-issue desk. 'Goddam these applications! We are already badly under-manned especially in your department. I have asked for extra staff but there are none to be had. We can't have bodies piling up in the corridors. Every camp is in the same boat. Too many sick, too few staff. I don't know exactly how many requests I've had for compassionate leave since this goddam flu started but it runs into hundreds. I've turned them all down – except for...'

'Yes, sir!' There was no need to spell it out – he knew what the captain meant. He was well aware that compassionate leave for the duration of the emergency meant that leave was only given to attend funerals. James stared woodenly ahead with no real sense of disappointment. He had expected nothing else but had felt obliged to try for Louise's sake.

'I'm sorry, Ferber, but I can't spare you – and it wouldn't look good if I did. Can't make exceptions to the general rule. You know that.'

'Yes, sir!'

'You're not really one of ours – only here for the duration of the epidemic – but I can't explain that to our lads. It would cause resentment if I were seen to show favours.'

Captain Stockwell leaned back in his chair and scratched the side of his face with long fingers. James found himself wondering what kind of farmer he would have made. 'Yes, sir. I understand.'

'God knows what we're supposed to do. We're fighting a war with one hand tied behind our back!' he told James. 'We're losing men as fast as we can get them into Europe. It would be a farce if it weren't a tragedy.'

James stared straight ahead. He would have to write to Louise's parents and suggest they employ a nurse to help them. Someone with professional knowledge had to care for them. By now young Toby might have succumbed. The thought made him shiver with apprehension.

The captain shrugged. 'So the answer's no, I'm afraid.'

'Yes, sir.'

'You can go.' He nodded in the direction of the door.

James turned and left the room, his heart heavy. Frustration welled inside him as he made his way back to the morgue, struggling with his over-vivid imagination. He couldn't allow himself to think of his wife ravaged by the disease because he knew only too well what it did to its victims. Instead he tried to think positively, imagining her recovery. He thought about her in happier times. He could dimly see her on their wedding day, twenty-two years old, slim and radiant in a cream gown of silk lace with a small circlet of flowers in her hair ... the same dress which still hung in the wardrobe with the occasional grain of rice falling from it.

'It will bring us luck, James,' she had insisted and until now it had appeared to do so.

With an effort, he remembered her paddling in the sea when she was eighteen, holding up her skirts with one hand while she tried to fill a brightly coloured pail with water for a little girl who was building a sand-castle but was afraid to venture into the waves ... That was the first time he had set eyes on her and he had known in that instant that she was the woman he would marry.

He had been walking along the beach with two friends from medical school who had teased him unmercifully about what they called his sudden infatuation. One of them had dared him to approach Louise, and needing no more urging he had done so.

'Can I be of help?' he had asked. 'You might get your skirts wet. Allow me.'

Surprised, she had blushed but handed him the pail and walked back the short distance to dry land beside him.

'Your daughter?' he had asked, handing

over the filled pail and praying that she was the child's aunt. She looked too young to be a mother and he could see no sign of a husband.

'Oh no!' She'd laughed. 'Just a little girl on the beach. I don't even know her name. She wanted some water for the moat but the waves bothered her. Her parents are over there.'

Filled with relief he had chatted to her and, abandoning his amused friends, had arranged to walk back with her to the hotel where she was staying with her parents, Alison and George, for a week. Alison had found him eminently suitable but George had only come round to the idea of an engagement later. He had never held a high opinion of the medical profession and made no attempt to hide it. When he had learned that James planned to join the army as a pathologist as soon as he qualified, he had protested.

'The army? Good God, man! I don't want my only daughter to become a widow.'

'If I do see active service, it will almost always be from the field hospital,' James had insisted, attempting to allay his future father-in-law's fears.

Now he paused to allow a squad of new recruits on a training run to pass him, then turned a corner which brought the hospital wing into view.

Smiling faintly, he remembered his wife in bed with newborn Toby in her arms. She had smiled up at him with such love and pride. Now she was somewhere between life and death and he might lose her. She would, he knew, be fighting for her life, desperate to survive to be with the two people who loved and needed her most. Would God look down and see what a sweet person she was? Would he save her?

He reached the morgue, went in and closed the door behind him, standing for a moment to take in the familiar smells – disinfectant, cold flesh, decay and blood. Did he only imagine the smell of helplessness? With his eyes closed he heard the familiar sounds – rubber trolley wheels hissing across the floor, the constant rush of swirling water, the occasional clatter of scalpels and the muted comments of his colleagues as they tried to lighten the atmosphere. Could he stay with this for the rest of his life, he wondered and was suddenly disenchanted with the army and its regulations. For the first time he began to doubt that this was for him. Maybe when the disaster had ended he would consider a change, back to civilian life.

One of the assistants stopped whistling and glanced up – Alan Dubois, a young man with a shock of ginger hair. He had not yet qualified but the army was desperate and had taken him on a short-term contract. From what James had seen he had shown very little aptitude for the work they did. 'Any luck, sir?' he asked James, swabbing down one of the tables with broad, careless movements that sent soiled water spattering on to the floor.

James shook his head and reached for a clean apron.

'Your wife might pull through, sir. Don't give up hope.' He twisted the cloth over a pail. 'My uncle pulled through and he's crippled with rheumatics. Weak as a kitten he is and has been for years. Lungs, too. He has to sleep sitting up in a chair so he can breathe. We all thought for sure he'd go but he proved us wrong!' He resumed his whistling.

James tuned out the cheerful sound and tied a mask over his mouth and nose. Not that he cared, he thought, with the beginnings of anger. If Louise died he wouldn't care if he followed her ... except for Toby. He must go on living for his son's sake, but if Louise was taken from them he knew that life could never be the same again.

The next morning's post brought a letter from Miss Harding to say that she was planning to move in with her brother and sister-in-law and would be returning to pack up her belongings. Fortunately she rented the flat so that did not present a problem. Eve read the short note:

...Would you be kind enough to lend a hand with the packing? I know it's a lot to ask but I should find it rather daunting on my own. I hope you and your mother are both well and free from the sickness. And that you have heard from your husband...

Eve read to the end and folded the letter. She was arriving today, the fourth of November. Eve frowned thoughtfully.

'I had intended to go round to the Beattys,' she told her mother. 'I haven't been round for a few days.'

'You'll wear yourself out! You've been very good to them already, Eve, taking all those things. Small thanks you got. They wouldn't even open the door to you.'

'It's up to them, Mother. I can't force myself into the house. Ellen knows what she's doing.'

'Let's hope so! And now it's Miss Harding.'

'I have to keep busy. I'll help Miss Harding to pack but I'm sorry she's going. I shall miss her.'

'You hardly know her,' Dorothy protested. 'How can you miss her? Really, Eve. You do exaggerate.'

Eve shrugged. 'We've shared things,' she said, remembering their abortive trip to meet the unfortunate Lewis, 'but I can see that being with her brother makes sense, especially in these dangerous times. And no doubt she'll be a comfort to them, since they've lost their son.'

Dorothy, reaching for her knitting, changed the subject. 'The post was late.'

'It was a relief man. The postman...'

'Let me guess!'

'Yes. He's off sick.'

Half an hour later Miss Harding arrived and after a cup of tea and a word or two with Dorothy, she insisted that they should make a start and, huddled beneath a large umbrella, they braved the drizzling rain and walked round to the flat. They were halfway up the stairs when the landlady appeared, wiping her hands on her apron. Small and anxious, Mrs Potter peered at them through spectacles which needed cleaning, and told Miss Harding how sorry she would be to lose her. Miss Harding thanked her and introduced Eve as 'a friend who is going to help me pack'.

The woman nodded her approval. 'You've been a very nice tenant, Miss Harding,' she told her. 'No trouble at all. I shall miss you but I can't do without the rent money so I've had to advertise for a new tenant. I've got someone coming later today. I hope you don't mind if I bring them up to see the flat.'

Miss Harding smiled. 'I don't mind but it won't look its best with just the furniture and no home comforts. No samplers on the wall, no vases or clock on the mantelpiece.'

'They'll have to take it as they find it,' Mrs Potter declared. 'Can I help at all – with the packing?'

'No, thank you. I'm sure we can manage.'

When the kitchen door closed behind the landlady, Miss Harding whispered, 'She's nice enough but rather nosy! I shall have my own room in my brother's house and they certainly won't snoop the way Mrs Potter does.'

The flat was surprisingly large for one person, thought Eve, as they walked down the hall and into a kitchen which was as neat as she would have expected.

Miss Harding took off her coat and hat, donned an apron and found one for Eve. 'All the china's mine,' she explained briskly, 'although the furniture goes with the flat. Just as well because there's no room for any more in my brother's cottage. Wrap the pots and pans and suchlike. The clock's mine and the kettle ... you can leave the table runner. Although I bought it I've never really liked it. There's a pile of old newspapers to wrap them in and there's a tea chest labelled KITCHEN. I'll be in the bedroom packing my clothes.'

Eve was astonished. 'How are you getting all this down to Devon?'

'I managed to find a carrier, although it wasn't easy. A Mr Groves. Everyone, it seems, wants to be gone from the city into the country, hoping to escape the flu. He'll be here around midday, so he says, but you know what these people are like!'

Eve tied on the apron and began her allotted task. She was rather surprised by Miss Harding's resilience and had expected some hint of regret that she was leaving her home. Maybe the loss of Lewis had left the family feeling bereft and needing the closeness and support of family. Eve opened a cupboard door and began to take down and wrap a variety of crockery – plates, cups, saucers and dishes. There was a gravy boat, several jugs, basins, egg cups, honey pot, teapot and strainer...

'This will take for ever!' Eve muttered. In the next cupboard she found glassware and in the next, jars of chutney and home-made jam. In the lower cupboards there were saucepans, frying pans, oven dishes and much more. It was already ten thirty-five. Eve could not see how they could possibly be ready by the time the carrier arrived at midday. 'So make a start!' she told herself and reached for the first sheet of newspaper and a small brown teapot.

Half an hour later Miss Harding came down the hall dragging a small trunk on castors. She left it in the hall and went back for a bulging carpet bag. Putting her head round the kitchen door, she said, 'Oh, wonderful! It's so kind of you. I'll make a start on the bookcase in the front room. All the books are mine and the ornaments. Would you like an aspidistra? I've never really liked them but it was a present from my aunt and she's long dead. I really don't want to take it with me.'

Eve declined but suggested that the landlady might appreciate it and this proved to be the case.

Eve was wondering how to break the news that Harvey was dead. Was it necessary? It hadn't occurred to Miss Harding to enquire about him so perhaps it would be better to let her leave without hearing the sad news? The old lady was being so determinedly brisk in the face of her own loss that to add to it might tip the balance and Eve had no wish to provoke sympathetic tears. Nor, if she was honest, could she guarantee that she herself would not break down if she spoke of her late husband.

Albert Groves, the carrier, arrived at

twenty past one with his sixteen-year-old son in tow. The son was sullen and unresponsive but he worked well and his father's cheerful chatter compensated for the boy's moodiness. They soon had all the boxes and cases in the back of his covered cart and Miss Harding paid them and handed over a sheet of paper containing the address to which the goods should be delivered.

It was going to take two days, she was told.

'Long way orf, Devon!' Albert Groves informed them.

'Yes, it is, but I shall be waiting. I'm going back by train later today.' To Eve she said, 'I've ordered a taxi to take me to the train station. My brother gave me the money and insisted. He's always been very good to me. Lewis was so like his father, he...' She checked herself as her eyes misted over briefly.

Too early to talk about Lewis, thought Eve, glad she had not mentioned her husband's death. She would write to Miss Harding eventually and break the news.

They watched the carrier's cart until it turned at the end of the road.

'You'd better come home with me,' Eve suggested, thinking of the denuded flat upstairs.

'Oh, no! I'm afraid I must wait here for the taxi,' Miss Harding told her. 'He had several other rides booked but he said he'd be here as soon as he could.'

Even as she spoke a taxi appeared and within minutes they had said their goodbyes.

'A new life,' Eve said, with forced cheerfulness. 'Do please write to me and let me know how you are getting along.'

Miss Harding nodded. 'No looking back.'

They exchanged a last shy hug, the taxi containing Miss Harding retreated and Eve found herself alone in the street.

'Well, that went like clockwork,' she muttered, astonished by the speed of events. She *would* miss Miss Harding. It dawned on her that she had expected a friendship to result from the events that had thrown them together. She sighed. Perhaps one day she would find her way to Devon and visit her. When all this ends, she promised herself.

Later that day, when Eve reached Number 20, Leopold Street she was dismayed to find a small group of people on the pavement outside and a car parked alongside the door. An argument appeared to be taking place between a very young police constable, an elderly woman and a man with an armful of papers, notebooks and cardboard files. Both men wore masks over the lower half of their faces.

Eve at first hung back about twenty yards from them, wondering whether she needed to become involved in whatever it was that was under discussion. As she hesitated an ambulance appeared and pulled up alongside. The driver dismounted and carefully tied a white mask over his mouth and nose before he joined the group. The elderly woman caught sight of Eve and hurried towards her and it was then too late to withdraw.

'It's not my fault,' she told Eve defensively. 'I went round twice yesterday because it was so quiet but they wouldn't open the door. Wouldn't even speak to me. I said to my hubby, there's something wrong and should I call the police, but he said I shouldn't interfere – and now look what's happened!' She blinked anxiously, crumpling her apron with her clasped hands. 'You can't blame me. I tried. They wasn't having any! The constable gave me a look like he didn't believe me. Sauce! Look at him. Knee high to a grasshopper. What does he know about anything?' She folded her arms unhappily.

Eve said, 'What's happened?'

'She's dead, isn't she?'

Eve gasped. 'Who's dead? Not Ellen?'

'Yes! Stone dead, when they found her, with Sam in her arms. And the girls, too. Locked themselves in the bedroom, they had.'

Eve put a hand to her heart which started

to beat uncomfortably fast. 'What – all of them – gone?' Her voice shook and her knees buckled so that she almost fell.

'Well, no. Not all of them dead. But Kate's real sick. She's going to the hospital. They'll be fetching her, but Mr Weston – ' she jerked a thumb in the direction of the man with the papers – 'he says there's no hope for her.' She sighed deeply. 'And Sam's dead. Poor little mite!'

'Dear God!' Only weeks ago Eve had been envying the little family despite their difficult circumstances. Now Jon and Ellen were both dead and the baby, too. Kate might die, also. It seemed impossible that disaster should have struck them so suddenly and so completely.

The neighbour wiped a tear from her eye. 'Poor little Sam wasn't long in this life, was he, bless him?'

'And the girls?'

'The two younger girls have been took away to an orphanage. Lucy and Amy. And we all know what that means! Not a very nice prospect, is it? Stuck in an orphanage. One step up from the workhouse, if you ask me, them places.'

Her face crumpled but she squared her shoulders, returning to the present with an effort. 'I know the girls, I told him.' She nodded in Mr Weston's direction. 'I'm Mrs

Annis from next door. The kids'll be OK with me for a day or two. But he wouldn't listen. Too big for his shiny boots, he is.'

'Poor Ellen!' Eve took two steps backward and leaned against the wall.

Mrs Annis eyed her warily. 'You all right?'

'I'll be fine in a moment.' In her mind's eye Eve saw Ellen at the window, shouting down, begging to be left alone. She had seen what might happen and had no doubt prayed to survive so that she could keep the family together. And poor little Sam ... Eve blinked back tears of frustration and regret.

'How bad is Kate?' she asked, desperate for some small hope to cling to.

The woman shrugged. 'Pretty bad. They thought she was a goner but then they saw she was still breathing.'

They fell silent as the constable and the ambulance driver carried out a body on a stretcher and manoeuvred it into the back of the vehicle.

'Taking her to the mortuary,' Mrs Annis whispered with a shake of her head.

'Who exactly is Mr Weston?'

'He's from the council. They're keeping tabs on the number of deaths – and he also has to deal with orphaned kids. Keep track of them, like. Bit of a stuffed shirt, he is. I told the constable the kids could stay with me over night while they tried to find someone to take them. He was all for it, the constable was, but then the other one showed up, miserable old sod, and said "No". Regulation number something or other. Oh, here comes poor little Kate, off to the hospital.'

Impulsively Eve stepped forward and tried to speak to the ambulance man who was carrying the girl in his arms. Her small, dark head drooped over one arm, her sharp little eyes were closed, her mouth was open. Her sticklike legs dangled over the other arm.

Eve cried, 'She'll be all right, won't she?'

The man gave her a quick, defeated glance. 'Don't ask me. I'm no ruddy doctor.'

Mr Weston glared at Eve.

'Out of the way, please!' he said sharply.

'If I ask at the hospital...?'

'Just keep away. If you're not family you won't be allowed in. You'll simply clutter up the place to no purpose. All visitors do is spread the infection.'

Eve watched as Kate was carried into the vehicle and it was driven away.

She said, 'The aunt lives in Exeter, I think. She would probably take the two girls.'

'That's my worry,' Mr Weston told her. To the constable he muttered, 'Too many do-gooders. They do like to interfere!'

The policeman looked embarrassed and Eve said furiously, 'If you don't recognize help when you see it, you shouldn't be doing your job!'

Mrs Annis's eyes widened at this show of defiance. 'You tell him!'

Mr Weston flushed angrily. 'You'd best get along home, whoever you are, and keep your opinions to yourself. We see too many busybodies in this line of work. This is a serious epidemic – a medical emergency. There are regulations in force. Proper procedures and ways of doing things. People like you should leave this to the professionals.'

Emboldened by Eve's stand, Mrs Annis glared at him. 'No need to take that tone. She was only trying to help.'

'I don't want her help – or yours.' His voice had risen and the police constable was looking anxious, wondering if he should take control of the situation but not knowing how.

Eve turned to Mrs Annis. 'I shall write to the Town Hall about this man,' she said in a calm clear voice. 'A true professional would have more consideration for people's sensibilities, especially at a time like this.'

She gave Mr Weston a quick glance and was pleased to see that her words had discomfited him. He looked shaken and opened his mouth to speak but thought better of it and fussed with his papers instead, pretending to look for something. Eve drew herself up, turned on her heel and walked away in the direction of home.

As Eve had expected, her mother, on Eve's return, was deeply shocked when she heard the news about Ellen and Sam Beatty, and was incensed by Eve's account of her argument with the officious Mr Weston.

'Full of his own importance,' she agreed from her seat at the kitchen table, as she sat watching Eve butter some bread for their tea. 'But how foolish not to accept help. The orphanages must be bursting at the seams with abandoned children. The idea of finding the aunt for the surviving children should have been welcomed. So much better for the little ones to stay with a relative instead of thrust among hundreds of other children.' She sighed. 'What must they be going through? The last week must have been a total nightmare. I wonder if they knew their mother was dead. Hopefully they imagined she was asleep or had fainted.'

'They probably knew. After all, they must have seen their father die.' Eve added a jar of jam to the table and set out two plates. The kettle began to whistle and she made a pot of tea. 'Knowing Kate I suspect she was in charge until she fell ill herself. I wonder if they will bury Ellen with Jon. I shall go to the morgue first thing tomorrow and tell them where he's buried. And little Sam, too. They should all be together. I heard talk a day or two back about a mass grave somewhere. I should hate them to be divided in death.'

'Go to church this evening, Eve. Say a special prayer for their souls ... and another for the three girls. If there's a God he'll surely spare them.'

'Good idea, Mother. I'll do that.'

'Remind me of their names.'

'Kate, in the hospital, and Lucy and Amy in the orphanage – wherever that is. I shall have to find out.'

They ate their tea in a subdued silence.

Seven

Overnight Eve had a better idea. She would pay for Ellen and Sam to be buried with Jon. She shared the idea with her mother who reluctantly agreed after some soul searching. She reminded Eve that they had no idea how they would fare financially now that Harvey was dead but, seeing that Eve's mind was made up, she eventually gave the idea her blessing.

As Eve set out on her way to the hospital the next day she was forcibly reminded of the date. Three young children waylaid her as she turned the corner and demanded, 'A penny for the guy!'

Eve was astonished. Was it already the fifth of November? And were the children still celebrating Guy Fawkes's unsuccessful attempt to blow up the Houses of Parliament all those years ago? The country was four years into a war and in the middle of an epidemic. Hadn't they had enough of death and destruction? It seemed not. On the other hand, perhaps it was a good thing that

137

children surrounded by so much grief, could distract themselves by maintaining the small excitements of normal life. They were so resilient.

She paused, examining the three children and their guy. The latter was crudely made from a stuffed sack with a large turnip for his head, on which a greasy cap rested at a jaunty angle. He sat in a crudely made cart, leaning drunkenly to one side. His eyes were holes gouged from the turnip. His nose and mouth appeared to have been drawn on with lampblack. He wore a patched oversized shirt that had seen better days and a yellow knitted scarf that needed a good wash.

Hiding a smile, Eve said, 'I hope the real Mr Fawkes looked a lot better than that!'

Taken aback, the children studied their guy.

The girl, bedraggled and with a slight squint, said, 'He's just been blown up, that's why!'

Eve laughed at the quickness of her reply and the children looked at each other hopefully.

She said, 'But they didn't manage to blow it up.'

The older boy, said, 'He's got the flu, then. He's sick.' Crouched beside the cart, he was scarcely better dressed than the wretch in the cart. His shoes lacked laces and his trousers were held up with string. He held up a jam jar which contained a single penny. 'Spare a penny, missus?' he repeated.

The younger boy said slyly, 'A very nice man gave us twopence!'

The girl's eyes widened. 'Ooh, he never! You're a liar, Tommy Trump. I'm telling Ma.'

'You shut up!' The older boy gave her a push and she pushed him back.

'Tommy is a liar! Tommy is a—'

Another push knocked her off her feet but she continued to taunt him. She wore a faded dress under a grimy pinafore but she had scuffed shoes on her feet.

The younger boy cried, 'Mollie is a muffin! Molly is...'

'We should have left her at home,' Tommy, the older boy, said resignedly.

'Ma said she was to come,' the other boy said. Molly stuck out her tongue at him and put a finger in each ear. 'Anyway we had to bring her – it's her scarf.'

She looked up at Eve. 'Tommy's lying. Ma gave us the penny.'

As both boys made a furious lunge in her direction, she ducked neatly, laughing defiantly. In the ensuing tussle the penny escaped from the jar and rolled along the pavement. While the boys chased it, the girl snatched up the guy, climbed into the cart and settled the guy on her lap.

Eve held out a threepenny bit and blinked back the tears. The children's artless prattle had reminded her of Kate, Amy and Lucy and the arrangements she hoped to make for their mother and baby brother. 'Here you are. There's a penny for each of you,' she said, dropping it into the jar.

'Thanks.' Molly shook the jar in triumph and shouted to the boys. 'Come back and see.'

Eve hurried away, her throat tight with a sense of foreboding.

'Don't die, Kate,' she whispered as she continued her journey. She tried to imagine the younger girls in the orphanage and hoped they had been able to stay together. She recalled what Mr Weston had said the previous day about 'the way things are done' and wondered whether she should pretend to be a relative when she approached the mortuary staff about Ellen and Sam. Would they bother to check her story? Suppose she claimed to be Ellen's sister ... and suppose they then agreed and insisted she remove the bodies from the mortuary?

Perhaps she was going about this in the wrong way. She slowed to a halt and stood still in the middle of the pavement, thinking rapidly. Perhaps she should find a willing undertaker first and then approach the hospital.

'First things first,' she muttered and changed direction.

She headed for a well-known firm of funeral directors – Wellin & Sons – but was surprised to find herself in a small queue. Hearing the three people in front of her being turned down she almost gave up but already there was another man behind her and it seemed this might occur at all undertakers. So I might as well try here as anywhere else, she thought.

'I'm here about friends of mine,' she began. 'The father is already buried and I want to bury the mother and child in the same grave.'

He rolled his eyes in a way that conveyed both regret and understanding. He was small and neat with spectacles. 'I'd truly love to help you, madam,' he told her. 'Our books are full for the next ten days and most people don't want to wait that long.'

'Ten days!' She wondered why she was so surprised. He had just offered similar information to the people who preceded her. 'Is there any chance that someone will cancel the interment? For any reason?'

He shook his head. 'And please don't think of offering to pay above the asking price. My father, George Wellin, is a God-fearing man and would never approve. You'd be surprised to hear how often...'

'I wasn't going to do any such thing! I doubt I could afford it even if I...'

'People are desperate to lay their loved ones to rest. Not all have the benefit of being in a mortuary, if you take my point, and the body needs to be dealt with promptly.'

Eve nodded. 'Well, thank you for your time.' She turned away and before she reached the door she heard the man behind her begging Mr Wellin to make an exception in his case.

'I'm sorry,' the woman told her, almost wringing her plump hands. 'We'd like to oblige everyone but it's simply not possible. We have three staff off sick and one died of flu. And I can't see an end to it.' She rubbed her eyes which were dark with exhaustion.

'But you wouldn't have to dig a grave,' Eve told her. 'There's a plot already where the father's been recently buried. Surely you could add the mother and baby.'

'There's so much paperwork, you see, and we're...' She glanced round as an elderly man entered. His face was wet with tears and he sank on to a chair as though his legs would not carry him any further.

He said, 'My wife...' and looked beseechingly at the woman behind the counter who held up both hands and shook her head. 'Oh God! Don't refuse me! You've known us for years, Nellie. Surely Albert would lay Beatrice to rest. One last small kindness for a lifelong friend. I've never begged you before but...'

'Harold, I have no more coffins,' she protested. 'This lady has just been refused a burial for a mother and baby. Do you think I enjoy saying no?'

Eve turned and left the shop, badly shaken. Of course everyone knew there was a flu epidemic but she had had no idea quite how severe it had become and how hopelessly stretched the resources were. What was the government thinking of, to let matters reach this stage, she wondered angrily. And more to the point, what could she do about Ellen and Sam?

For more than twenty minutes she wandered unfamiliar streets in search of another undertaker and finally found one in a small back street. The area was unprepossessing and she hesitated. The small window was grimy with years of dirt on the inside and soot on the outside, and only a small curling sign that hung in the window announced that it was, in fact, an undertakers.

'Mr Jack's Funeral Parlour,' she muttered. Please, *please* say yes, Mr Jack, she hoped.

Inside, the office-cum-shop was empty and there was an air of faded gentility. To her surprise the young man who appeared in answer to the jangle of the doorbell, was cheerful and tidily, if shabbily, dressed. His fair hair was neatly cut, he was clean shaven and showed no sign of weariness or despair.

'Good morning, madam. I'm Mr Jack's son Robert. How can I be of service?'

From the rear of the tiny room Eve could hear sawing and guessed that coffins were being put together as fast as possible. She explained her needs and he listened with his head on one side.

'We've a waiting list,' he said briskly, 'but we could do you a nice burial the day after tomorrow. How would that suit?' Without waiting for her answer, he reached for a notebook and pencil. 'We could collect your loved ones later today and keep them until the appointed time when we would deliver them to the churchyard of your choice.' Seeing her mingled surprise and relief he added, 'We are a large family, and we have been called together to deal with this emergency. Six brothers, in fact. I'm actually a clerk in my uncle's clothing firm but he's had to close temporarily. Sales are down. Nobody's buying clothes – except black day wear, and we specialize in nightwear.'

Another young man appeared, handed a mug of tea to Robert and nodded to Eve. He looked very like Robert and she guessed he was another of Mr Jack's relations.

Glancing over Robert's shoulder, he asked, 'How many more for today?' and they consulted the page together. 'Ah! Three will do it.'

'Has the timber come?'

'Not yet and Pa's getting agitated but they did say midday.' He grinned at Eve. 'If this flu lasts much longer they'll be running out of trees!'

Robert smiled at Eve. 'He's a milkman by trade. Helping out here in his spare time. Not that they let him do any sawing but he can polish and screw on the handles.' He handed her a business card. 'That's our address. The hospital mortuary will need that. Tell them we'll be along later this afternoon.'

Eve hesitated. 'Where will they be kept?'

'Don't you worry about that, Mrs Randall. We've got a nice quiet room, black drapes, black candles. All very respectful. You can see it, if you like, but it's not looking its best because of the number of coffins awaiting collection.'

Eve shook her head. She felt instinctively that she could trust the young man. He mentioned a price and Eve paid him and said, 'Goodbye.'

As she walked towards the hospital she had doubts about the 'respectful' part. Obviously the room would be crammed with coffins but this was the best she could arrange. She was lucky to have found someone to bury Ellen and Sam and she was truly thankful for small mercies.

In America, on the ninth of November, the small white clapboard church was bright in the sunshine as Louise's funeral party, bearing her body, made its way through the churchyard towards the newly dug grave. For James, the date would always be recalled with a deep sense of loss. Louise had been the perfect partner – loving, generous, a good mother, a dutiful wife. He could not see how he could ever love anyone else and was wondering how he would face his lonely future.

He felt sorrow for her mother who stood beside him as they gathered round the grave, her face still pale with shock, her eyes haunted by memories. She, too, was devastated by her death. Young Toby would soon be old enough to understand what had happened and have to come to terms with the loss of his mother.

Despite the sunshine, a cool breeze disturbed a few remaining dead leaves and fluttered the parson's dark clothes. The sky was a deep blue with a few scattered clouds but the mourners, maybe fifteen in all, paid scant attention to the weather. He knew that many people had chosen not to attend.

Gatherings of any kind were dangerous in the midst of an epidemic. Close friends with young children had stayed away, sending flowers and letters of regret, and he understood their reluctance.

James Ferber held his son's hand while Louise's mother, Alison, walked close beside him, watching the child anxiously. So far Toby had apparently been unaffected by funeral service, standing or kneeling obediently when the congregation sang or prayed. Toby was very like his father, slightly built with the same brown hair but with his mother's grey eyes. James was pleased that his wife would be buried with her father in the family plot because new plots were hard to come by.

When he returned to Camp Devens, his son would be well cared for by Alison until he could arrange his discharge from the army – which he expected would be sooner rather than later. The long war was drawing slowly but surely to a close. Bulgaria had signed an armistice more than a month earlier and other German powers were said to be hoping to do the same. Germany had a new Chancellor who was eager to bring the war to an end.

The mourners listened as the parson repeated the familiar words of the burial service. They had been lucky, James knew.

Louise's family had been established members of the small community and Alison had called in favours. Louise had been laid to rest in a superb mahogany coffin lined with pleated white silk and had been lowered into the ground above her father's coffin. There had been organ music at the service and a small choir, and the church had been decorated with tasteful displays of flowers. No expense had been spared, he knew that, but it meant so little. He had lost his beloved Louise. She was gone from him. Their plans for a future were finished, but three and a half years ago she had given him Toby and he was determined he would never lose him. He could be a pathologist anywhere, he told himself. Anywhere that he could make a new home for himself and his son.

Toby said, 'G'andma?'

Alison turned instantly. 'G'andma's here, baby!' To James she whispered, 'Let me have him. He knows me better than you. He'll be worried with all these strangers.'

Reluctantly James noticed how willingly the boy clutched her hand and leaned against his grandmother's leg. It was true, he reflected. Toby had seen him very rarely over the past months while work at the camp kept him away from home. He must get closer to his son, he decided, now that Louise was dead.

Closing his eyes he mumbled the final prayer and listened to the blessing. Someone passed him a single red rose and he leaned forward and dropped it gently on to Louise's coffin. A deep and painful sense of loss welled up in him and he covered his face. He stood there in silence while one by one the mourners drifted away. They were making their way back to Alison's house where the maid was waiting to serve the refreshments and the maid's husband was opening bottles of wine.

Alison laid a hand on his arm. 'I'll go back, James, to see to things. You follow when you're up to it. Toby will be fine with me.'

When they had all gone, he lowered his hands but remained there, desperately trying to raise his wife's image in his mind. An image of happier times, hopefully, but all he could see was the slim ravaged body in the white gown lying silent and still inside the coffin. Suddenly, unbidden, he remembered the letter he had written to Harvey's widow, before he had understood a fraction of her pain. He began to imagine how she must have felt when she read it ... and then he groaned aloud.

'I did send it ... didn't I?' Appalled, he tried to remember but had no recollection of slipping the envelope into the post box on the base. The more he thought about it, the more his guilt deepened. He *hadn't* sent it! So where was it? Still on his desk?

Eve Randall had never read the words of comfort and regret he had put together so sincerely. Was it too late to send it? He had certainly dated it. The poor woman would wonder about the delay. Perhaps he should write another letter, telling her about Louise's death and possibly writing with more understanding. God knows he knew more about the desperation of loss than he ever had before. Nothing in his whole life had prepared him for the sense of desolation that gripped him.

With a sigh, he whispered a final farewell to his wife and began to make his way back. It would be so easy to give way, but he had their son to think about. Somehow – he had no idea how – he must turn their lives around. Louise would want them to be happy. But how was it to be achieved?

Back at his mother-in-law's house he found the usual subdued murmur as the mourners seated themselves around the extended table and were served with a meal of soup, cold ham and salad followed by Alison's famous lemon tart with cream. For a moment he stood in the doorway watching the proceedings, feeling strangely set apart from everyone else. His mother-in-law caught his eye and indicated the spare chair next to her but he shook his head, unable to face anything to eat. Alison's brother Bernard appeared with two tumblers of whisky and thrust one into James's hand.

'Terrible thing!' he said. 'Terrible. Takes a bit of getting over, a blow like this.' He was a small stout man in his late fifties, with a red face and small bulbous blue eyes. James had seen a photograph of him with Alison as children and Bernard had looked very similar then, only smaller and with a paler face.

James could only nod. He sipped the whisky without enthusiasm.

'Nice service though, James. Very nice. One thing I'll say for our preacher man – he does a good service.'

'Yes, he does.'

James and Bernard had never been close, in fact they rarely met, and when they did James found him pompous. Louise had always found him overbearing, too, and had recalled him from childhood as an uncle to be avoided on his infrequent visits.

'He used to pinch my cheek,' she had told James with a shudder. 'And ask me questions to make me look a fool in front of whoever else was present. Once he asked me to recite the names of all the books in the Old Testament and when I didn't know, he reeled them off and laughed and said whatever was my teacher thinking of!' She'd smiled. 'I used to lie in bed at night and imagine him as a St Bernard dog, with a barrel tied round his neck. One of those dogs they send up mountains in Switzerland to rescue people who are stuck in a snowdrift!' She had shaken her head at the memories. 'I don't think my mother liked him either because he was Grandmama's favourite and could do no wrong in her eyes.'

Now Bernard cleared his throat purposefully and James knew at once what was coming. Being a member of the medical fraternity had one severe disadvantage.

'What I can't figure out, James, is why you fellows can't get to grips with this damned flu? Not that I'm speaking personally, of course. I know you aren't a scientist. But you're all in cahoots, if you see what I mean. You get together at conferences. You confer. Doctors, scientists – you're all in the same line of business, so to speak.' He sipped his drink, watching the effect his words were having on James, relishing his feeling of superiority. He had never been at all academic, and James had always known that Bernard resented his medical achievements. Now he had a chance to berate James for science's failure. 'You publish all these treatises on this, that and the other,' he went on, 'and you theorize. You try to blind us mere mortals with science. And all this money spent on research, millions of dollars, *our* dollars...'

James gave him a stony look. He was becoming used to the public's hostile attitude towards anyone who worked in the medical arena. Doctors, researchers – they were all being blamed for the disaster.

Biting back a sharp reply he said, 'We simply don't have the necessary equipment – the technology – needed to discover the bacterial agent. Medical discoveries can only happen when we have the right tools and so far our very best microscopes are not powerful enough. To make it simple, it's like fighting with your hands tied behind your back.' He spoke slowly, as if to a child, but the snub went over Bernard's head.

The bulbous eyes were fixed on James accusingly. 'But I thought – at least, I read somewhere – that this Pfeiffer had found the bacillus or whatever it was. It was in all the papers. That was years ago but it worked then.'

'It worked for that specific strain of the disease. It keeps changing. His bacillus does not work against this new strain.' James thought of Harvey Randall, earnestly trying to explain to him what the problems were and apologizing for their lack of progress. He recalled the many promising leads which

briefly raised their hopes only to lead nowhere, leaving frustration and depression in
their wake. How glad James was that he was
not a scientist.

Bernard's wife Janet now left her seat at the
table and hurried across the room. She was
a slim woman, probably in her mid-fifties,
still pretty and very feminine. Louise had
been fond of her aunt.

She said, 'Bernard! You're keeping poor
James from his lunch.' To James she said, 'I
hope he's not on his hobby horse again.
Bernard loves to rail against authority of any
kind. Don't you, dear?'

Bernard's expression hardened as he looked at his wife. 'Don't talk such nonsense,
Janet. You do love to talk about things you
don't understand. James and I are having an
interesting, somewhat challenging, medical
discussion about—'

Her face flushed at the insult. 'About the
failure of the best medical brains to put an
end to all this,' she interrupted. 'I'm beginning to know it by heart!'

'He's part of it!' Bernard protested hotly.
'He has to take some responsibility.'

'He's a pathologist, Bernard. For heaven's
sake!' She touched James's arm. 'Don't let
him upset you, James. Why don't you come
and eat. Alison is getting fretful and the soup
is finished. You shouldn't starve yourself at a

time like this.'

James smiled at her. Hardly her fault she had married the man, he thought. She must have been young and impressionable at the time. Now she had her own cross to bear. 'I'll be with you in a couple of minutes.'

He turned back to Bernard who said, 'Women! One thing my wife hates is an intelligent argument.' With a sour expression on his face, Bernard watched her return to the table. ' So-o ... What do we do, eh? Just ride out the storm? Or have you got a secret cure up your sleeve? Going to dazzle us any day now, are you?'

James resisted an urge to punch the self-important face that was thrust so close to his own. He would have liked to do it for Louise's sake but he was not a violent man and deep down he sympathized with people's disappointment. 'Since we can't yet find the cause it's difficult to create a suitable serum,' he explained. 'In laymen's terms, we are looking for a serum that will subdue this particular infection by aiding and abetting the body's own immune system.'

Bernard gave a short derisive laugh. 'Well, frankly, I don't get it!'

'I wouldn't expect you to, Bernard.' James hoped his expression was hard to read. 'The medical complexities of this research are far beyond the average mind but don't feel too badly about it. There are, unfortunately, thousands more just like you.'

He thrust the empty whisky glass back into Bernard's hand and walked away. That was a cheap jibe, James, he told himself but Louise would have enjoyed it and he couldn't begin to pretend he was sorry.

The following Monday, the war came to an end with the long-awaited signing of the armistice at 5 a.m. It would take effect later that same day – at the eleventh hour of the eleventh day of the eleventh month of 1918. It brought four years of bitter hostilities to an end and many people would be able to rejoice. Others would not. They would be the unfortunate millions who had lost their loved ones during the fighting or those who had lost family and friends to the other, more recent scourge.

For James, Armistice Day passed in a blur of grief and regret and it was not until the following day, when he returned to his duties at the camp, that his colleagues convinced him that the world was at peace and for that at least they should be thankful.

For Eve and her mother the news was welcome but overshadowed by Eve's personal day-to-day problems.

Dorothy said, 'There'll be victory parades,

no doubt.' There was a noticeable lack of enthusiasm in her voice. 'Street parties, most likely, for the children. Some of the youngest were born in war and will find peace hard to understand.'

'It's a big step in the right direction,' Eve agreed. 'At least the poor wretches in the trenches can come home, but I won't be happy until we've beaten the flu. A medical breakthrough. Now that would be the icing on the cake!'

Dorothy tutted mildly. 'Really, Eve. God has answered one of our prayers. You should at least be grateful.'

Eve stared at her. She thought of all the heartaches, pain and misery of the past four years and couldn't bring herself to answer.

Later that day, Eve was pitting her wits against bureaucracy at the South London Home for Orphaned Children. She sat in front of a desk, hands clasped in her lap, and prayed that Mr Weston would not put in an appearance. He knew she was not a family member and he might also recall the clash of personalities on the doorstep of the Beattys's home.

At present she was dealing with a Miss Rosely who was evidently working long hours with little reward and looked thoroughly jaded. She reminded Eve of her one-time geography teacher – pinched features surrounded by frizzy hair and a pleated skirt with blouse and a cardigan that had been neatly darned at one elbow.

'So your name is...?' Miss Rosely looked up enquiringly.

Eve spelt it out for her.

'And you are enquiring after...?'

'Lucy and Amy Beatty from Number Twenty Leopold Street. Their parents are dead but I know of a great-aunt who would take them in.'

'Her name is...?'

Eve only knew her as Aunt Biddy but had decided to gamble on a few lies. Hopefully Miss Rosely would be too thankful to place two of the orphans and wouldn't enquire too closely.

'Miss Biddy ... I forget her surname for the moment but I can find out for you,' she said. Had she ever heard it? Surely Ellen must have mentioned the aunt's name. 'She lives in Devon. A village called ... Somewhere near Exeter ... Todleigh. Yes, that's right.'

'Somewhere?' Miss Rosely raised her eyebrows. 'If you don't mind me saying so, you do seem rather vague on the details, Mrs Randall.'

'Biddy Franks,' Eve invented. 'I think it was Franks.'

Miss Rosely's pen moved again then stopped abruptly. She frowned. 'Now just a moment ... I seem to recall...' She riffled through a stack of documents which were piled on one side of her desk. 'I think we lost Amy Beatty. Let me see.'

'*Lost* her? Lost Amy? You mean she died?' Eve protested. 'No, that can't be right. She was fine. They both were.'

'She developed the flu soon after she came in ... Very unfortunate. We had to isolate her ... Ah, yes. Here we are. Came in on the fourth incubating the disease and died two days later. I'm so sorry to be the bearer of bad news. Cause of death ... influenza followed by pneumonia exacerbated by malnutrition.'

'But...' Eve stared at her. 'They were both well. The neighbour said the girls were...'

'She was obviously not as well as she looked, Mrs Randall.' She gave Eve a reproving glance. 'Looks can be misleading. Influenza can take time to show itself, you see. The girl looked well enough but she was incubating the disease. Obviously in the early stages. It's a wonder Lucy hasn't contracted it but I think the danger has passed as far as she is concerned.'

Eve, shocked to the core by the news, was engulfed by a wave of despair. Was there no end to the tragedy? The sooner she installed Lucy with her aunt the better. Hopefully she would be safer there away from the over-crowded streets of London.

Aware of Eve's distress, Miss Rosely softened a little. 'I'm sorry. I'm sure we did everything we could to save her. We have a very dedicated staff here and a fully functioning sick ward. A body needs to be very well nourished if it stands any chance of beating the disease and sadly many of the poorer people are not well fed. It's a fact of life. It is a very virulent disease.'

'I *know* it's virulent!' Eve cried. 'It *killed* my husband.' She realized she was almost shouting and she could feel her pulse speeding up. Shock at the news of Amy's death, a growing sense of frustration and a feeling of help-lessness was undermining her self-control. *Stop this, Eve!* she urged inwardly. *You have to remain calm or you will get nowhere with these people.* 'I'm sorry,' she said quickly. 'That was quite uncalled for. How could you have known? We've all lost someone ... That is, I expect you...'

Miss Rosely did not lift her head but stared fixedly at the page she was writing on. 'I have no one to lose,' she said, her voice flat. 'I finally begin to think I am fortunate in that respect.'

Mortified, Eve stammered an apology but Miss Rosely appeared not to hear and continued with her questions.

'Is Miss Biddy Franks coming to London to collect the child – that is, Lucy Beatty?'

'Er ... no.' Eve thought quickly. 'I said I would collect them ... I mean Lucy and travel with her to her aunt.' Poor Amy, she thought, dying alone in a strange place.

'Just a moment...' Miss Rosely was frowning. 'I have a note here about the existence of a third sister. Kate Beatty.' She glanced at Eve. 'She is still in the hospital but making a good recovery.'

'She's recovering? Kate's going to live?' Eve hardly dared to believe it. 'Are you sure? I mean...' A broad smile lit up her face. Suddenly the world seemed a better place. 'That's the most wonderful news!' It meant that Lucy was no longer the lone survivor of the family. 'Does Lucy know?'

'Most certainly.'

Eve hesitated. 'You are sure?' She thought she could hardly bear it if somehow this was a false hope.

Miss Rosely gave her a thin smile. 'I do know my job, Mrs Randall. I can assure you that I have been notified of her recovery. Contrary to your obviously low opinion of our service, we do have the children's welfare at heart and I have arranged for Lucy to be reunited with her sister as soon as possible.' She allowed herself a sly glance at Eve and then, relaxing, continued. 'Sadly only two of the children survived but I'm sure you'll agree that is better than none.'

'Oh, it is! Thank you for such amazing news. My mother will be thrilled, too.'

Miss Rosely returned to her form filling. 'So has the great-aunt been notified of your arrival with the two girls?'

'I've sent a letter.' It was another lie. Eve knew only the name of the village but was sure someone in the post office there would point them in the right direction. 'She doesn't believe in the telephone and a tele-gram would alarm her.'

'And she will be willing and able to care for them? How old is she?'

'No one is allowed to know!' Eve risked a smile which they shared.

'And she will have the wherewithal to feed and clothe them adequately?'

Eve nodded then added, 'Yes. She has means.' Doubts began to surface as the lies continued. Suppose the old lady didn't want the girls or couldn't afford to take them in ... Firmly she pushed the concerns aside. She would deal with them if and when she met them. One thing at a time. Her main aim was to prevent Kate and Lucy from being drawn into the system and her best chance to do this was to act while the organization was groaning under the extra load, while matters were chaotic and errors could be made and overlooked. She felt guilty but told herself that, in this case, the end justified the means.

Fifteen minutes later the paperwork had been completed and Eve was told she would be notified when Kate was released to the orphanage. Providing that Lucy was still well, Eve would be allowed to collect them.

Eight

That evening Eve sat upstairs with her mother, nursing a throbbing headache. Dorothy was in bed with a folded newspaper, doing a crossword puzzle. She had always claimed to be successful with crosswords but tonight she was only giving it half her attention.

'I'm not surprised you have a headache, Eve,' Dorothy chided gently. 'You've taken too much on yourself at a time when you should be resting and recovering. You should not underestimate the blow it's been to your body *and* mind to lose Harvey. The doctor said that rest was the best way to recover your strength but here you are, chasing about, looking after everybody but yourself.'

'Mother, I know you mean well but...'

'Eve, I'm saying this for your own good, dear. I know what you're doing and it won't work.'

Eve groaned inwardly. 'I'm just trying to save what's left of Jon's family. And I did manage to have them buried together –

except for poor Amy...'

Dorothy held up her hand. 'Now stop there, Eve. You are not a miracle worker. You didn't know she was dead and you couldn't have intervened. She's dead and buried and there's nothing you can do now. Accept it, Eve, and don't start blaming yourself.' She shook her head. 'Now you're planning to rush off to the middle of a godforsaken moor with two girls you hardly know, in search of a phantom aunt...'

'Todleigh is not a moor, Mother, and—'

'You know what I mean, Eve. Devon and Cornwall are wayward counties...'

'And Aunt Biddy is not a phantom. I shall find her.' Eve rubbed her forehead, willing the headache to recede but it clung on doggedly behind her eyes as an unforgiving pressure. She was consumed with weariness and cast a surreptitious glance at the small bedside clock. Ten past five. She realized with dismay that it was four hours before she could decently go to bed. The thought of cool sheets and a soft pillow were very tempting but Eve felt she owed it to her mother to give her some company since she had spent so many hours worrying about others. She knew Dorothy hated to be alone for too long. Eve had once suggested that a cat would be company, but Dorothy disliked the idea of cat's hairs in the bedroom so the notion had been abandoned.

Dorothy stared at the list of clues. 'Seven letters, third letter is "s", and the clue is "Twice in a hot place".'

'Try biscuit.'

'Biscuit?' She lowered her head slightly and peered at Eve. 'How d'you make that out, dear?'

'The word comes from either French or Latin and means twice cooked.'

Eve closed her eyes and sank further into the small armchair.

'Well, who's the clever one?' Dorothy huffed. Although she frequently asked for help, she actually preferred to discover that her daughter didn't know the answers either. 'It would fit,' she admitted reluctantly. 'I'll put it in lightly so that I can rub it out if need be. Now let's have a look. Seventeen down is "moggy might use this". Eight letters. The last but one letter is "l".'

Eve said nothing.

'Eve, did you hear me?'

Eve sat up slowly. 'I fancy a glass of cold milk. Can I get you anything? A cup of tea, perhaps.'

'That would be nice. And a biscuit. You could think about this while you're down-stairs.'

'About what?'

'The moggy clue. I had a school friend

once. We called her Moggy but her name was Margaret. The girl from Wales. I told you about her. You must remember. We used to play hopscotch together in the playground. I must have been about ten, I suppose. Margaret Thomas. That was it. They moved away and it...' She frowned. 'Are you all right, dear?'

'Just tired. My back aches.'

Dorothy tutted. 'I'm really not surprised, dear. All that traipsing about. You're overdoing it, Eve. I keep telling you but it's water off a duck's back! You simply will not listen to me.'

Eve levered herself up from the chair and made her way slowly downstairs. In the kitchen, she stood for a moment staring round the familiar room and trying to remember what it was she wanted. She felt dizzy and somehow disconnected from the familiar surroundings.

'Oh, yes!' It came to her at last. 'Tea for Mother and milk for me.' She slid the kettle back on to the hob, poured herself a glass of cold milk and sat down to drink it. It was wonderfully cold and soothing to her throat which seemed uncomfortably dry. Having finished it, she immediately refilled the glass and sipped it more slowly. When she had quenched her thirst she stood up, with an effort, to make the tea. She laid a tray with a small teapot, cup, saucer, sugar, milk and cinnamon biscuits and carried it upstairs. She would tell her mother she needed an early night and would go to bed about eight.

'Oh, thank you, dear.' Dorothy balanced the tray with practised ease and poured herself a cup of tea.

Eve sat down. 'That clue – I think it might be catapult.'

Dorothy stared at her. 'Catapult? Hardly, Eve. I mean, how on earth could a cat use a catapult?'

'I think it's supposed to be a twist. A joke. Cat – apult.'

'A joke? Oh, I see. Not very amusing but I think you may be right. Let me see...' Her face brightened. 'Yes, it is catapult because the other word will fit ... How clever of you, dear. Moggy as a cat and not as Margaret. Well, they certainly are obtuse, these clues, but it gives one so much more satisfaction when they're solved. I've always been rather good with clues. Your grandfather commented on it more than once. He liked me to do crossword puzzles because it kept me quiet. Catapult does fit ... and that gives me a "p" there. Where's your milk, Eve?'

'I've already drunk it. I was thirsty.'

'Aren't you going to have a biscuit?'

Eve shook her head. 'Mother, I'll make you a sandwich later and there's a slice of that

168

Dundee cake. I think I'll have an early night. I'm running out of energy.'

'Very sensible of you, dear. A sandwich will be quite sufficient. But not cheese, Eve. Is there any ham left?'

'I don't know. I'll have a look. If not there are some potted shrimps.'

'Potted shrimps in a sandwich? Really, Eve! What's got into you? If it has to be the shrimps, I'll have them with some thin bread and butter. Do we have any brown bread?'

Eve snapped, 'I don't know!' Knowing she sounded waspish she added, 'I'll use brown if we have any. If not it will have to be white.'

'There's no need to take that tone, Eve. I was only asking.'

'I'm sorry. I told you, I'm not quite up to par today. Everything is such an effort.'

Dorothy glanced across at her daughter. 'You do look a bit peaky, dear. An early night will certainly do you good. I shan't be late myself tonight although I've promised myself another chapter of my book.'

Eve closed her eyes and lay back in the chair. Her headache was much worse, tightening painfully around her skull. She felt shivery and glanced again at the clock. Only half past five. The early bed time she had promised herself seemed a long way off. She imagined the moment when she would slip between the sheets and slide in to a deep refreshing sleep but with the image came the reminder that she would sleep alone. Never again could she rest with Harvey's loving arms around her or feel his soft goodnight kiss on her hair. She would never again hear him whisper, 'Sleep tight, darling.' The other side of the bed would be forever empty and there would be no comfort for her there. The spectre of loneliness was beginning to haunt her.

She wondered where Harvey's body was buried and hoped it was not a shared grave. The army would know. They would keep records and she must get in touch with them as soon as the crisis eased. If Harvey had not shared a grave then what, if anything, was written on his tombstone? The army would never use terms like 'Beloved Husband' or 'Dearly Missed'. If there were no tombstone it would be as if he had disappeared – or had never lived at all.

She smothered a groan and put a hand to her head but the troublesome questions persisted. Perhaps when she no longer had to care for her mother, she could summon up her courage and go to America in search of him. She could have a tombstone en-graved with his name on it. Maybe she could have him moved into a separate plot. She sighed. Fine plans but in her heart she knew she was a nervous traveller and the trip would be a huge expense. Would she be able to go to America and seek out his last resting place?

At least he was at peace now, she reminded herself, but the thought did little to soften the knowledge that, for her, the world was an empty place. Closing her eyes, she could no longer hold back the tears and they slid silently down her cheeks.

Dorothy, intent on her crossword, pressed the blunt end of her pencil into her chin as she wrestled with another clue. 'Seventeen across: "The end of the road?" Five letters, second letter's probably "e". I thought of "home" because when you get to the end of the road you've arrived home – but there aren't enough letters and the "e"s in the wrong place.' She shook her head. 'And it ends with a question mark. I do hate it when they do that. How can it be a question? "The end of the road?" Second letter "e"...'

Death, thought Eve wearily, but by that stage, she was quite beyond speech.

When Eve awoke it was dark and there was no moonlight to brighten the gloom. Her eyes felt heavy as she forced them to stay open. She longed for a drink of something cold but her limbs felt leaden and even changing position in the bed caused her discomfort. Her back still ached and her arms and legs now felt heavy and un-cooperative. For a moment she lay there, considering whether or not she was able to get out of bed and make her way downstairs to the kitchen. The answer was a definite 'No!'

The pain in her head had worsened and now drummed intensely, causing her to screw up her face in pain. For what seemed like hours she lay there in the darkness, trying unsuccessfully to summon some energy. Utterly exhausted, aching all over, Eve tried to concentrate but her mind was woolly and thoughts came and went without remaining long enough for her to capture them. Was she too hot? With an effort, she threw off the bedclothes.

Minutes later she felt the heat drain away, and began to shiver. I'm ill! she thought, sur-prised, but even that thought slipped away as she slid into a half conscious state.

Through the long night she tumbled be-tween waking and dreaming and the dreams were more like nightmares. Harvey appear-ed, calling to her, but when she tried to move toward him he became faint and disappear-ed. She heard his voice – or thought she did – and struggled to make sense of what he was saying. Young Kate Beatty spoke to her, from behind iron bars, her dark eyes flashing with anger. Ellen drifted past in the new hat

Jon had bought her. 'Every woman should have a new hat before she dies!' Had she heard those words? Was she dreaming? Crying out, Eve awoke and found herself in her bedroom.

Dorothy was leaning over her. 'You called out. Was it a nightmare?'

Eve tried to answer but no words came to her. Instead she groaned. Her mother's expression changed.

'Oh Lord! She's ill!' Her hand covered her mouth but her eyes regarded Eve fearfully.

'Harvey! He came...' Eve said, closing her eyes. When she opened them she was alone. 'Mother,' she cried feebly. Or thought she did. Had she spoken? Would anybody hear her?

It seemed a long time before her mother was once more standing beside her bed, shaking her awake.

'Sit up, Eve. Just try, for my sake. I've crushed up two aspirins in some jam, the way you liked them when you were little. I want you to sit up – I'll help you ... Good. Now swallow this ... All of it ... Good girl! Now wash it down with a few mouthfuls of warm milk. That's the way. Now you can go back to sleep and I'll be here all night. I shall doze in the chair. I'll be fine.'

Eve felt a kiss on her cheek and tried to smile. 'If I die...' she began.

'Die? What nonsense. You most certainly will not die! Who will help me with my crosswords if you die?' The words trembled but Eve took heart from them as she slipped back into her confused world, somewhere between sleep and waking. Her only link with reality was the touch of her mother's hand on hers, willing her to survive the night.

When Mrs Banks turned up on Tuesday to do the ironing, she was met at the door by Dorothy who wore a dressing gown over her nightdress.

'You mustn't come in, Mrs Banks,' the old lady told her. 'My daughter is ill and I think it's influenza. I want you to take this note round to the doctor in the hope he will call round.'

'Influ—!' Mrs Banks stopped mid-word. She had decided that if she never uttered the word, she might somehow keep it at a distance. 'Oh, my giddy aunt! I was here yesterday for the washing. Ooh!' Her eyes widened fearfully. 'I might have caught it.'

'Well, we'll have to hope you haven't. I want you to take this round to the doctor. Then I have one more errand and...'

'I'd rather not come in the house, Mrs Collett, if you don't mind.' Panic was setting in.

'Of course not. I want you to stay out of harm's way but first I need the doctor.' Dorothy indicated the note.

'But you said the doctor wasn't making any more house calls because his wife was taken sick.'

'That was some time ago. She may have recovered or she may have died. Either way the doctor might be resuming his house calls now. I need to know one way or the other because if he's not coming, I shall have to find another doctor. Now, please do hurry, Mrs Banks. In the meantime, I shall get myself dressed.'

Ida Banks made her way to the doctor's house, her mind busy with the startling news of Mrs Randall's illness and the questions arising from it. Firstly she wondered if she, herself, might already be infected. Secondly she wondered, if she was *not* infected, how would she manage for money if she was not able to do the work she was paid to do. She also worked for a Mr Towney who so far had shown no sign of becoming ill but she only worked for him one day a week and that money would barely cover the rent. Her husband was a plumber but he didn't have much work at the moment for some reason. He blamed it on the flu but Mrs Banks didn't see how the illness could have affected the pipe work.

When she knocked at the doctor's door it was opened, after a long delay, by a frail-looking woman dressed similarly to Dorothy ... in a nightdress and dressing gown.

'Yes?'

'I've a note for the doctor.'

'I'm his wife. I'll give it to him.' She held out her hand.

Mrs Banks stared at her in amazement. 'I thought you had the – I thought you were ill.'

'I did, but, God be praised, I'm on the road to recovery. We don't all die, you see.' She managed a smile.

'No-o.' Mrs Banks thought it nothing less than a miracle.

The doctor's wife regarded her earnestly. 'Most people fail to take the Lord into consideration when they face catastrophe.' She held the collar of her dressing-gown closer to her thin neck. 'They rely on worldly remedies, you see – hot drinks, herb teas, cinnamon milk, salt of quinine. My husband swears by epinephrine to counteract the pneumonia...'

'Epin ... what? I've never heard of it.'

'Epinephrine ... and then there're some who recommend cold packs to the head.'

'Is that so?' Mrs Banks looked flummoxed. Packs of what? She was trying to commit all these remedies to memory in case the worst happened. 'What do you think works best? Because if I catch the you-know-what, I mean, my husband – good soul though he is – won't have the faintest idea how to get me better and he's not one for saying prayers so I'll have to write it down for him before-hand. Because I might be so ill that I'm delirious.' She regarded the doctor's wife earnestly. 'I've heard about that. It means you can't think straight, can't remember things and you get all muddled in your head. Is there one above all the others? One best remedy?'

'Why prayer, naturally. If the world has turned to sin and is punished by a scourge of sickness, then we should all be down on our knees, praying for forgiveness! I prayed and God saved me.'

'I see.' Mrs Banks looked doubtful but managed a nervous smile. Surely being mar-ried to a doctor was of some help. 'Well, I'll remember that – and I'll pray for Mrs Ran-dall because she's very poorly. Is there going to be a reply to that note? It says that Mrs Randall is ill and her mother thinks it's the...' She bit back the awful word.

'The flu. Of course.' The doctor's wife straightened up. 'Everyone jumps to that conclusion. You can tell them the doctor is now doing house calls again and I'll give him this note when he comes home. He'll call on you as soon as he can but I can't say when that will be.'

'Thank you. And ... you take care of yourself!'

She smiled. 'I am in God's hands.'

'And the doctor didn't catch it from you.' This was important, thought Ida, because surely it meant that although Mrs Banks had been in Mrs Randall's house doing the washing the previous day she need not have caught anything. Perhaps God *was* watching over her even before she started on the prayers. Perhaps he considered her one of 'the just'. Whatever they were.

'No. The Lord was merciful. Never forget the power of prayer, Mrs Banks. They do say the good Lord smiles on the just.'

'Right.' Not entirely convinced by the logic, Mrs Banks retraced her steps thoughtfully. Careful to remain well back from the doorstep, she repeated the message to Mrs Randall's mother who was now dressed and appeared to be in good health.

'Thank you, Mrs Banks. Now here is your last task. It's a list of groceries, and a few things from the chemist. Here is some money.' She handed Mrs Banks a purse. 'If you would fetch those things I shall be most grateful. I won't expect you to re-enter the house until my daughter has recovered but if you would call by each morning to see if there are any errands, you will be paid your usual wages at the end of the week.'

'Oh!' That was a relief in more ways than one. 'Right you are then.' She hesitated. 'The doctor's wife says she was saved by prayer because she put herself in the care of the Lord.'

Dorothy smiled. 'I'm sure a few prayers do no harm at all,' she said, 'but I'm a firm believer in the saying "God helps those who help themselves!" I shall boil onions with vinegar, strain it and sweeten the liquid with honey. It's not exactly pleasant but it's drinkable and it saved my life when I had pneumonia as a child. Congestion of the lungs, they said it was, but my mother knew better. It's pneumonia, she said. I can hear her saying it now.' She smiled at the memory. 'Funny what you remember, isn't it? Now, where was I? Oh, yes. Three or four spoonfuls first thing in the morning plus a small glass of sweet sherry last thing at night.'

'Ah! It all sounds very good ... I'll be off then.' She was handed a shopping basket. 'I shall pray that Mrs Randall doesn't die,' she promised.

'Die? *Die?*' Dorothy drew herself up to her full height. 'Do I look the sort of woman who would let her daughter die?'

'Well, no ... I suppose not!'

Chastened, Mrs Banks went on her way,

full of information and thoroughly confused.

Eve lay in bed that night, bathed in perspiration as the fever took hold of her. She was vaguely aware that her mother had sponged her down with cool water, but exactly when that had been she had no idea. It might have been an hour ago or five minutes. Her throat felt as if it was on fire, raw and rough. Her headache had never lessened and her body was a mass of aches and pains so that the thought of moving to a more comfortable position was out of the question. Nothing would ease the discomfort, though she had obediently sipped her mother's remedy.

The curtains were closed but when she forced her eyes apart for a moment, she could tell it was dark but since she dozed and woke intermittently, she had no idea of the time and cared little. At times she thought she was dreaming but at other times she felt she was wide awake and hallucinating. Strange and frightening shadows surrounded her, unfamiliar voices whispered in her ears and disorganised thoughts darted in and out of her mind.

Somewhere a church clock struck one and shortly after she was aware of her mother beside the bed.

'Head up, dear, that's the way ... slowly does it.'

Eve obeyed, her body moving sluggishly. She felt a warm flannel wiping her face and then her damp pillow was removed and a clean one was tucked under her head. A cool hand smoothed her tangled hair back from her forehead. 'That's better, isn't it? Go back to sleep now. I'm not far away if you need me. Only in the next room.'

Eve tried to speak but nothing came out. The small movements had exhausted her and she allowed herself to sink back into the dark confusion that passed for sleep.

Next morning, abandoning her role of invalid, Dorothy was up and about extraordinarily early. By ten to eight she was washed and dressed and writing a letter. She wrote carefully in her flowing hand, recalling with pleasure the prize she had won at school for her handwriting when she was nine years old. The school had awarded her a certificate but her father, delighted by her success, had bought her a thin gold bracelet. Dorothy had never been a clever child – words and numbers were never her strong suit – but, as her reports made clear, she was painstaking and persistent and good with her needle.

To the matron or whom it may concern,
    Mrs Eve Randall is indisposed with the
    flu and unable to collect Kate and Lucy

Beatty as arranged but she will notify you as soon as she is better. Please do not send the girls away anywhere as there are plans for them to rejoin their great-aunt. I (Eve Randall's mother) will try to call in at the orphanage in a day or so to check on the girls' health and well being.

Yours faithfully,

Dorothy Beatrice Collett

In fact, Dorothy had no intention of visiting the orphanage for she had been housebound for too long and the thought of venturing outside made her nervous. However, there was no need for staff at the orphanage to know that. If they thought she was likely to appear at any moment, they would surely take special care of the Beatty girls. Dorothy was not at all sure that her daughter had any right to take the children to the great-aunt but she was no longer prepared to interfere. Eve took after her in some respects and had inherited her stubborn streak, although it had rarely been obvious until now.

Dorothy's doubts had remained unspoken but they remained. Suppose the elderly maiden aunt didn't want the children or was too frail to care for them on a permanent basis. Bringing up two girls would be a huge responsibility. She knew from bringing up

Eve that one child could be a strain, not only emotionally but financially. How old was this great-aunt? Did she even *like* children? Presumably she could stand them for a short visit because Eve had said the mother took all three girls when she went up there to give birth to Sam. And would it be good for the girls to be brought up by such an elderly woman? Suppose she took ill and died on them!

We'll have to hope for the best, she thought, sealing the envelope. She wondered how long she would have to wait for Mrs Banks and glanced at the clock. I'll take the onion and honey drink up to Eve, she decided. If Mrs Banks turned up it wouldn't hurt her to wait on the doorstep for a few minutes.

Mrs Banks duly appeared at the door twenty minutes later. She wore her best coat and shoes and had wound a scarf around the lower half of her face. Whether to keep out the November weather or to resist germs, Dorothy wasn't sure.

Dorothy stared at her. 'You look very smart, Mrs Banks.'

Mrs Banks lowered her voice confidingly. 'I thought I should even though it isn't Sunday because I'm going to church after I've done your errands. I shall pray for Mrs Randall as well as for me and my hubby. I'm not going to a service because of all those people coughing and sneezing and spreading germs. It did say in the newspaper to stay away from crowds so I thought I'd just slip in when nobody else is in there and, you know, say a few prayers. How is Mrs Randall? What sort of night did she have?'

'Not well and she was very restless but she has the flu so I don't expect anything else. The doctor didn't call.' She regarded Mrs Banks accusingly.

Mrs Banks tutted. 'I gave his wife your message. I wonder what happened?'

'Called away to someone more urgent, I daresay,' Dorothy said with a shrug. 'Anyway I have this letter which I want you to take to the orphanage. It's about twenty minutes walk from here and you can't get there easily by bus so...'

'I shouldn't dare get on a bus. All those people squashed together.'

'Yes, well...' Dorothy couldn't decide whether Mrs Banks was being exceptionally prudent or becoming paranoid. 'I've drawn you a little map to help you find it. You must hand it in and—'

'I'd rather not go in, Mrs Collett.'

'Then post it through their letter box. Somebody must see it, that's what matters. You may see someone going in. If so, ask them to deliver it to someone in authority.'

She handed the envelope to Mrs Banks who took it gingerly. 'It won't bite you! It hasn't been in the sick room. It's not contagious.'

'Right. So is that everything? No groceries? Nothing from the chemist?'

'That's all. And thank you.'

Dorothy closed the door, muttering to herself, then made her way into the kitchen where Eve's nightdress soaked in suds in the large sink. She squeezed it thoroughly, rinsed it in clear water and took it outside. After putting it through the mangle to remove the surplus water, she pegged it on the line, thankful for a stiff wind which would quickly blow it dry.

It was nearly midday before the doctor called. Any ill will Dorothy had been feeling towards him vanished when she took a first look at his face. He looked grey and drawn and sank gratefully on to the chair she offered. He looked defeated and, rubbing his eyes, made no attempt at conversation – not even to enquire about the patient's progress.

Without a word, Dorothy poured him a glass of sherry. 'Drink this, doctor,' she told him. 'You look as though you are barely functioning.'

He nodded and, without protest, drank half the sherry. Then he leaned back in the chair and said, 'You have no idea, Mrs Collett. No idea at all!'

Dorothy nodded. 'Allow me to start then. My daughter has the flu. I recognize the symptoms because I had it myself as a child. Eve has come through the second night and has a high fever with some delirium but no signs as yet of developing the second more dangerous stage. I have it under control. Now tell me what has reduced you to this low state.'

He raised his eyes to hers. 'I've been battling to save a young mother and her newborn baby girl. She was three days into the flu when she went into an early labour. She wasn't due for another three weeks but she fell getting out of bed in the middle of the night. An hour later her contractions started. I was with her when your message reached my wife, but of course I couldn't abandon her.'

'Most certainly not! Poor young woman.' Dorothy hesitated. 'I'm afraid to ask what happened.'

The doctor shook his head. 'The baby died an hour later. I did what I could but...' He drew in a long, wretched breath.

'Drink up your sherry, doctor. I think you need something stimulating and then a good long sleep.'

He swallowed the sherry obediently and handed her the glass.

'Mabel will look after me. Fortunately I'm

blessed with a good wife.' He sighed deeply. 'The mother is in deep shock ... I shall call on her again this evening but first I must snatch a few hours rest.'

He stood up. 'Shall I glance in at your daughter, Mrs Collett?'

Dorothy shook her head. 'I know there is nothing else that can be done. I really don't think you could climb the stairs – the way you are. Go straight home and into bed.' She resisted the urge to help him along the passage to the front door. 'And don't dwell on your failures, doctor. The whole country owes your profession a huge debt of gratitude for all you've done these last months.'

'You're very kind but ... it's never enough, is it?'

She took his hat down from the hat stand and handed it to him.

He murmured, 'Goodbye' and she watched him stumble wearily back along the pavement.

There's always someone worse off, she thought. That unfortunate mother had just lost her child! Closing the door she made her way back into the kitchen, spread an ironing blanket over the table, took the iron from in front of the stove and began to iron Eve's newly dried nightdress.

Nine

The orphanage playroom had a high ceiling with large windows placed far up in the white-washed walls, and gas lights set equally high to be out of reach of children. The windows were shut against the cool November weather and the air smelled stale with a hint of disinfectant. The large room appeared smaller because of the excessive number of children it now contained. Intended for, perhaps, fifty at the most, it now held nearer to seventy of varying ages, with the exception of babies who were housed in the adjoining nursery.

On this day, boys and girls sat or stood or wandered about in varying stages of confusion. There was a large table but too few chairs, so those that chose to sit sat on the floor, many staring dazedly ahead or watching the antics of the others. One child, a boy of about seven, sobbed quietly beside an older girl who was trying to comfort him. There were few toys – push-along animals on wheels, four or five dolls, several teddy bears and a large doll's house which was entertaining three young girls. The amount of noise was surprisingly low because the children, parted from their parents so abruptly, were trying to come to terms with what was happening to them and behaved cautiously within the new environment.

The three adults did their best to comfort the tearful children – two young women and an older woman. Each of these women had at least two children clinging to their skirts. Below the apparently calm atmosphere was a sense of deep bewilderment.

Kate and Lucy sat close together on the floor against one wall, watching with narrowed eyes. Their knees were drawn up, their hands clasped round them defensively.

Lucy said, 'When are we going home?'

Kate put an arm round her. 'We can't go home. I told you. There's no one there.'

'Why not?'

'I told you and told you! They've gone to heaven. They're having a nice time with the angels. You don't have to be sad.' She turned her head away and wiped away a tear. 'One day we'll see them again.'

'Tomorrow?'

'No!' To change the subject, Kate pointed suddenly. 'See that boy there. He's going to be bright.'

'Is he?' Distracted, Lucy followed the

direction of her sister's finger. The red-haired boy was holding a ball which he turned over and over in his hands with intense concentration.

'Like Sam,' said Kate. 'Sam was going to be bright.'

Lucy looked at her hopefully. 'Am I going to be bright? Amy said I was. She said I was clever. I can say my ABC.'

'Go on then. Say it. I bet you can't.'

'I can. A, B, C!'

'That's not how you say it. You have to say a,b,c,d,e,f,g,h,i ... You have to say *all* of it.'

A plump girl of about Kate's age came up to them. Her fair hair was plaited into two short braids. 'D'you want to be my friends?' she asked.

Lucy, unsure, looked to her sister for guidance and Kate shook her head.

'No. Go away,' Lucy said.

'Can I sit with you then?'

'No,' said Kate. 'We're sisters. We don't want to play with anyone else and we don't want to sit with anyone.'

The child seemed unabashed by the rejection. 'Why not?'

Kate put an arm round Lucy. 'Because we have to stay together. We want to sit here and talk about our family.'

'My ma is dead and my pa is a sailor. One day he'll come home and collect me.'

Lucy looked at Kate, who said, 'We've got an aunt.'

'My name's Beatrice,' the girl told them. Then she turned abruptly and walked over to another girl and asked if they could be friends. The answer was 'Yes' and the child with braids sat down next to her.

Lucy sighed. 'Why don't we want to be friends with anyone?'

Kate said firmly, 'Because we ain't staying here so we don't need any friends.'

'So, are they staying here for ever?'

'I expect so. Some of them. They haven't got any family but we have. The lady said that we're going to stay with Aunt Biddy. We're going to live with her for ever. She's our family. She's...'

She was distracted by another woman who walked into the room with a pile of books in her arms. To Kate all the women were interchangeable and she didn't bother to learn their names because she wasn't staying. This lady was pretty, Kate thought. She had dark wavy hair, a bright red smiley mouth and big eyes. She reminded Kate of a princess she had seen in a book.

'Now then, children,' the woman began cheerily. 'There are some nice books here for you to look at.' She put them on the table. 'Come and have a look.' Nobody moved but all eyes were on her, carefully assessing her motives. She continued to smile cheerfully. 'I'm Miss Pringle and I've brought you these lovely books. Miss Stobart will be here later and she's going to tell you a story about ... a fairytale, but for now you can look at the books for yourselves.' The children still did not move but they exchanged glances among themselves. She held up a book chosen at random. ' It's called *Animal Tales* and it's all about animals. Now who'd like to read this – or just look at the pictures?'

There was still no response.

She picked up another one. 'Oh, goodness! Look at this lovely book. This is about castles and dragons and all sorts of exciting things.'

Lucy glanced at Kate who shook her head.

Miss Pringle admitted defeat. 'Well, they're here if you want to look at them. They've been given to us by some very kind people.'

All eyes watched her retreat.

Ten minutes later her place was taken by another lady-in-charge, a middle-aged woman who carried a sheet of paper.

'Kate and Lucy Beatty?' she called looking around.

Kate narrowed her eyes suspiciously. She was slowly gaining confidence but what was going to happen now? When she had come round, after the bout of flu that had nearly killed her, she had found herself alone in the hospital ward filled with sick and dying

patients. No one explained ~
be there. No one ca~
bothered to tell her a.
plight of the rest of th~
been utterly terrified. N
short years of life had pre~
feeling of being alone, ad~
world. Only once she had
here, to be reunited with Lucy,
explain that her mother was dea
her an orphan, and so were Sam ~

Now she lowered her eyes and
wordlessly at the floor, stricken wit~
frightening suspicion that, for some na~
less reason, she and Lucy were going to \
separated. Keeping quiet seemed the safes~
option. Lucy, however, stood up.

The woman consulted her list. 'Are you
Lucy Ann or Katharine?'

'Yes, miss.'

'Which one?'

Slowly Kate stood up. 'I'm Kate.' She took
hold of her sister's hand.

'Come with me, both of you.'

Lucy stepped forward but Kate pulled her
back.

'Where to?' Kate fixed the woman with a
hostile look.

'Just to the office. There's a message about
you. It's nothing to worry about.' She nodded impatiently. 'Come along.' She turned

he room.

vo girls eyed each other.

said, 'We'd better go.'

trailed nervously after the woman,

a seemingly unending corridor and

y ended up in an office.

grey-haired man sat behind a large desk

peered at them over the top of his spec-

les. He wasn't wearing a white coat so

ate thought he was not a doctor but 'a man

n charge'.

'Thank you, Miss King. Wait for them, will you, please.'

'Yes, Mr Forbes.' Obediently Miss King sat on a chair by the door, crossed her ankles and folded her hands in her lap.

The man in charge consulted his notes. 'Lucy and Katharine Beatty, I presume.'

'I'm Lucy.' She smiled winningly.

Kate tugged at her arm, determined to take charge, not trusting Lucy to say the right things. As firmly as she could she said, 'Mrs Randall is going to take us to our Aunt Biddy in—'

'We have been notified by letter that Mrs Randall has been taken ill but asks that you remain in our care until such time as she is recovered.'

At the words 'Mrs Randall' and 'ill', Kate's insides lurched with shock.

'She's taking us to Aunt Biddy,' she in-

sisted. *But suppose she died?* she thought. She forced herself to ask the question even though she dreaded the answer. 'Is she ill with flu?'

He nodded. 'But we shall assume a complete recovery and proceed accordingly until or unless we are informed to the contrary.'

Kate didn't know what he was talking about. Was it good or bad? Her hand tightened round Lucy's. 'We're going to Aunt Biddy's,' she repeated.

'Ye-e-s. But where exactly does your aunt live? We need a few more facts for our records. The number of the house, perhaps, and the name of the street?'

Kate felt a new flutter of anxiety. More problems she couldn't deal with.

'Mrs Randall knows,' she said firmly. 'The biscuit lady. She'll tell you all that.'

'I know. It's a long way on a train,' Lucy said. 'We went there when Sam was born and Aunt Biddy let us help her make some jam tarts and she said mine were the best.'

'She did not!' Kate turned to her, dismayed by the betrayal.

'She did so.' Lucy's lips trembled.

'She did *not*, so shut up,' hissed Kate. 'Anyway, I'm the oldest so I have to say it all, not you.' She lowered her voice. 'You might get it wrong.'

'Girls!' Mr Forbes frowned over the top of

his spectacles. 'Thanks to an unwarranted amount of bureaucracy, we cannot simply write to "Biddy", can we?' He smiled at Miss King. 'There are blanks on the page that have to be filled.'

'All very time consuming,' Miss King said.

'Indeed.' He returned his attention to the two girls. 'The lady, your relative – she must have another name.'

Undeterred, Lucy piped up again. 'It's "Aunt". Aunt Biddy.'

He rolled his eyes then looked at Kate.

'I think it's Towner because Ma used to write to her and I posted the letters and they were addressed to Miss B Towner – and she lives in Exeter.'

'Well done, Katharine.' He scribbled something down.

Kate, beaming, whispered, 'See.'

'Do you know whereabouts in Exeter?'

Kate frowned. 'There's a farm next door with cows and chickens and...'

'Cows and chickens? In Exeter? I doubt it. Any buses, Katharine? Any big buildings? Any rows of houses?'

Kate's frown deepened.

'No? Never mind.' He glanced at Miss King. 'It is maybe a nearby village. This Mrs Randall will presumably know.' He put down his pen, folded his arms on the desktop and leaned forward. 'So, the situation is this. This is a place where children come when they have no mothers or fathers to look after them. So we look after them instead. Some children stay here until they reach sixteen. Some, like you two, stay for a few days and then go to live with someone else. You, it seems, will live with your aunt. I hope that is all clearly understood.'

'I want to go home,' said Lucy. 'Why can't we?'

For a moment his expression softened. 'It isn't your home any more, Lucy. There is no one to pay the rent. Someone else will be living there soon. A different family.'

Lucy's eyes filled with tears which rolled down her cheeks and fell on to her pinafore. Kate gave her a fierce hug. 'Don't cry. You've still got me!' She turned to the man behind the desk. 'I'm going to look after her, even when we get to Aunt Biddy. Lucy's bright. I'm going to teach her things. She doesn't know her ABC yet but I'm—'

Lucy rounded on her, suddenly shrill, her tears forgotten. 'I do know it! You're telling lies! I'm telling Ma!'

Kate said gently, 'You can't tell her anything, Lucy.' Her voice shook. 'Not any more.' She turned to the man in charge. 'She's too young. She still doesn't understand.'

He was taken aback by the small show of

emotion. 'That's quite enough of that,' he said gruffly. 'Off you go with Miss King. And behave yourselves. I feel certain your mother and father would have wanted you to be properly obedient while you are with us.' He swallowed hard.

Lucy brightened. 'Our pa's a grave digger and he earns a lot of money and he bought Ma a new hat with ribbons and feathers.' Her eyes shone at the memory.

'It was brand spanking new!' Kate added with quiet pride.

For a long moment he stared at her and then at Kate, then he shook his head, pressed the fingers of one hand over his eyes and waved a dismissive hand in Miss King's direction. She rose obediently and led them away.

On the same day, but on the other side of the world, James Ferber was sitting on the swing seat in his mother-in-law's house. It was nearly seven and he'd been into Toby's room to tell him a bedtime story and settle him to sleep. He had no idea how he would have survived the days since Louise's death if he had not had Toby to consider.

He heard the door open behind him and hoped that Bernard was not going to join him. He and Janet had been invited to dinner – a small celebration Alison arranged each year on the fourteenth of November, to remember her late husband's birthday.

'Ah! Here you are!' Bernard stood in front of him, blocking out the thin afternoon sun, his shadow thrown across the porch. 'Mind if I join you?' Without waiting for a reply he pulled up a deck chair and sank into it with a sigh of pleasure.

James opened his eyes and forced a smile. 'I'm just rearranging the world!' he mocked. 'Trying to sort out a future.' This was true but he didn't expect Bernard to understand or sympathize. It was simply something to say.

Bernard crossed his legs and squinted up into the sun. 'Alison mentioned that you were making plans.'

'Trying to.'

'She seems to think you're going to leave the army. Bit of a change for you, isn't it? I mean we've always thought you loved the army. I mean I know you're not a fighting man – but it's still a career.'

James detected a hint of criticism. 'I've had enough of it. After I'd done my medical training I wanted a bit of a change and the army recruiting was very seductive. A man's life! See the world! That sort of thing. I thought it sounded more of an experience than going straight into a mortuary or hospital ... Now it takes me away from the family and without Louise I have Toby to think about.'

Bernard turned to him. 'Alison says you've always had this wanderlust. You're talking about going to Europe now that the war's finally over – although you won't be seeing it at its best. Hardly the way I'd want to see it. The war must have knocked it about. Buildings in ruin, the economy shot to hell. It's going to take years to restore Europe to its former glory.' He shrugged. 'I thought about that myself, once upon a time, but family ties – you know what I mean. Never did go. Should have done it while I was young and carefree. I talked about it with my friends and we were all keen but somehow we never quite got it together. Big step and all that and our parents were nervous about the idea. Then I met Janet...' He shrugged.

'Do you regret it?'

Bernard hesitated. 'In a way but ... No, I don't really think so. Janet would never have wanted me to go without her and like most women she was nervous of travelling abroad. She's never been out of state, let alone abroad. And then she does have a weak stomach and worries about foreign food.' He shook his head. After a long silence he said, 'Alison says she's offered to look after Toby for a couple of months while you go gallivanting to England. She wants you to have the opportunity. That's how she put it.'

'Yes, she did offer. It was very generous of her.'

'To be quite honest, Janet and I don't think she's up to it at her age. I think she loves the idea – she adores her grandson and would love to look after him – but a child that age can be a handful. He's only two and very lively.'

'He'll be three in a month's time.' James fought down a rush of resentment. *What right had they to interfere?* 'I didn't ask Alison, you know. It was entirely her idea. She offered and it took me by surprise. That's what I mean by saying I'm trying to make plans. Considering all my options. Louise and I thought once upon a time that we might make a home in England for a time but...' He shrugged. 'The war came along and everything was put on hold. What did Alison say when you told her you thought she would find Toby too wearing?'

Bernard's blue eyes darkened with alarm. 'Oh, now don't get me wrong, James. We're not trying to meddle. God no! We haven't spoken to Alison about it. Just thought ... Well, thought we'd put it to you first. We mean no harm. Wouldn't want her to know, actually. She might take it the wrong way. Might be offended if she thought we thought she couldn't cope with the boy.'

He was rattled, James could see, and wondered if, in fact, this was entirely Bernard's objection. 'I'll maybe talk it over with Janet,' he said thoughtfully.

Bernard's alarm grew. 'Er ... I'd rather we kept this between ourselves, if you don't mind.'

'But if you two have already discussed it...' he said innocently.

Bernard frowned. 'To be honest, James, we haven't actually discussed it. Not specifically. Just "like minds", if you know what I mean. I know how she'd feel about it.'

So Janet had not been in agreement, thought James. This *was* Bernard's idea. Was this merely envy? Did Bernard resent the fact that James, being forced to take stock of his life and his future, was possibly going to do something adventurous? Something many Americans talked of doing. Europe. The old world with its quaint ways and mysterious challenges? Something Bernard would have enjoyed. He began to feel sorry for the older man though he couldn't say why. Bernard still had the woman he loved and a comfortable home and enough money. He was a happily married man with a grown-up family whereas James was newly widowed with a motherless son to care for.

His irritation fading, he said, 'I'll bear in mind what you say, Bernard. Thanks for mentioning it.'

'And you won't say anything to Alison or Janet? Just a heart to heart between the two of us...' His voice trailed away.

After he'd gone inside the house, James gave serious thought to what he had said. Was it really a good idea to leave Toby with his grandmother? Was it fair to Toby to leave him so soon after Louise had died. Would the boy feel that he had lost both parents? Perhaps ... a new idea crept slowly into his mind. Perhaps he should take Toby with him!

Late that same evening, the daylight faded and heavy clouds plunged London into a dark and sombre night with no chance of a moon. As Dorothy lit three candles and closed the curtains she sensed that her daughter's illness had reached the critical stage. Eve was almost constantly delirious and her temperature rarely fell below 104 degrees Fahrenheit which was way too high for safety. Dorothy had heard of people who had fits when their temperature edged up to 105 degrees. She had talked to people and read accounts in the newspapers and was ready for anything. As she looked down at Eve, her hair wet with perspiration, her skin unnaturally red, her mouth slack, Dorothy felt a frisson of fear. This sad, sick creature was not the daughter she recognized, merely a gaunt, fretful shadow of her former self.

For all her brave talk, Dorothy was suddenly frightened. The next ten or twelve hours would either see an improvement as the fever broke, or a gradual deterioration into the deadly stage of pneumonia from which so few people recovered. Even her son-in-law had died of it.

She leaned over the bed. 'I'm going to sleep in this room with you tonight, Eve dear,' she said loudly. 'I'll be right here with you. I'm going to watch you every minute of the night so you can rest easy.'

She sat down on the bedside chair before her legs gave way under her. The past few days had been a greater strain on her own resources than she would ever admit. After so long being semi-bedridden, the effort of each full day had shocked her but also surprised her in a way that was entirely unexpected. Her days, she realized, were more interesting than when she was confined to bed, and when she did go to bed at the end of each day she had a feeling of satisfaction which had been missing for some years. She was quietly proud of the way she had managed the house and her daughter albeit with the help of Mrs Banks who was still running errands for her. It had occurred to Dorothy that one day she might even venture outside herself and see how it felt to be in the outside world again.

As she sat beside Eve, she breathed deeply, trying to conserve her strength and decide on a campaign of action. How was she going to deal with her patient? What was Eve going to need?

'You won't be lying down, that's for sure!' she told her silent daughter. 'There's no way I'm going to let bloody fluid collect in your lungs.' She had studied everything written about the disease and felt that she was now something of an expert on the subject. 'You'll be sitting up, my girl, propped up with pillows ... and you'll have plenty of nourishing chicken soup...' If the time came, she amended, that Eve could take in soup without allowing it to dribble out again. At present that was barely possible.

She covered her face with her hands and prayed – for the third time that day. 'Please Lord, look down and pity my daughter who is already in such distress from the loss of her husband, which you thought fit to allow!' What was He thinking about, she wondered, disturbed by his apparent lack of compassion. Wasn't God supposed to be all-loving? 'If these terrible things are sent to try us, then we have been sorely tried. If they were meant to punish us, don't you think we've been punished enough? I know the war has ended – the armistice was wonderful – but we still have another battle on our hands. When is it going to end, dear Lord?' She uncovered her face but her eyes remained closed.

The truth was, she was losing patience with Him. If He could not save Eve then perhaps she should make a pact with the devil ... Sell her soul in exchange for Eve's life. She would willingly do so, Dorothy told herself. More than anything else in the world, she wanted her daughter to recover from Harvey's death and somehow make a new life for herself. If dying would bring about her daughter's eventual happiness, she would be willing to give up her life. She had enjoyed it so far but it would all be for nought if Eve was going to spend the rest of her life alone and unhappy. Being a widow had little to recommend it. Dorothy felt a huge responsibility for Eve's welfare and always had. A pact with the devil? How would one go about it? She had no idea.

With a jolt, she opened her eyes. *Pull yourself together, Dorothy,* she reminded herself sharply. *You're wandering!* She glanced at the clock. Quarter to nine! Time to give Eve a gentle wash down with a soapy flannel. It might not be medically proven as beneficial but she knew from experience that it could be calming – a sign of tender, loving care that could soothe the unconscious mind as well as the body.

What else? She had to keep busy. Anything to keep the fear at bay. The chicken soup was simmering on the hob ... and she must prepare a makeshift bed for herself in the armchair. A pillow and blanket would do and she could prop her feet on the footstool her grandmother had given her for her birthday all those years ago. The frame and legs were of oak and had been lovingly polished for many years. The padded seat had been covered with a cross-stitch design on hessian, showing her name – Dorothy Mary – in bold red lettering and her age – seven years – in blue. It had been a labour of love. Maybe her grandmother would look down on them and, seeing the trouble they were in, would intercede on their behalf. Dorothy smiled at the fancy. Then she straightened up, stiffening her resolve. No matter how long and fearful the coming hours of darkness, Dorothy would be ready for it, she told herself, and together she and Eve would somehow survive the night.

The hours ticked by and Dorothy stayed wakeful, but by three fifteen in the early hours she dropped into a fitful sleep from which she was awoken by a loud groan from her daughter. Sitting bolt upright, Dorothy threw off the blanket, slid from her chair and lit another candle.

'Eve!' With horror she saw that her daughter had slipped sideways and was almost on the floor. With her heart racing, Dorothy rushed to the other side of the bed, put her arms round Eve and tried to lift her back into bed. After a struggle she managed it and was able to look at Eve's face. The colour had fled and she looked almost lifeless. Her head lolled, her eyes were closed, her limbs seemed not to function. She looked to Dorothy like a sad rag doll.

'Eve! *Eve!*' she screamed. In a panic, she slapped her daughter's face and shook her with as much energy as she could muster. 'Eve! Don't do this! Open your eyes! You are not going to die!'

She propped Eve back against the pillows and pressed her own face against her heart to listen for a heartbeat. She heard one but it was faint and erratic.

'Oh God! This mustn't be the end. Listen to me, Eve, I beg you! Open your eyes. You have to stay awake. You can't simply slip away. Eve, do you hear me!'

What should she do? She hesitated, her mind a terrified blank.

Eve groaned again which meant she was still alive. Dorothy almost wept with relief but there was no time for rejoicing. Somehow she knew that her daughter's life hung in the balance. Had she tipped over into the second stage of the illness? If so, her lungs might already be filling with liquid. With an effort she dragged Eve as far up the bed as she could and pushed pillows behind her head and back in an effort to keep her upright. She brought up her knees as a kind of anchor and pushed her own pillow against Eve's feet to try and prevent further slides into a prone position.

'You have to stay upright,' Dorothy said loudly. 'You must not slide down into the bed. Don't fight me, Eve!' Scenes from Eve's childhood slid into her mind – Eve as a child trying to run away down the street and fighting Dorothy's efforts to restrain her. Eve refusing to wear her new shoes because she hadn't been allowed to have the unsuitable pair she had wanted. Eve closing her mouth and refusing to eat whenever Dorothy tried to persuade her to try a new vegetable. Eve had occasionally been very wilful and had proved a stubborn adversary.

But this was different. Eve was not consciously defying her mother, she genuinely did not have the strength to comply. Sitting up was beyond her. Dorothy stepped back and regarded her daughter. Still Eve's head tilted to one side and her body threatened to follow it. She would topple over again the moment Dorothy's back was turned.

'Oh Lord!' Did she have no control over her body, Dorothy wondered anxiously. Was she unconscious? Was she, perhaps, slipping into a coma? The dreadful thought galvanized her. She climbed up into the bed alongside her daughter and put both her arms around her. It was uncomfortable but that was a good thing, she told herself. She would be quite unable to fall asleep and would be able to monitor Eve's progress. Dorothy's one aim would be to hold her daughter upright until such time as she regained her senses and could control her own movements. If it took all night, so be it.

Throughout the rest of the night Dorothy talked loudly to Eve about the things she might recall from her childhood days. Anything to keep herself awake and to hopefully penetrate the blankness in which Eve seemed to be immersed.

'Do you remember the first time you saw the Punch and Judy, Eve? You were five and we had gone to Southend for the day. You were so determined to watch him but then you were frightened and your father had to carry you away! Afterwards you insisted that you liked the crocodile best.' Her voice was growing hoarse but she persisted, afraid of the silence that would follow if she gave up –

a silence which would allow Eve to be taken from her. 'And there was a little ginger kitten once that belonged next door but you were always trying to coax it round to our house, so in the end we bought a kitten for you and although it was a tabby you called him Ginger!'

As the hours passed, the candles spluttered and, one by one, went out. Around five o'clock Dorothy's arms and shoulders were aching and the constant strain had given her a headache but she refused to give up. Now and then Eve gave a slight sigh which Dorothy took to be a good sign. Abruptly, just before six, Eve opened her eyes, blinked and closed them again. A few minutes after seven she lifted her head, opened her eyes again and slowly took in her surroundings. She looked dazed but she was definitely regaining control of both mind and body. And there was no gurgling within her lungs, no painful cough, no ominous red spittle. Dorothy uttered a silent prayer and knew that the worst was over.

Later that morning Dorothy took another small step towards reclaiming her life and preparing herself for the future – whatever that might be. She dressed warmly and stepped outside into the street. After so long as a semi-invalid she felt almost nervous as she took her first walk in what she considered 'the outside world'. She had forgotten how gloomy the streets of London could be on a dark day. The pavement was wet and she walked gingerly past the houses. A group of children shouted at each other, a scrawny dog barked, a coster pushed his barrow, his face drawn, his eyes sullen. A baker's cart passed her, drawn by a blinkered horse and a young woman with a toddler lowered her eyes as she passed Dorothy.

After a few hundred yards, Dorothy decided she had seen enough of this miserable street and, turning abruptly, she made her way slowly home and closed the door thankfully behind her.

Ten

Several weeks later, at the South London Home for Orphaned Children, the large dining room was set out with rows of trestle tables with wooden forms for the children to sit on. It was a far cry from the old workhouses, being bright and airy and smelling of soap and water. Many of the workhouses still existed but the buildings of others had been requisitioned and turned into hospitals or asylums for the mentally ill. Through the windows the overcast November sky could be seen.

The wooden tables were covered with large sheets of paper which would be removed and burned after each meal. Normally the meals would be taken in two sittings – older and younger children – but because of the influx, three were now needed.

On this day, the twenty-eighth November, Kate and Lucy sat side by side at one of the tables, waiting for their food to be placed on the plates before them. Both girls wore second-hand clothes – their own having been removed and fumigated on arrival in an effort to avoid bringing in more infection. They would be returned when, and if, the children were claimed. Lucy fidgeted in a jumper that was too tight and regarded her sister's too large dress with envy. She thought about her own clothes that her mother kept back home, remembering especially the green best dress that her mother had made for her from one of her own old skirts.

'When are we going home?' she asked, knowing that the question would annoy Kate but needing to ask it anyway. If she kept thinking about home perhaps it would be there, waiting for them, and Kate would be wrong. If they never spoke about it, it might well disappear.

'We're not going home,' Kate said wearily. 'I've told you. Drink your milk.'

The mugs had already been filled with milk poured from large jugs. Lucy sipped obediently.

'She's not coming,' she whispered. 'The biscuit lady – she's not coming!'

'She is. Stop saying that.'

They both knew Lucy referred to Mrs Randall, otherwise known as 'the biscuit lady'.

'Then where is she?'

Kate regarded her with exasperation. 'They told us. She had the flu, like me. Like

Ma and Pa and...' She swallowed back the rest of the list. 'They said we had to be patient. She's coming to fetch us when she's better.'

'P'raps she's dead.'

'She's not!' Actually Kate *was* starting to doubt but she was not going to admit aloud anything so frightful. 'I had it and I didn't die so why should she? Anyway, if she was, somebody else would take us to Exeter.'

'Who?'

'Mrs Randall's mother.'

'But she's old and she lives in bed.'

'She'd get up.'

'Suppose they don't bother. They might say we have to stay here.'

'We won't. I told you – if we don't go to Aunt Biddy we'll run away.'

'Where to? Where will we go?'

'Somewhere nice. Somewhere where we can do whatever we like and...' Kate stopped in mid-sentence as a thick slice of bread and jam was put on to her plate with a pair of large tongs. She watched carefully as her sister's slice appeared. 'You've got more jam than me!'

'You had more yesterday.' Lucy licked her slice. 'It's marmalade. What's yours?'

'Same.' They ate in silence, slowly, making it last. A small boy sitting next to Kate began to cry and they stopped eating for a moment to look at him.

'What?' asked Kate. 'What's the matter?'

'I d-don't like marmalade.' He scrubbed at his tears. 'I like jam.'

Lucy said, 'So do I,' and took a large bite to establish ownership.

Kate turned round to take a look at what the children in the row behind them were eating. Their bread was spread with raspberry jam. She leaned across. 'Anyone like marmalade more than jam?'

A girl with fair braids nodded. Kate stood up, reached over without a word, took her slice of bread and exchanged it for the boy's bread and marmalade. The children on the table waited in horrified silence. Kate had committed a cardinal sin. 'Messing with the allotted food' was not allowed. On the far side of the room, the lady in charge said sharply, 'What's happening over there?'

'Nothing, miss,' came from half a dozen throats, and six pairs of innocent eyes widened. The children held their breath. On one occasion a slice of cake had been withheld as a warning against further misdemeanours.

Fortunately the moment passed. The little boy smiled at Kate, rubbed away his tears and began to eat the bread and jam.

Kate grinned back.

Small things were becoming increasingly

important as the days passed. The routine was the same every day except Sunday when they were taken to the nearby church, walking in twos in a long crocodile. Kate knew the routine by heart. Get up, wash, make the bed, say grace, have breakfast of porridge and a rusk and milk. Go into a large room and be taught tables and rhymes, copy things from the blackboard on to a slate, then listen to a story. Playtime outside with balls and hoops and beanbags for twenty minutes, if it wasn't raining, then more lessons until the midday meal. The dinner varied. Sometimes it was bony fish and potatoes and sometimes it was gristly meat and potatoes. If they were very lucky it was minced meat pasty. Then a long walk round the streets and back to the playroom to enjoy the toys and look at the books or crayon on the paper until a tea of bread and jam or marmalade and a piece of cake. And then bed.

Kate bit into the bread and jam. 'It might be cherry cake,' she said hopefully.

'It might be caraway seed!'

'Ugh!' They screwed up their faces in disgust.

Lucy said, 'Aunt Biddy makes lovely cakes with nuts on the top.'

'She makes lovely pancakes and lovely rice pudding and...'

'Lovely everything!'

They exchanged secret smiles. Having Aunt Biddy made them feel very superior to the rest of the orphans whose futures were less than dazzling. Aunt Biddy had a large garden with a swing in it and an elderly dog called Binky and an apple tree and a wardrobe that smelt of camphor balls and a fire that was always smoking when the wind was in the wrong direction and a well with a bucket on a chain that went up and down when you turned the handle.

Aunt Biddy herself might be elderly with grey hair and spectacles that were never cleaned and hands that were knobbly but – and it was a big but – she was theirs. She was family. Kate and Lucy had family!

A slice of cake was put on to Lucy's plate and she sampled a corner of it. 'It's lemon,' she announced.

They relaxed. Lemon was acceptable.

'Aunt Biddy isn't dead and she *is* coming for us,' Kate said cheerfully, and bit hungrily into her slice.

The next morning began as usual when the lady in charge walked into the dormitory and clapped her hands. The children got up and queued to wash in tepid water in the row of china basins, with a piece of hard soap and a thin square of flannel. They dressed and then made an attempt to make their beds the way they had been taught, tucking the corners in and smoothing out the creases. They were on their way to the dining room for breakfast when Kate and Lucy were withdrawn from the line of children on the stairs by one of the ladies in charge.

'Come along, Kate and Lucy. Mrs Randall is here for you.'

The two girls exchanged shocked glances, unable to believe that it was really happening. The moment they had waited for and the words they had hoped, but never quite expected, to hear. *Mrs Randall is here for you.*

Silently, proudly, they followed the woman down the stairs, under the envious eyes of the other children. Inside the office, 'the biscuit lady' sat waiting on a chair. Kate regarded her with narrowed eyes. She looked different. Thinner, paler, sad. But she *was* the Mrs Randall they knew. A familiar face. Her heart thumped inside her chest. Mrs Randall smiled at them and Lucy returned the smile. It was no trick. There was no mistake, thought Kate. Mrs Randall was here. Belatedly, Kate smiled also.

Mrs Randall said, 'I'm sorry you had to wait so long. I wasn't well but here I am!'

'We thought you were dead from the flu,' Lucy said.

'No we didn't.' Kate gave her a warning nudge. 'You did. I didn't!'

The lady in charge tutted. 'Now, now, children. Is that a nice way to greet Mrs Randall? Say "Good morning".'

The girls chorused the words.

'Children these days are rarely taught good manners. It's sad the way standards are slipping.'

Mrs Randall said, 'Kate and Lucy are usually very polite girls. I expect they're a little overwhelmed. They've been through a great deal.' She looked kindly at the girls. 'We'll have some breakfast when we get back to my house. We just have some paperwork to deal with here. You must wait patiently and then we'll be off.'

Kate and Lucy stood together, holding hands, in a torment of anxiety that, even at this late hour, something would go wrong and the long-awaited prize would be snatched away from them.

The lady in charge (they had never managed to remember any names) sat at her desk and wrote in her book.

'Perhaps you would be kind enough to confirm in writing when the girls have been safely delivered to their aunt,' the woman said, turning to Mrs Randall. 'If for any reason that is not possible, please notify us and return them promptly.'

'Certainly, but I don't anticipate any problems.'

'Good...' She poised, her pen in mid-air. 'It was Exeter, wasn't it?'

'Todleigh. A small village near Exeter. On the outskirts of the town.'

Kate closed her eyes. Every minute was an agony.

'In Exeter there's a big church,' Lucy said, 'and we went in it and saw Jesus on the cross, because that's where he lives, but he didn't say anything. I think he was...'

Kate tugged at her hand. 'Ssh! Don't interrupt.'

Lucy ignored her. 'I think he was dead because he must have seen us but Ma said ... Ouch!'

Mrs Randall said, 'What's the matter?'

Kate went pink in the face. 'I stepped on her foot. By mistake.' She gave Mrs Randall a look of deep entreaty.

'Of course Jesus is dead,' the lady in charge said. 'He died to save all sinners, Lucy. I'm sure they taught you that at Sunday school.'

Lucy looked baffled.

The lady behind the desk stood up and handed an envelope to Mrs Randall, who put it into her large purse.

'And if you would sign each of these papers...'

Mrs Randall signed. Kate held her breath.

Signing things sounded very important.

'Well, that's that – except for the girl's clothes, of course. They are in that paper bag on the chair. Washed and ironed. We'd be grateful if you'd return the ones they are wearing in the same condition as soon as possible. We are still receiving a fair number of children each day. I've never known such a time.' The lady held out her hand and Mrs Randall shook it. 'And you two girls be good for your Aunt Biddy. She's very kind to offer to look after you.'

Mrs Randall said, 'Say "Thank you", girls.'

Kate did so.

'But Jesus did see us,' Lucy said, 'and I smiled at him but he was so dead he couldn't talk so...' Kate nudged her. 'What? Oh! Yes. Thank you.'

Kate took hold of Mrs Randall's hand and after a moment's hesitation, Lucy did the same with the other hand. It seemed to take for ever to find their way out of the building and on to the street. Lucy looked around her and a broad smile lit up her face. Kate gave a small cry and burst into tears.

'Oh, Kate, dear! What's the matter?' Mrs Randall knelt beside her. 'Don't you want to come home? Tomorrow we'll go to the station and find the train and go to see Aunt Biddy.'

Kate sobbed, muttering incoherently and

then flung her arms around Mrs Randall's neck in a frantic hug.

Lucy's smile faded as she regarded her sister doubtfully. 'She's upset.' Her voice quavered.

Mrs Randall held out her free arm and included Lucy in the hug. When eventually they set off again for 'home', they walked together, hand in hand.

As the train drew into Exeter station with a rush of steam and squealing brakes, Eve was aware of conflicting emotions. For the past few days, the children had been part of their lives and she was thoroughly exhausted by the experience. Were children always so demanding, she wondered, or were Lucy and Kate worse than most. Her mother had done her best to help but had finally retreated to her bed the previous afternoon 'to regain her sanity', as she had put it. It seemed that for the children, everything became a major challenge, excitement or dispute. She had done her best to keep them interested yesterday, a shopping trip for new shoes and a walk to the park where they could play on the swings and the slide. She had bought them jigsaw puzzles and had played Snakes and Ladders with them, and Dorothy had read to them. All to no avail. By bedtime the girls were still wide awake and could not be settled to sleep before nine o'clock.

The day, to Eve, had lasted twice as long as usual and her head was still spinning from the unfamiliar strains on her patience. She wondered more than once how Aunt Biddy would cope. Perhaps the elderly aunt had 'a way' with children and would withstand the constant clamour, the arguments, the laughter, the sudden tears – the apparently inevitable highs and lows.

Eve knew she would miss them but she had decided to keep in touch by writing to them. She knew the house would seem empty when she returned but told herself that that would come as a relief.

'We're here!' Lucy's voice was high with excitement as she stared out of the window.

'Will Aunt Biddy be waiting for us on the platform? She was when we came with Ma.'

'I don't know, Kate. I expect she will. I told her the time of the train when I wrote. We'll get down and you can look for her.'

'The first one to see her is the winner,' cried Kate, already struggling to unlock the carriage door.

'Allow me.' An elderly man stepped forward, removed her firmly and opened the door. He stepped out, looking, Eve thought, very relieved. The children had been fidgety on the long journey but the train was so crowded there had been nowhere else for him to go. She wondered how Ellen Beatty had managed the train journey with three lively children while she was expecting her fourth child.

There was no sign of an elderly lady searching the faces of the passengers and for the first time she became uneasy. Biddy Towner had never answered her letters but Eve knew that some people could not read easily and, if they could read, might not be able to write back. She knew next to nothing about the children's aunt except what she had gleaned from the children and from Ellen's casual comments when they had met in the churchyard. She sighed. How long ago that seemed ... and what a lot had happened in the interval.

Crestfallen, Kate cried, 'She's not here. She hasn't come to meet us!'

All around them people were being greeted by friends and relatives.

'Well, sit on this seat and wait for ten minutes,' Eve said. 'She might be late. I said we'd meet her on the platform.' She frowned. 'Will she come into Exeter by bus, Kate? Can you remember?'

'A man fetched us with a horse and cart,' Lucy answered for her. 'He smelled funny and Aunt Biddy said he was a bit too fond of the you-know-what!'

Kate tutted. 'She means gin.'

'You've got a good memory, Lucy!' Eve said.

Kate nodded. 'She's going to be bright.'

Ten minutes passed while the girls raced up and down the platform with shrieks of excitement and Eve's worries intensified. When fifteen minutes passed she stood up. 'Come along, you two! She has obviously been delayed. We'll have to make our own way to Todleigh.'

It was easier said than done. They were told that the carrier had already left and the next bus was an hour away.

'We'll have to take a taxi,' Eve told them. That meant joining a short queue but after a lengthy wait it was their turn. They clambered into the vehicle and, after a discussion about the fare, were on their way.

'Where to in Todleigh?' the driver asked over his shoulder.

'I'm not quite sure. You had better put us down at the post office. I have to make enquiries there. We don't know the exact address.'

'Bit of a rum do, innit?'

'We're doing the best we can,' Eve told him, more sharply than she intended. 'We expected to be met from the train.'

The more Eve thought about their predicament the more she began to doubt the wisdom of trusting her letters. Suppose they had been lost in the post? Or Aunt Biddy had mislaid them and forgotten the date of their arrival?

The driver added to her worries. 'You little girls want to be careful,' he warned them. 'They do say Todleigh is haunted! That when it gets to dusk the ghost of the lone horseman rides the...'

'What is a ghost?' Lucy asked, intrigued.

'Don't ask!' cried Kate, putting her fingers in her ears.

'Ah! They do say this one rides about on his ghostly black horse and goes about his wicked ways with...'

Lucy screamed.

'Please stop that!' Eve told him. 'You're frightening them. Lone horseman indeed! Do you want to give them nightmares?'

He broke into hoarse laughter. 'Just my joke, missus.'

'I don't find it funny.'

Lucy said, 'What is wicked ways?'

'Nothing,' Eve told her. 'He's just being silly.'

The countryside was living up to its reputation, thought Eve. They were driving past fields, a small copse of trees, and the occasional cottage. An isolated farm consisted of a couple of barns, a farmhouse and what she presumed to be cowsheds. A glimpse of a small stream revealed a man fishing with a brown dog sitting beside him, apparently watching intently for the first sign of a bite on the man's rod.

'There's a horse in the field near Aunt Biddy's house and he eats carrots and apples and the farmer let us feed him. Is he wicked?'

'Certainly not. He's probably a very nice horse.'

Cautiously Kate unblocked her ears. 'Are we nearly there?'

As if to answer her question, the taxicab drew to a halt outside a small village store. The post office sign swung over the door. The children scrambled out and Eve settled the fare. She watched the taxi reverse and drive back the way it had come, then led the children into the post office which also served as a general store.

A large black cat slept on top of a half-empty sack of corn and a dog, sprawled in front of the counter, wagged a greeting without getting up. There was no sign of a post-mistress and Eve took a moment to look around the store. Rows of tins and jars stood neatly on rows of wooden shelves. A variety of utensils hung from hooks in the ceiling – a watering can, a bundle of door mats, a lantern, small kettles and three trowels. Other goods were piled against the walls, and on the counter Eve saw a pair of scales.

At the far end of the shop there was a corner dedicated to the postal service and this consisted of a small counter and, behind it on the wall, a board with dusty, curling notices pinned to it.

Kate spotted a small brass bell and snatched it up and began to ring it while Lucy woke up the cat and tried to make friends with it.

'The cat's called Blackie,' she informed Eve. 'See! She remembers me. She's smiling.'

'Smiling?'

'Yes. See how her whiskers are curling. That's how cats smile.'

A thin woman appeared through a doorway at the rear of the store. She wore a serviceable apron over her dress and was wiping her hands on a cloth. She threw up her hands with pleasure when she recognized the children. 'Well, by all that's holy! Haven't you two grown.'

'Mrs Piggot!' cried Kate. 'We've come to live with Aunt Biddy because she's our family now. We'll live here and go to school here and everything.' She glanced anxiously at Lucy who had finished petting the cat and was now crouching beside the dog, whispering into his ear.

Mrs Piggot looked round the shop. 'But where's the rest of you? Isn't your ma with you? And that bonny little boy...' She caught sight of Eve's face and faltered to a stop. Eve mouthed the word 'flu' and the woman frowned. Then her eyes widened as she guessed Eve's meaning. 'Not ... You don't mean ... Oh, no! Not all of them?' She put a hand to her mouth to hide her dismay. 'Oh dear Lord! Why, that's ... I just can't reckon to that!'

'Is your dog still deaf?' Lucy asked.

Mrs Piggot turned slowly. 'What, dear? Is he still deaf? Oh, yes, my lovey. He'll always be deaf but he don't mind, see.'

Kate had missed nothing of the exchange. 'We were in a big house full of children. They had no families so they had to stay there. They were orphans. We have Aunt Biddy.'

Mrs Piggot leaned on the counter, struggling for words.

Eve introduced herself and then said, 'Kate and Lucy have been very brave and sensible.'

Mrs Piggot still appeared to be dumbstruck.

'I knew their parents. I was a friend.'

'Mrs Randall, you said? Should I remember you?'

'No. We haven't met. I'm – Jon Beatty worked for me and I knew Ellen and the children. I'm just bringing the children down. I'm catching the last train back tonight to London. We were expecting Miss

Towner to meet us but she wasn't at the station. I wonder if you could let me have her address.'

Mrs Piggot still stared at her, seemingly at a loss for words. 'Did you ... write to her, recent like?'

Eve nodded.

To her surprise the woman's face crumpled, her eyes filled with tears and with a muffled cry she turned and disappeared through the door into the private rooms behind the shop. The uneasiness Eve had felt earlier returned. What had the letters to do with anything?

Lucy grew tired of the dog and pointed to a row of jars of sweets. 'Aunt Biddy lets us have a lollipop when we've been good and we have been good. We were good on the train and in the taxi.'

Kate was staring at Eve. 'Why is she crying? Is it because we're orphans?'

'I ... I expect so, Kate. It was bad news and she's upset.'

'She'll get over it.' Lucy regarded her seriously. 'We have to. When Pa died Ma told us that. She said life isn't a bag of cherries and we have to get over things.'

'Cherries!' Kate said. 'Ugh! They're sour!'

'They are not!'

Eve said, 'Oh! Well then ... I expect Mrs Piggot will get over it.'

They all turned as a man appeared. Eve saw that he looked flustered. She presumed he was the woman's husband. He was as tall as his wife but heavily built with a lined, leathery face. He wore a tweed hat that had seen better days and a waistcoat that had seen too many dinners.

'Sorry about my wife,' he said. 'She's that soft-hearted. Always has been. They used to tease her at school. Told her sad stuff just to see her cry! You know what kids are like.' He carried an unopened letter which Eve recognized as he handed it to her. 'We didn't know what to do with it,' he explained, 'seeing as it couldn't be delivered ... on account of...' He drew a long breath. 'On account of Miss Towner being expired. Died in the hospital ten days ago. Went in right as rain with an abscess on her jaw but it went bad. Septic. Turned septic and the poison just raced through her blood. That's what they said. Blood poisoning.'

Stunned, Eve clutched the letter.

Sharp-eared Kate cried, 'Is she dead? Is Aunt Biddy dead?'

'Yes, dear, she is,' Eve told her, struggling to maintain her composure in the face of such dire news. 'Poor Aunt Biddy.'

'Was it the flu?'

'No, Kate, it was a bad tooth.'

Mr Piggot looked uncomfortable. 'The

wife's making you a cup of tea. She says you're to come in and sit yourselves down – and the girls must have a lollipop each.'

'Ooh! A lollipop!' Lucy hopped from one foot to the other with excitement at the prospect of this treat. 'We have to choose,' she told Eve. 'We always do. I choose...' She closed her eyes while she made the decision. 'I choose yellow ... No, red. Yes, I choose red.' She looked at Kate. 'What do you choose?'

Kate was staring fixedly at Mr Piggot.

Eve, leaving the girls in the shop, was slowly coming to terms with the enormity of the blow. She walked slowly through the doorway and sat down heavily on the chair indicated by the postmaster's wife. 'I don't know what to say!' she muttered. 'Or quite what to do! I should have realized something was wrong when she didn't answer my letter but I thought perhaps ... she couldn't read. That sounds a dreadful thing to say but...' She shrugged.

Mrs Piggot stirred the teapot and poured lemonade into two glasses for the children. 'Miss Towner could read and write well enough. Oh, yes! She was very clever. Years ago she used to write school books – history books they were. In lots of schools. She was an expert on Roman and Greek history. She earned a good living from her books.' She poured tea into three cups for the adults. 'Sugar and milk? Help yourself. Oh, yes, we were all very proud of Miss Towner in the village.' She smiled. 'Not that she was above herself. Oh, no! Not a bit of it. Very down to earth, she was. A pretty woman but crossed in love.' She shook her head at the memories. 'He was from outside the village – you know the type.' She nodded disparagingly. 'Poor Miss Towner was head-over-heels, she was, and then a few days before they were to be wed, off he goes with another woman! A brazen hussy she was and no mistake. Then her poor old mother passed away and Miss Towner was left to care for her father, old Ted Towner. Miserable old devil, and no mistake. But being the only child...'

As she talked, Eve tried not to listen. She was wondering what time the next train back to London would leave Exeter. They would have to go home and Kate and Lucy would have to go back to the orphanage. Her heart sank at the prospect. Could she do it? Could she walk them back to the orphanage and leave them there? Could she face their expressions of betrayal as she turned to walk away? She didn't think she could. But what else was to be done? They couldn't stay with her ... Could they? She shook her head. She needn't think that far ahead, she told herself.

'Take it one step at a time, Eve,' she told herself.

She glanced at the clock on the mantelpiece. Nearly one o'clock. By this time she had expected they would all be sitting in Aunt Biddy's cottage, enjoying some of her home cooking. She had looked forward to seeing the children's faces when she greeted them at the station. She had anticipated leaving them with their aunt – all three waving cheerfully from the gate as she departed. Now none of that was going to happen. Kate and Lucy were coming back to London with her. What would her mother say? The more she thought about it, the more she told herself it was out of the question but so was the alternative. Surely she would never be able to abandon them?

She recalled the stricken expression on Kate's small face when she heard Mr Piggot's news. There was a haunted look in the dark eyes and the small mouth was pinched in fear. Luckily Lucy was too young to have immediately grasped the full significance of what had happened.

Mrs Piggot was still talking. 'We all marvelled at the way Miss Towner coped. A lesser person would have become bitter but she carried on, same as always. She had other offers, but wouldn't take them. Her first love was her only love. Sad, that was.'

Mr Piggot came in with the two girls, each sucking a lollipop.

'There's a drink of lemonade each for you when you've finished those lollies,' Mrs Piggot said. 'You can go out the back and look at the hens if you've a mind.' She pointed to the back door and they went out willingly enough. 'Kiddies do love to see animals, don't they? Specially town children.'

Mr Piggot cleared his throat. 'You might be able to help us out, like. We've had the solicitor in here asking about relatives and we only knew of the Beattys and they didn't answer the letter regarding the will. There's the house – that was left to Miss Towner by her father. Why don't I telephone him, the solicitor I mean, and tell him you're here with the children – with what's left of the family?'

'But I'm only a friend of the family. I couldn't sign anything or make any decisions.' Instinctively, Eve shied away from the added responsibility. 'And there really isn't time. We shall have to find a suitable train and...'

'Stay overnight, why don't you? The house is there. Miss Towner wouldn't object. It's cosy enough with a bit of a fire.'

A mumbled voice from the back door said, 'Can we? Please?'

Kate, lollipop in mouth, was staring at Eve,

her gaze unblinking.

'Oh, Kate, I don't know,' Eve protested. 'The thing is ... We ought to go back to London. My mother will be expecting me – and we don't have a telephone.' She drew a long breath. 'Let me think for a moment.'

Mrs Piggot smiled. 'Yes, lovey, you have a quiet think. We won't bother you. We'll feed some corn to the hens, Kate. Come along.'

Kate removed the lollipop and stared at Eve. 'Ple-e-ase!'

The postmaster said, 'You go along now, Kate.'

When he and Eve were alone, he sat down opposite her at the table and drew his teacup towards him and took a sip. 'I know you need to think about this – it's all been a bit sudden, like – but let me put a few things to you first.'

Eve nodded, grateful for any help she was offered for she felt hopelessly out of her depth.

'You'll be all of a dither, I know,' he said, 'but this is a good opportunity to help the children. They may be orphans and they may have nobody but Miss Towner always said she'd leave her house to the Beattys when she died. So you being here and the solicitor being only a few miles away in his office ... See what I'm getting at? You should at least talk to him, for the kiddies' sakes. He could be here in ten minutes or so – or we could have a bite to eat and he could call by afterwards. Plaistow and Barrett. That's the firm – and one day, no doubt, Mr Scayne will be made a junior partner when old Mr Plaistow retires.'

Eve hesitated, aware that she was being drawn in against her will. But what he said made sense. Who else would deal with the affairs? There was no one else.

'You'll like Mr Scayne,' he said. 'He's a real gentleman. He's only young but his head's screwed on right and he's qualified. He'll help you sort things out for them.'

It was the least she could do, she acknowledged. *Why not agree to see the man? If it would help the girls she shouldn't refuse.* She smiled. 'That makes a lot of sense, Mr Piggot. Thank you. I'll see him.'

'And you'll stay overnight? I could get a fire going for you in the cottage and you could take a few hot bricks for the beds. Not that the cottage has been empty that long. It shouldn't be damp. The girls would love it and you would be here first thing tomorrow in case there was anything outstanding that...'

Eve felt happier. 'I'm beginning to think this is a conspiracy, Mr Piggot,' she joked. 'Am I ever going to see London again?'

'Oh, Lord! Forgive me, Mrs Randall.' He

stood up. 'I'll just telephone Stanley Scayne and arrange for him to come over, say around two o'clock. That'll give us time to have a bit of something to eat. My wife's a dab hand at rustling up food. She says that's why I married her.'

They both laughed. Eve was beginning to feel slightly more hopeful at the thought of some expert advice from Mr Scayne.

'If I could let my mother know we were staying...'

'Haven't you got a neighbour with a telephone? Someone who'd take a message and pop across to your mother?'

Eve thought about it. 'There's Mrs Jackson at Number Eleven. She has a telephone because her health is so bad and she often needs to call out the doctor. Maybe she would take a message.'

Within minutes, it seemed, it was settled. Stanley Scayne would call at two thirty and Mrs Jackson had agreed to tell Dorothy what was happening in Devon. Eve began to feel as if she were on a roller coaster, but with so much well-meaning support she could hardly resent being helped on her way.

Eleven

Stanley Scayne was probably in his early twenties, Eve realized, and she thought he was very charming. He had an eager, boyish manner but he seemed well-informed and she summed him up as a wise head on young shoulders. He was of average height, stockily built with curly brown hair, and had hazel eyes in a pale face, with a ready smile. He laughed a lot despite the fact that it made him breathless, and Eve warmed to him immediately. Discreetly he took control of the situation and she felt the pressure lift. Nothing seemed as worrying as it had done before his arrival and Eve began to relax.

Within minutes of arriving, the two of them were sitting in his motor, outside Biddy Towner's home, waiting for the estate agent to arrive with the key. Kate and Lucy were still at the post office with the Piggots, playing with a large but ancient set of wooden farm animals.

Stanley Scayne produced a file and riffled through the sheets. Eve watched the way his slim, well-manicured hands handled the papers. 'The will,' he said, 'leaves everything to the Beatty family, which now means Kate and Lucy. It includes the cottage and its contents. There are no savings of any kind. Somehow Biddy Towner managed on what remained of her parents' savings plus, of course, her own earnings.'

In some ways, thought Eve, Stanley Scayne reminded her of a younger, less serious version of Harvey. They shared the same enthusiasm for their work, Eve decided, a characteristic which always impressed her in a man and, like Harvey, he made her feel less anxious. Ever since she was a child, her mother had been telling her not to worry so much. 'It will all come out in the wash!' had been one of Dorothy's favourite maxims. Now, remembering Harvey brought back Eve's sense of loss and changed her expression from one of interest to something darker.

Stanley Scayne paused. 'Am I going too fast, Mrs Randall? You must stop me if I'm not making myself clear.'

'No! It's not you. My mind was wandering. I'm sorry.'

She saw him glance at her left hand where she still wore her engagement ring and wedding band but she said nothing about Harvey's death. She still found it hard to describe herself as a widow without the risk of breaking down and at present it was hardly relevant. She saw that he wore no wedding ring – so he was not married. Unless he, too, had lost his spouse which seemed unlikely if his cheerful attitude to life was anything to go by. Perhaps he was one of the fortunate few, so far untouched by a death. She wondered why he had not served during the war as the postmaster had told him that the young man had been in Devon.

As if reading her mind, he said, 'You're wondering why I'm not in the army.'

'Oh, no!' she protested, embarrassed by his perception.

'People always do. It's natural. The trouble is I suffer from an inherited heart problem. None of the armed services would take me.' His gaze was frankly appraising with no hint of resentment.

She felt herself blushing. 'Please forgive me. I had no right...'

'Nothing to forgive. I was equally curious about you. We humans are inquisitive animals.'

Eve decided she liked his humorous smile. 'That's a nice way to put it, Mr Scayne.' After a brief hesitation she shared her own situation. 'My husband was a scientist. He died recently of influenza.'

'How appalling for you! I'm so sorry.'

To prevent any further talk of Harvey she said quickly, 'I should have been concentrating on what you were saying. Please go on.'

Obediently he repeated his earlier comments and continued to explain the position in which the Beatty children found themselves. 'They weren't a large family. It seems that means Jon and Ellen Beatty had few relations and the war and influenza have reduced the numbers. Since only the girls remained of the family, they would each inherit a share when they reached twenty-one. First Kate and later Lucy.' He frowned. 'The thing is, what to do about Myrtle Cottage. It's in need of repair and it won't do it much good to let it stand empty until Kate is old enough to be involved. Should it be sold, the money could be invested. Or the house could receive some refurbishment and be rented out. Of course, the children could move in and live in it if they had suitable carers.'

Eve looked at him, startled. 'I hope you're not asking *me* to make a decision! I wouldn't feel at all competent. I'm simply what some people would call a "do-gooder". A friend of the family trying to be helpful.'

He grinned. 'You've caught me out, Mrs Randall. I was hoping you might have an opinion, but I agree, it's hardly fair. What is going to happen to the girls, Mrs Randall? As they are orphans might they be classed as wards of court? Do you have any idea?'

'I'm afraid not,' Eve admitted. 'Technically, they should be returned to the orphanage – that was the understanding on which I withdrew them, because I have no legal claim on them whatsoever. Even if I had...' She swallowed. 'I think, had my husband still been alive, we *might* have considered adopting them. We did plan to have a family but ... that's out of the question now. Not that we had ever envisaged adopting because we still hoped ... but then all this hadn't happened.' Under his intense gaze Eve felt herself floundering. 'I'm a widow with an ailing mother to look after and possibly half a pension to live on.' She spoke bluntly, hoping not to sound self-pitying. 'So I would hardly be the ideal candidate financially if I applied to adopt anyone.'

'You're being very frank, Mrs Randall. I appreciate what you're telling me.' His expression changed. 'I'm truly sorry about your husband.'

Eve shrugged helplessly. 'Ironically he was a research chemist, working for the army in America, trying to find a cure for influenza but ... it felled him along with the thousands of other poor wretches.'

He nodded. 'They say it's proved devastating over large areas of the world but, with the news restrictions due to the war, nobody is getting a very clear picture. You probably know more about it than most of us. Where was your husband when he died?'

'He was working in an army camp where the disease was rampant. One day I hope to go across and see where he's buried.'

For a few moments they were both silent and before either could speak, a pony and trap came into sight and the horse was pulled to a halt beside them.

Stanley Scayne brightened. 'Ah! Here's Peter Nicholls, the estate agent.' He climbed out and had a few words with the elderly man who, clutching the reins, made no attempt to alight. Eve watched Stanley Scayne, more impressed than she cared to admit to herself. She found him relaxed but confident for someone who looked so young. Surely, she thought, any young woman would find him attractive. Perhaps he was devoted to a mother who relied on him in some way. Eve could imagine him putting an elderly parent first. He looked so full of life she found it difficult to believe his heart problem could kill him.

Nicholls tapped the horse and drove off, but not before belatedly acknowledging Eve with a brief smile and a wave of his hand.

Stanley walked back to her. 'He's desperately late for another appointment so sends his apologies but here's the key. Let's take a look at Myrtle Cottage.'

The so-called cottage was surprisingly spacious. Seeing Eve's surprise Stanley Scayne told her that Biddy Towner's parents and grandparents had been comfortably off, due to a small business making uniforms of all types. 'Every time a war came along they would be thriving. In between wars there were always the steady earners – school uniforms, police uniforms and so on. They sold the business a few years ago to a distant cousin who died shortly after and it passed into other hands.'

'Myrtle Cottage is bigger than I expected,' Eve admitted, taking in the four downstairs rooms and a wide staircase to the upstairs accommodation. There was a large kitchen with an enormous table that had been well-scrubbed over the years so that the top was a paler colour than the legs. A motley collection of pots and pans covered every shelf and the rugs which covered the tiled floor were faded and frayed at the edges. There was a deep sink with one tap.

'Well water,' Mr Scayne said. 'Biddy Towner didn't believe in newfangled ideas. But I'm told the water's from a spring and good enough to drink.'

The large walk-in pantry was lined with

jars of home-made jams and pickles, and a large dresser groaned under a huge array of mismatched mugs and plates and saucers of all sizes.

The hallway was dark and Eve noticed gas mantles on the wall.

Mr Scayne said, 'I seem to remember there's a small, rather primitive, ice house in the garden.'

There was a small room referred to as 'the boot room' and a small office-cum-study overflowing with books and papers. The large living room was comfortably furnished but with a distinct air of what Dorothy would call 'shabby gentility' and Eve could see why Kate and Lucy had enjoyed their visits to Aunt Biddy. A sofa full of cushions, a large rocking chair, smaller chairs and footstools and a polished wooden table for dining at on special occasions.

'Peter Nicholls had a surveyor look it over and it does need work,' Mr Scayne admitted. 'The larger bedroom has a large damp stain on the ceiling, the steps to the cellar are rather unsafe and most of the windows need repair. Follow me up the stairs but don't worry about the creaks and groans. The stairs are sound, just old.'

Upstairs there was a passage with rooms leading off. Four bedrooms, a very ancient bathroom and a box room crammed to the ceiling with cast-off furniture, old toys and various items of bric-a-brac. Eve stood in the main bedroom and looked out of the window at a large but neat garden with rows of vegetables and colourful flower beds. There was even a small pond. She pointed it out.

He laughed. 'There were fish in it at one time until a hungry heron descended and ate them all. Miss Towner didn't care for fish so she never restocked it.'

'You seem to know her very well.'

'It's a small community here. I used to live in Todleigh and my aunt still does. Ida Bloom. She and my mother were sisters and very close My aunt was very friendly with Biddy Towner. Everyone knew Biddy. Since we have handled the estate, I've learned more. You can see that the garden was Miss Towner's pride and joy.'

Eve nodded. How wonderful it would be, she thought, staring out of the window, if the children could grow up in this cottage that was already like a second home to them.

Stanley Scayne touched her arm and she turned a little too quickly. He said, 'Are you thinking what I'm thinking – that it would suit the girls down to the ground?'

Eve nodded. 'Exactly! But how could it be done?'

'That's the problem, isn't it?'

'How urgent is it that you settle the estate? I'd like to have time to think it over. There might be a way but I can't see it at present.'

'No real urgency except – when do you have to return the girls to the orphanage?'

'I'm supposed to give them a declaration signed by Biddy Towner to say that I've handed them over but I suspect they're so overworked just now that they won't notice for some time if it doesn't happen.'

'Where will the girls be during that time?'

Eve closed her eyes. Was she really going to say this? 'I think ... that is, I suppose they'll stay with me. I'll have to talk to my mother and I don't know how we'll survive them – they're so lively! – but ... Yes, I think that's the only answer. They can stay with us for a week or two while we try and find a solution.'

'That's very public-spirited, Mrs Randall. Being sent back to the orphanage after discovering their aunt is dead. Well, it would be adding insult to injury. They seem cheerful enough but it's impossible to know how deep their grief must go.'

'I couldn't do that to them, Mr Scayne. My biggest nightmare is that they might eventually become separated. If a couple wanted to adopt one of them but not the other ... Kate can be very fierce and overprotective of her sister. She's deep and it's hard to know exactly what she's thinking. Lucy is sweet and I think what you see is what you get. I think she would be easy to place with an adoptive couple. Kate would be more of a challenge but I admire her courage.'

'You are obviously very fond of both of them.'

Eve was startled. 'Fond of them? Perhaps I am. Intrigued, certainly. I have no experience of children. They are something of a mystery to me.' Warning bells started ringing in her head. Getting fond of them would be a mistake. Loving and losing was such heartache.

She changed the subject. 'Do you have any children, Mr Scayne?'

He shook his head. 'My heart problem is...' he started to say. 'It seems wrong to take a wife and have children knowing that you might die and leave them to fend for themselves.'

'But you might not. Think how much you will miss.' Eve tried to speak lightly.

'Perhaps I'll give it some more thought,' he said quietly but Eve thought he looked a little wistful.

Eve and the children spent the night in Myrtle Cottage. Eve felt more relaxed now that Mrs Jackson had agreed to take a message to Dorothy, and the King's Head, urged on by Stanley Scayne, provided a meal for them in a small back room. Reluctantly, the cottage had to be closed up again the following morning and Eve took the children back to London.

Dorothy was up and dressed when they arrived home and was eager to hand Eve a letter which had come from America. 'It might be about your pension,' she told her. 'And about time too. What do they think you've been living on all this time? Thin air?'

While the children told Dorothy all about their trip to Devon, Eve took the envelope into the front room and steeled herself to open it. Inside was a folded sheet of paper and another letter sealed in a second envelope. She unfolded the first letter, which was in a hand she didn't recognize.

Dear Mrs Randall,

I owe you a deep apology for not forwarding the enclosed letter from your husband when he died. I had promised him that I would do so but life in the camp is so desperate that I kept forgetting to post it. Not much of an excuse but I hope you will forgive me.

I also lost my wife Louise recently to the damned disease and can totally understand your loss. Harvey was more than a colleague – I like to think we were friends

– and I felt his death keenly. He wrote the enclosed letter while he was still fit and I guess we both hoped I would never need to forward it to you. Please believe that you were always in his thoughts – but you don't need me to tell you that. His illness, though severe, was short, and before he became delirious he talked of no one but you. I hope his letter brings you some comfort.

When the war ends I shall no longer be in the army as I have a small son, Toby, to think about and have resigned my commission. Somehow, when the current situation has eased, I have to create a new life for us. I plan to travel to England with him at some stage and would like to contact you if you felt you would like to meet.

I shall look forward to hearing from you.

God bless you and keep you safe.

Yours regretfully and with respect,

James Ferber

Eve refolded the letter. Could she bear to meet this man, she wondered. No doubt he would be willing to talk about Harvey's last weeks and his final days but that might be painful. The question she most longed to have answered was the whereabouts of her husband's grave. Did this man know the answer to that question? If so, he hadn't mentioned it in his letter. Did that mean that Harvey might have been buried alongside others in the same plot? She must reply to the letter, she told herself, when she had time.

Harvey's letter had brought tears to her eyes even before she had read it. Just to hold it meant she could imagine him pouring out his heart, putting pen to paper and knowing that she would only read the letter if he died.

My dearest Eve,

What a sad task this is – writing a letter yet hoping you will never read it. I am very much aware that life here at the camp, as well as elsewhere in the world, is a frail business while this influenza rages undiminished. I pray I may live through it and will once again hold you in my arms. That is my dearest wish and if He is merciful we will be together again...

'Oh Harvey!' she cried. 'We never will! The very worst has happened. I've lost you ... We've lost each other.' Unchecked, her tears flowed and it was some time before she could see clearly enough to go on reading.

But if I should die I want you to remember how much I loved you and how much joy you brought into my life. It grieves me that we shall never have the family we wanted. I know how disappointed you will be, but, dearest Eve, understand what I am going to say now. I would hate you to spend the rest of your life alone. You deserve to be happy and when another man comes into your life who can love you as I do, you must marry again and hopefully have children. I want to rest easy in my mind that my memory will not prevent you from making a new life for yourself.

I will always be a part of you because I know you will keep me in your heart...

Here an ink blot appeared and Eve imagined the pen slipping from his weary fingers.

I am so desperately tired. Forgive me if I stop now and snatch a few hours sleep.

With all love from your adoring husband,

Harvey

Underneath there was a row of kisses. Eve held the letter to her chest, closed her eyes and tried to conjure up her husband's image but it remained obstinately indistinct. She wiped her eyes and took several deep breaths then carried both letters upstairs and put them with the rest of her letters.

From downstairs she heard childish laughter and wondered what her mother was doing to entertain them. She would have to go down and face up to her new problems, she told herself. There was no time for self-indulgent grief. She had lost Harvey but the girls had lost almost everyone they loved.

Later that evening, while the children shared the bed in the spare room, Eve and Dorothy had a chance to discuss the recent developments.

Dorothy said, 'We are agreed, then, that we won't return them to the orphanage?'

'I couldn't face it, Mother, and that's the truth. I would feel that we were betraying them. I think they trust us to do the right thing by them and now they have a chance of staying in their own home. Mr Scayne seems sure he can come up with a solution but in the meantime...' She shrugged.

'I know, dear,' said Dorothy. 'They have to stay here.'

'Would you mind, Mother? It might not be for long. If only they could re-open the school they would be there most of the day.'

'Not much chance of that, Eve, until the flu has really ended. I doubt they have enough staff for one thing.'

'But less pupils!'

'True.'

Eve sighed.

'In the meantime we have to find a way to keep them usefully and quietly occupied. I've been thinking we should prepare a routine that they can enjoy. When you were a child and the school holidays came round, I used to give you a little schooling each morning for an hour and a half. If you worked hard, you earned a lollipop or a stick of barley sugar. You could choose. It gave the days a shape and, I daresay, a little discipline. Do you remember any of that, dear?'

Eve smiled. 'Vaguely. Is that when I learned to sing "Widdecombe Fair"?'

Dorothy beamed. 'It was! Well, let's just say it didn't do you any harm.'

'Mother, it's a wonderful idea.' Eve thought rapidly. 'We could dream up some words for them to copy – making it easier for Lucy, naturally ... and some numbers and simple sums. They could each have a little notebook. If we give them lots of praise they'll enjoy it.'

'We could give each other a break.' Dorothy suggested. 'I spend my mornings in bed while they do their "lessons" downstairs with you, then after lunch they come upstairs with me and we do knitting or I teach them some verses or a little song – or read to them...'

'Then I take them to the park about three, weather permitting...'

'While I get up, come downstairs and make tea for all of us!'

They looked at each other with unfeigned relief.

'I'm beginning to think we can do it without the nervous breakdowns I've been anticipating!' Eve said.

They were still laughing when they heard footsteps on the stairs and Kate appeared.

'Lucy's asleep,' she announced.

'So why aren't you?' Dorothy asked.

'Cos I'm too thirsty.'

Eve said, 'You can have half a glass of water.'

'I won't wet the bed. I never do.'

'No, but you'll want to use the potty in the middle of the night and you'll wake up Lucy and then...'

'Where are our clothes?'

The disconcerting change of subject was something Kate did rather well, thought Eve. It always managed to keep her off balance. Now, while she hesitated, Kate pressed on.

'And where are our toys?' She gave Eve one of her fierce looks, dark eyes flashing. 'We had lots of toys. Are they still at our house?'

'I don't know, Kate.' Eve thought about it. They had probably thrown everything out because of the risk of infection but she didn't want to assume anything. 'We could go round tomorrow and ask. Would you like to do that?'

'Yes, because I had a doll and Lucy had a teddy and we had a bat and ball and a box of dominoes and I had a best dress and so did Lucy but mine had lace and hers only had ribbon ... And Lucy had some little black boots and Ma said she has to wear them in the evenings when she's getting tired because the doctor said she's got weak ankles and that's why she keeps falling over but Lucy forgets and I have to remind her.' She tossed her head.

Somehow Eve kept her face straight. 'We'll go round tomorrow and ask. They may have kept them but don't be too disappointed if they've gone. Now help yourself to some water and...'

Kate grinned. 'I'm not thirsty any more.' She disappeared upstairs.

Eve looked at her mother with raised eyebrows. 'Kate at her most devious!'

Dorothy smiled. 'You'll get used to it, dear. We were all children once remember – and you were no angel!'

True to her word, Eve took Kate and Lucy back to their old home to see if any of their belongings remained. The man who opened the door to them was a Mr Braggs – a small shapeless man who might have been any age between thirty and fifty. He looked at them nervously when Eve explained the reason for their visit then pushed back his cap and scratched his head.

'Your stuff? We had to clear it all out. It's all in the shed – at least what seemed worth saving is. There was a lot of useless clutter...'

Kate opened her mouth to protest but Eve silenced her with a warning glance.

He went on. 'My wife wanted to burn it all – you know, because of the germs and the flu and them dying, and in case we got it but I said, "Let's give them a week or two", even though we heard from Mrs Annis next door that some of the kids was in the orphanage. You from there, are you?'

Eve hesitated. 'From the orphanage? Er ... not exactly. This is a semi-private visit.' She hoped he wouldn't become too inquisitive. 'Would it be all right for us to look through what remains?'

He nodded without speaking and led them through the house and out into the back-yard.

Kate stared round and bristled immedi-ately. 'Where's our mangle?' She pointed accusingly at an empty corner of the yard.

'Sold it,' he told her. 'Didn't fetch much but we had one already. Our was better than yours.' He opened the door of a ramshackle shed. 'Help yourself but don't blame me if you go down with the flu!'

'I've had it,' Kate told him loftily. 'And I went to the hospital and they made me better and she's had it too.' She pointed to Eve and Mr Braggs hurriedly stepped back. Kate followed Lucy into the shed which housed a selection of flowerpots, rusty garden tools and a sagging shelf piled with paint pots, brushes and dirty rags. They also found several large sacks and a few boxes filled with the Beattys's belongings. Eve had no intention of filling up her home with worthless bric-a-brac, but she told the children they could choose five things each and they had ten minutes to search through the remnants of their previous life – although she didn't put it into those words.

'The rest can be burned or destroyed,' she told Mr Braggs who was loitering a yard or so away from her, nervously holding a handkerchief to his mouth. 'A person who has recovered is no longer infectious,' she said, with an attempt to reassure him. 'That's what the doctor told me.'

'I never have trusted them doctors. Think they're blooming God, they do. I know folks who have gone into hospital and never come out! That's doctors for you, that is!'

Kate found her doll and her best dress, a

book of fairy tales, a musical box and the new hat that Jon had bought for Ellen.

'But it's all squashed,' she told Eve, her mouth trembling. 'The feather's broke. It was brand spanking new, that hat, and Ma loved it! Pa said she looked like a queen. I wanted to wear it but he's ruined it.' She gave Mr Braggs a venomous look which might have withered a lesser man. 'He's horrible, he is!'

Mr Braggs's sharp ears caught this outburst. 'I never touched it,' he told her. 'It was like that already.'

'It never was!' cried Kate.

Lucy paused in her own search to support her sister. 'It was brand new when Pa bought it!' She glared at Mr Braggs, thin arms akimbo.

In the face of the sisters' united front he crumbled. 'Then must have been my wife what done it cos, hand on heart, it wasn't me.'

Eve examined it. 'I think we could steam it back to shape, Kate, and maybe find another feather. When we finish with it, it will be as good as new.' Aware of Mr Braggs's impatient frown she turned to Lucy. 'Are you ready?'

Lucy picked up the items she had chosen – an armful of soft toys and a baby's rattle.

'A rattle?' Eve laughed. 'Aren't you too big

for a ...'

Kate turned on her. 'It was Sam's. She can have it if she wants!'

'Sam's? Oh, Lucy!' Eve felt terrible. 'Of course you can have it. I'm sorry. I didn't know it was Sam's. Now let's...'

Kate said, 'Where are the boots?'

Lucy's mouth set in a tight line. 'I don't like them. I don't want to wear boots, so there!' and stuck out her tongue.

Before Eve could decide whether or not to initiate a fresh search, Mr Braggs decided he had been patient long enough. 'Right, time you were off, then!' he said. 'I said time's up! Out of there. Come on!'

They left reluctantly and he closed the door to the shed.

Eve said, 'Say "thank you" to Mr Braggs.'

Kate said, 'We need to find the black boots...'

'I said time's up!' He slid the bolt home.

Eve reminded them of their manners and Lucy, free of the boots, thanked him with a demure smile. Kate scowled and muttered something unintelligible, still apparently smarting about her mother's hat or the sale of their mangle.

As they retraced their steps in the direction of 'home', their arms laden with the spoils of their search, Eve watched them surreptitiously, wondering if the visit to their old home had, after all, been a good idea. But the girls seemed none the worse for the somewhat sad reminder of their former life and chattered cheerfully enough. I've learned something else about them, Eve realized. Children can be amazingly resilient.

Twelve

The letter from Stanley Scayne came a week later. It arrived on Monday, the ninth of December and was dated the previous Saturday. Eve read it several times with mounting confusion before she took it up to show to her mother. Her first thought was an outright rejection of his proposal. Slowly she read it through again, trying to think rationally.

> ...and my suggestion is that you and your mother might like to become tenants of Myrtle Cottage which would remove the need, at least for the present, of selling it or renting it out to strangers. If you were willing, the children could live with you thus removing the threat for them of a return to the orphanage...'

Eve found herself trembling with anxiety at the idea of such a commitment; there were several reasons for this. If the experiment to become the children's carers were to fail for any reason, Kate and Lucy would be distraught. Also she and her mother would have relinquished the rented flat in London – she drew a long breath and tried to calm herself – and she would feel a complete and utter failure. It would do no one any good, she argued silently.

Fine for you, Mr Scayne, to see this as an answer, she thought. It would solve his problem very neatly. But what about Eve and Dorothy? Her mother had already brought up her family and Eve had no experience whatsoever – if she discounted the last few weeks. And how would they like living in the country? She and her mother were Londoners and proud of it. They were 'townies, born and bred'. A half-smile softened Eve's face.

'I like living in London!' she told the absent Mr Scayne. 'I like being near the City and the West End. There's a certain busyness about town life.'

Of course, the war and the epidemic had changed everything but now that the war was over normal life would resume. Not that it could ever be the same for her without Harvey, but London would once more become the centre of entertainment, commerce and culture and the familiar bustle would return. She sighed wistfully, the letter forgotten for a moment in her hand.

With an effort she recalled what little she

had noticed of Todleigh. Was it a village or merely a hamlet, she wondered, and wished she had paid more attention to it. She could remember a church and a sign which said 'School Lane' so there must be a local school where Kate and Lucy could attend. She had vaguely noticed a small shop that sold knitting wools and a man had called at Myrtle Cottage in the morning after they arrived, pushing a bicycle with a box full of fish on the front. Was there a butcher? A library? Probably one bus a day into Exeter and none on Sundays. A village fête would be the highlight of the year and a runaway cow the biggest excitement! It all sounded very uninteresting and yet ... in her mind's eye she saw Myrtle Cottage in all its shabby 'glory' and remembered the children's glowing faces as they re-explored the house. Myrtle Cottage was the nearest thing the children had to a home now and it was the only link to their happy past, to a time before tragedy struck.

Stanley Scayne had thought of everything.

Because we would no longer need to pay for a live-in housekeeper to care for Kate and Lucy, it would be fair to reduce the rent you and your mother would pay and, of course, we could produce something in writing – a formal contract of some kind, to ensure that your interests as well as those of the children were safe-guarded...'

He was so proud of his plan, thought Eve, and she gave him his due. It was clearly a possible solution.

It's brilliant, actually, she conceded, but whatever would her mother have to say about it? Her peaceful retirement would go straight out of the window if Kate and Lucy moved in with them for a long stay. But then, if Harvey and Eve had had children of their own, presumably Dorothy's life would have been just as tempestuous. She would still be living with them and there might have been grandchildren.

Later that night, when the children were in bed, and she and Dorothy were relaxing in the front room, Eve handed the letter to her mother after a brief warning. 'We don't have to say "Yes", Mother. Read it and think about it. It might work. It might not. We mustn't let Stanley Scayne ambush us!'

She sat silently, staring into the fire, while Dorothy read the letter twice then glanced at her daughter.

'Well, this is unexpected. Rather unsettling, actually.'

'It is, isn't it? I almost wish he hadn't written this way. I know he's trying to be helpful and on paper the idea is a good one but, from our point of view ... Well, I don't know what to think, Mother.'

'The trouble is, Eve, everything is happening so quickly – one thing after another! So many decisions to make and we have so few facts to help us make them. From the financial point of view it's tempting. I have very little money left and you have to find out about your pension from Harvey – if there is one. To stay at Myrtle Cottage almost rent free would be very helpful.'

'And the cottage is quite large – much bigger than this flat. The children would love it...'

'But, Eve, would we be committing ourselves to Kate and Lucy for ... for a very long time? We could hardly change our minds. Children grow up and can be very difficult.'

'Mother, if Harvey and I had had a family, *our* children might have proved difficult.'

'Most certainly they would, Eve. You'd have had all sorts of problems and trials – enough to test your patience or even your sanity.' She smiled to soften the warning. 'But you would have had Harvey with you. You'll only have me, dear, and I may not live to see them grow up. If you don't marry again you—'

'Mother! I shall never remarry. How can you think that I could ever find another man like Harvey? No one can ever take his place.'

'Never is a long time, Eve. Would he want you to stay alone for...?'

Eve suddenly remembered that she had not shown her mother Harvey's last letter and she hurried upstairs to fetch it, then sat silent while Dorothy read it.

'There you are then, Eve,' her mother said with quiet satisfaction. 'He wanted you to make a new life for yourself. He was a good, generous, loving man. Every young widow should be prepared to start afresh.'

'You didn't!'

Dorothy hesitated. 'I was much older than you are now when your father was taken from us. I felt I had had my share of married life.'

For a few moments they both sat and thought about Edgar Collett. With a sigh, Dorothy reached out and patted her daughter's knee. 'I know it's early days, but when I die I should like to know you have someone to love you.' She handed back the letter. 'Keep that safe, dear. You will always treasure it.'

Eve took the letter and kissed it. 'I wonder what Harvey would have advised. He did always say I would make a good mother.' She laughed, a trifle self-consciously. 'He did want us to have a family.'

'But they would have been your own flesh

and blood,' Dorothy protested. 'Kate and Lucy are not your children.'

'They are nobody's children now!' Eve cried, with sudden passion. 'That's the whole point, Mother – they belong to nobody. They're orphans! They're adrift but hopefully too young to realize the full extent of their predicament.' She took a quick breath. 'They have no mother – and I have no children. I keep wondering if Fate ... but that's ridiculous.' Agitated she ran her fingers through her hair. 'Forget I said that. It's nonsense, I know.'

For a while they sat without speaking, each one busy with her own thoughts.

At last Dorothy shook her head. 'We could have a trial period, perhaps. See how it works out.' She sounded uncertain as she handed back Stanley Scayne's letter.

'I thought of that but – how would it seem to Kate and Lucy if after a few months or a year we changed our minds and abandoned them? I'm so impressed with them and the way they've dealt with this disaster. But I wonder how many more shocks and disappointments they could survive without being damaged in some way. They're only young ... and Kate's been so brave and Lucy remains so sunny...'

Dorothy watched her as she struggled with her dilemma, unwilling to influence her one way or the other but aware that she had to make a decision.

Eve said, 'And I don't know if I could bear to live in what Harvey used to describe as "a one horse town".' She shrugged. 'Todleigh is so limited. No ballet, no theatres, no decent transport, no—'

Dorothy raised her eyebrows. 'I don't recall you ever going to the ballet, Eve. And rarely to the theatre.'

'Maybe not but they are available, Mother. We could go. Harvey wasn't too keen on indoor entertainment. He liked motor racing and fishing and ... and the rodeo.'

'The rodeo? Good heavens!' Dorothy rolled her eyes. 'He wouldn't find many rodeos in this country. We eat our cattle. We don't ride them.'

'He enjoyed them over there.' Eve tried to think of something more civilized. 'And he enjoyed sailing.'

'Well, I can see that Brockley must have lacked appeal – rows of sooty houses, regular London pea-soupers, noisy trams, traffic fumes.' Dorothy smiled. 'Harvey must have hated our part of London. But you're not being fair, Eve. Todleigh is near Exeter and Exeter is an important market town. I don't think much of your arguments. I don't think Todleigh is the real problem.'

Eve looked at her reluctantly. Her mother

was usually very perceptive. 'What do you think is the problem?'

'I think you're afraid, Eve, and I don't blame you. Taking responsibility for two children is an enormous risk. A huge commitment.'

'And if I let them go – if I return them to the orphanage, I shall live with it for the rest of my life. I shall always wonder what happened to them and if they're happy. I shall never forgive myself.'

Dorothy said softly, 'Why don't you say what's in your heart, Eve? I think I know but I won't say it for you but I will say this. Whatever you decide, I'll support you as long as I'm able.'

They looked at each other. Eve's heart began to race. 'I want to look after them,' she said shakily. 'I think I might even ... I probably want to adopt them!'

Dorothy held out her arms. 'Then let's make a few enquiries, Eve. One step at a time.'

It seemed wiser not to allow the children to know what was in Eve's mind for their future in case there were unexpected problems. For three days Eve could not even bring herself to answer Stanley Scayne's letter, afraid to put her big idea into words. She knew she was trying to delay the finality of her plan and she spent long hours in the darkness of the night, restlessly trying to imagine how their lives would change. She imagined herself taking the children to school in the mornings and collecting them at noon for their midday meal then back again to school ... or perhaps they were already old enough to go to and fro unescorted. There was so much she did not know.

She would have to nurse them through the various childhood ailments – measles, chicken pox, diphtheria. Suppose one of them had an accident or died. The thought paralysed her momentarily. She wouldn't always be able to rely on her mother's experience and her own judgement might not always be sound. Would she be a good mother? Could she look after them well enough?

'You'll get used to it gradually,' she whispered. 'You'll learn as you go along. And how many mothers are perfect parents?'

She told herself that there was no need to aim for perfection. That way she needn't feel like a failure. All she could aim for was to do her very best for them. And it would be equally unfair for her to expect the children to be perfect. Of course that was out of the question, too. They would be awkward, argumentative, difficult in ways she could only imagine but she remembered her own childhood which, in her eyes at least, had been far from plain sailing.

One factor in the equation was one that she hardly dared consider and that was the totally unexpected but unmistakable attraction she had felt for Stanley Scayne. His very positive attitude to life had impressed her and if they moved to Myrtle Cottage she might see him from time to time. He had said his aunt lived in Todleigh and he might visit her. It was an attraction which bothered her. She was a very new widow and had never expected to be drawn to any man other than Harvey and certainly not so close to his death. Despite her mother's words on the subject, Eve felt guilty.

Shame on you! she scolded herself. *You are embarking on a big adventure that will require all your energies – and all your love. Your present way of life will disappear and the new life won't be easy. The last thing you need is the distraction of another man!*

On the fourth day she got up early and wrote to Stanley Scayne accepting his suggestion. Later in the morning, as she slipped the letter into the pillar box, she knew she had started something she would never be able to stop and as she walked home, her insides fluttered anxiously.

You're afraid! Better get used to the feeling! she warned herself. Then managed a small but oddly triumphant smile.

The next few weeks were confused but exciting as the arrangements for the move slowly fell into place. Their own flat was relinquished with the usual four weeks' notice and the landlord quickly found a new tenant. Myrtle Cottage was checked over by an enthusiastic Stanley Scayne who drew up a list of repairs that needed immediate attention and hired a suitable handyman to deal with them. The blocked gutters were cleared, a crack in the main chimney was filled, a broken window pane was replaced and a few broken roof slates were replaced. The outside privy had not been forgotten, either, and had been cleared out and a new wooden seat purchased.

Ida Bloom, Stanley Scayne's aunt, had agreed a small fee to come in and do some cleaning. Having been a friend of Biddy, she set to with a will to make the cottage homely and welcoming for the newcomers. She cleared the rooms of Biddy Towner's personal items, scrubbed floors, cleaned windows and relined cupboards with newspaper. She also remade the beds, saw to the laundry, and dusted and polished the furniture.

The day before Eve was planning to tell the children about the imminent move, Kate button-holed Eve when Lucy wasn't near enough to overhear the conversation.

'What's happening?' she demanded. She had folded her arms defensively and her expression was unreadable. 'Because I know something is. Is it about me and Lucy? Because I want to know.' Despite her somewhat grim stance, Kate's voice shook slightly.

Eve, taken by surprise, forgot the little speech she'd been planning and asked, 'How did you guess?'

Kate shrugged her thin shoulders. 'Secrets and whispers, and names I don't know, and things you don't tell us about.'

And you listening at keyholes, Eve thought, hiding a smile. On three occasions Kate had been discovered outside the living room door, long after they had been tucked into bed. Her excuses were varied – she needed a drink of water or had a 'tummy ache' or had had a nightmare.

Kate went on. 'But I know about Mrs Bloom because she came to tea one day and Aunt Biddy told her how to make carroway cake so that it wasn't all dry and horrible.'

Eve realized that she had been well and truly ambushed. She smiled. 'Go and find Lucy and I'll tell you both the secret.'

Dorothy also joined them, unwilling to miss the girls' excitement when they heard the news.

'We are all going to live in Aunt Biddy's cottage,' Eve told them. 'We're moving the day after tomorrow.'

Nobody spoke. Kate stared at Eve while Lucy looked at her sister.

'All of us?' Kate asked at last.

'Yes.'

Lucy tugged at Kate's sleeve. 'That's good, isn't it?'

Kate's gaze remained fixed on Eve's face. 'Is it true?'

'Yes, Kate, it's true.'

'So we're not going back to ... We're not going anywhere ... We're coming with you?'

Eve nodded. 'We were going to tell you tomorrow so you could help us with the packing. The furniture men are coming to take some of our furniture but the rest will be sold after we've gone.'

Kate glanced towards Dorothy who said, 'That's right, Kate. It's true. Are you pleased?'

Both Dorothy and Eve had expected great rejoicing and the reality was unsettling.

Kate looked at Lucy. 'We're going to live in Aunt Biddy's house,' she said. She turned back to Eve. 'For how long?'

'For as long as you want!'

'Like a holiday?'

'No. Like a home where we all live.'

'For ever?'

'If that's what you want. It will be your house – yours and Lucy's. Aunt Biddy gave it to you when she died.'

Kate looked at Lucy. 'For ever,' she repeated. Her face began to crumple suddenly and tears shone in her eyes.

Lucy said, 'What? Live with the biscuit lady? And Mrs Collett?'

Kate could only nod.

Eve said, 'It's worth a big hug, isn't it, Kate?' And then Kate stumbled into her arms and sobbed with a mixture of joy and relief.

Seeing that Lucy now stood alone, Dorothy reached for her and gave her a kiss. 'Won't it be exciting?' she suggested and finally Lucy beamed with delight.

Ten minutes later they were celebrating. Kate and Lucy each had a barley sugar stick and Dorothy and Eve were enjoying a cup of tea and a biscuit.

Eve was learning already. It would be difficult, she knew, to get the children off to sleep when bedtime came around.

Christmas at Myrtle Cottage was fairly chaotic but Eve, mastering the ancient stove, managed to cook a large chicken and a piece of boiled ham and Dorothy made a plum pudding. They had tea with Ida Bloom and her husband Walter who were both in their seventies but looked fit as two fiddles. Ida gave each of the girls a crocheted collar and she promised to teach Kate how to use the crochet hook when she was older.

Stanley Scayne appeared on Boxing Day with a picnic basket and, thankful that they had had no snow, they trekked half a mile into the nearby wood and sat down on a large rug to drink hot soup and eat warm meat pasties which his mother had made for them. Only Dorothy was missing from the impromptu feast – she had opted laughingly for a couple of hours of peace and quiet.

Ten days later the village school reopened its doors and Kate and Lucy were enrolled in the little school. According to Kate, her teacher, Miss Farraday, was known to the children as 'the dragon' and woe-betide any child rash enough to displease her. Whispering in class, spitting on a slate to get rid of a mistake, tugging the girls' plaits or wiping a nose on a sleeve were all crimes punished by having to miss playtime. Anything worse resulted in being kept in after school or writing out twenty lines. Kate immediately began an undeclared war with her.

Lucy's teacher was a pretty young woman named Edith Anstey, who taught the little ones their alphabet, encouraged them to add up and take away and rewarded children who tried very hard with a toffee from her 'sweet box'. Like every other child in the class, Lucy adored her.

By the time Easter arrived the 'family' had settled in to their new life. For Kate and Lucy it was rather like an extended holiday and, to Eve's relief, they seemed to thrive on country life.

Dorothy found village life quiet compared with London but missed Brockley less than she had expected. It was, of course, less than peaceful when the children were around and she secretly relished the times when she withdrew from the hurly-burly to the safety of her own bedroom and could enjoy her solitude.

Eve found life as a mother totally exhausting but never dull, but she was still haunted by the death of her husband and found the children a welcome distraction from more sombre thoughts. She still deeply regretted the fact that she had never been able to see her husband's resting place or say a final farewell.

Outside Todleigh the rest of the world was coming to terms with peace and people in Britain were thankful that the influenza pandemic had apparently done its worst. Men and women clung to what remained of their old lives or tried to build new ones. As a result of the high death rate from the war there were plenty of women for the surviving young men to marry but it meant that many widows would remain alone and would struggle to raise their young families. Thousands of unmarried women despaired of ever finding a husband to give them the family life they had been led to expect.

At Myrtle Cottage birthdays came and went and high days and holidays broke up the seasons of the year. In March, Kate was nine, in May, Lucy was five. Eve settled into her new role and gradually found mothering the two girls at once daunting and rewarding with never a dull moment. There were minor crises and conflicts when she briefly wondered that perhaps she had made a mistake but these were quickly forgotten. They were compensated for by the times when Kate and Lucy finally unlocked those memories which had been too hard to bear and began to talk comfortably about the family members they had lost.

'Amy would have been six today!' Kate announced one day in April. 'She would have been bright, Amy would.' She spoke without a trace of sadness, as though she had accepted that her sister had gone.

On another occasion, Lucy had said, 'My black boots would have fitted Sam one day – if his ankles were weak.' She had suddenly realized that the lost boots would no longer have fitted her. 'And they might have been weak. Pa said that weak ankles run in the family.'

Kate had grinned. 'And then we all giggled at the thought of all the weak ankles running about by themselves and Pa said not to be silly and that made us giggle even more until we couldn't stop and even Ma giggled!'

She'd looked at Lucy and both girls had fallen into peals of laughter at the cheerful memory.

Ellen's new straw hat that Kate had rescued now had pride of place in the girls' bedroom. Kate put it on from time to time, looking at herself in the mirror and claiming wistfully, and quite untruthfully, that she was the image of her mother. Lucy's soft toys – a rabbit, an ancient teddy and a rag doll had been joined on the deep window sill by a knitted duck from Ida Bloom and a blue felt mouse from Stanley Scayne's mother. Lucy slept with Sam's rattle in the bed beside her.

By mid June it was becoming difficult for Eve to remember her earlier life with Harvey and she resisted the temptation to imagine how they would be living if he had survived the influenza. She was not trying to shut him out of her life but it seemed that he was withdrawing from her as the days passed into weeks and months and daily life in Todleigh came between them. On June the third, however, something unexpected was about to happen which would bring back all the sad memories.

When the children came home from school they were full of excitement. Both tried to talk at once as they told Eve about the motor car.

'It was parked outside the post office,' Kate cried, 'and there was a man getting out of it and he had a little boy with him and he went into the post office...'

'And on the back seat there was a bunch of flowers and a – what was it, Kate?'

'A suitcase and a box and the car was black...'

'It was not! It was blue!' Lucy's voice rose in protest.

'It was black,' Kate said, 'and it had a little lamp on the front and there was no roof and...'

Eve, laughing, put her hands over her ears and begged, 'One at a time, girls, please.'

Kate said, 'Aunt Ida was at her gate and she said he must be an American because he spoke so funny.'

Lucy abruptly lost interest. 'I had a toffee from Miss Anstey's box. Because I can say my ABC.'

'How clever you are, Lucy!' Eve gave her a quick kiss and then gave Kate one as well.

'We don't have toffees,' Kate said. 'We're

too old for toffees. Miss said so.'

'But you got the cane,' said Lucy.

'I did not! Anyway, it didn't hurt.' Kate glanced quickly at Eve to see if she had registered this slip.

Eve raised her eyebrows humorously and Kate sighed.

'I pushed Tom Belling over,' she admitted, 'but it serves him right. He keeps saying we talk funny.'

Lucy said, 'Perhaps we're Americans like the man in the motor car. Aunt Ida said he spoke funny.'

Kate shook her head. 'We're Londoners, silly, not Americans. How could we be Americans? We don't come from America, do we?'

'I don't know and I don't care!' Lucy tossed her head – a habit she had recently learned from Kate.

A knock at the front door interrupted this conversation and Kate rushed to answer it. A man and a small boy stood on the steps and behind them was 'the motor car'. For once Kate was too surprised to speak. Eve and Lucy followed her to the door.

Eve recovered quickly. 'Good afternoon.'

The man was a little taller than Eve with brown hair and blue eyes. The boy beside him had soft brown hair and looked up at Eve with grey eyes under long dark lashes.

The man lifted his hat. 'My name's James Ferber and this is Toby, my son. We are looking for a Mrs Randall, Harvey Randall's widow.' He smiled suddenly. 'Have we finally found her?'

'James Ferber?' Eve whispered, as a bewildering mix of emotions raced through her. The name was familiar. Of course! This was the man who had written to her, enclosing Harvey's last letter. As she stared at him, frightful images floated into her mind of the two men, hopelessly engaged at the far off military camp, in a struggle to save lives. 'Please...' she stammered, remembering her manners and opening the door further. 'Please come in, Mr Ferber. You're most welcome.'

The two girls backed away to allow them in but Eve saw the gleam in Kate's eyes.

Kate held out a welcoming hand. 'Come in, Toby,' she said promptly. 'I'm Kate and this is my sister, Lucy.'

The little boy stared at her nervously then turned and clung to his father.

'He's a bit shy,' James told them, 'but he'll come around.' He knelt beside the boy. 'These people are our friends, Toby. I guess they want to show you their toys.'

Kate said, 'And we have a pond in the garden.'

Not to be outdone, Lucy said, 'And an

apple tree but there aren't any apples on it.'

Still Toby shook his head and Kate looked at Eve for help.

'Let's not hurry him,' she suggested. 'Maybe he's thirsty.'

Eve led the way into the front room, wishing she had polished the furniture and attended to the dusting.

James had a sudden brainwave. 'Toby will show you the motor car if you like. He knows all about cars, don't you, Toby?'

Toby, distracted by this suggestion, turned abruptly to the girls. 'I want to work with cars when I grow up.'

Surprised to finally hear him speak, Kate and Lucy regarded him with admiration.

Kate said, 'We'd love to see the motor car, wouldn't we, Lucy?'

Lucy nodded dutifully.

James said, 'We'll give you a ride in it later.'

Startled, Kate fixed him with a stern look. 'Is that a promise? You mean it? We can all ride in the motor car?'

James glanced down at his son. 'What do you think, Toby? Is it a promise? Shall we take them for a ride?'

The little boy's face lit up. 'Yes, Papa!' He smiled shyly at Kate and then Lucy.

'Will it go up hills?' Lucy asked.

'If we can find a hill, it certainly will.'

He and Eve watched as the three children

hurried out into the hall on their way to examine the exciting machine that now stood outside Myrtle Cottage.

'They won't do anything silly, will they?' Eve said. 'I mean, it couldn't run away with them?'

James shook his head. 'It takes brute strength to turn the engine over with the handle and they can't get at that even if they wanted to. They'll be quite safe. There's no need to worry. They can simply look at it and sit inside. Perfectly safe, but of course we must keep a close eye on them.'

He sank gratefully into the chair Eve indicated which faced the window and stretched out his legs. 'When we found you had left London, I began to think we'd never find you,' he admitted. 'I hope you don't object to being tracked down!'

'Not at all,' Eve told him. 'I shall enjoy talking to you but first I must get you some refreshment.'

He held up a hand. 'We stopped at a tea-shop in Exeter not long ago and had some scones and cream. Do please sit down, Mrs Randall. We have so much to talk about. For a start, I'd love to know how you come to be tucked away in the depths of the country. I always assumed, from my too brief chats with Harvey and the address he gave me for the letter, that you were town people and lived in London.'

Eve laughed. 'I thought we were!' She went on to tell him what had happened to change her mind.

She noticed that he listened intently as she explained about the Beatty family.

'Your neighbour told me simply that you had decamped to the wilds of Devon with a couple of orphans! It took me a while to get my head round that.'

'It was all very strange. Making any kind of decision on my own without Harvey to advise me ... but I needn't tell you that. Somehow you decided to come to England. And with Toby, too. That must have taken some thinking about! I was reluctant to come here at first and yet ... It felt as if a determined Fate was nudging me along a certain path. I should say "nudging us". My mother is asleep upstairs. She is widowed and lives with me and helped me make the decisions which weren't easy.'

She stood up again to take another look at the children. Turning from the window, she asked, 'And how about you and Toby? How long do you intend to be in England?' She was surprised to discover that she hoped his stay would not be too short. She sensed a kindness in him which reminded her of Harvey.

He shrugged. 'I don't know. We were in

northern France for three weeks before crossing the Channel. I meant to travel more in Europe but it's so dispiriting. It was a shock, Mrs Randall, to be honest. We read and heard so much about the war and we sent our boys over but ... the reality is terrible. So much damage, so much heartache and bitterness. The truth is it depressed me.'

'London suffered, too.'

He gave a weary smile. 'I was glad to get away, to be honest. As to how long we shall stay, I'll wait and see. Unlike you I have nobody to help me make decisions and am actually living from day to day. I have Toby to consider. Should I make a home for us in England? We – that is my wife and I – had sometimes thought of settling here but now I'm not sure what will be best for Toby.'

Eve saw the children in the distance, sitting in the back seat of the motor car, talking animatedly. 'The girls will love having Toby here,' she told James. 'They lost their brother Sam to the flu as well as their sister and parents. Here in the country I think they are recovering.'

She sat down again, somewhat sobered by the reminder of the terrible experiences they had all suffered.

'I think I might spend some time in Exeter. We might all be able to spend a little time together, perhaps. Toby would love it. He's been a rather lonely boy. He's not used to other children and they can be boisterous. He's easily frightened.'

Eve glanced at the clock. 'I hope you'll stay for tea. Where are you staying in Exeter?'

'I found a very pleasant but small hotel near the town centre. I've got a room with a double and single bed so Toby will be near me at all times.'

The innocent mention of a double bed, something that neither of them could share with the person they had lost, caused an awkward silence to descend.

Would she, she wondered, ever share a bed again? She missed being married and no doubt James was missing his wife. All over the world there were widows and widowers left from the war and the influenza. There would be lonely times ahead for so many people. She was impressed to think that James had come all this way from America to see her and share Harvey's last moments with her. She owed him a great debt of gratitude. The silence lengthened but was broken at last by Dorothy's bell ringing upstairs.

Eve jumped to her feet. 'Mother has woken up,' she said. 'If you'll excuse me I'll go up and help her. She'll be so thrilled to meet you.'

★ ★ ★

290

The rest of the day passed in a cheerful whirl. The three adults found plenty to talk about and the three children enjoyed each other's company. James kept to his promise and bundled them all into the motor car with the exception of Dorothy, who declined the offer. When Toby's bedtime loomed, it was arranged that he and James would spend a day with them later in the week.

'We're going to visit a couple of estate agents,' James told them. 'Wherever we go, I check out the area and consider the prospects of settling there for a few years. Exeter is no exception. We'll go to Kent and maybe Hertfordshire.'

'You must talk to Stanley Scayne,' Eve told him, a little too quickly. 'He's very professional and likeable – and trustworthy, of course. He was tremendously helpful when we first came here and now we consider him and his mother and aunt good friends. You'll be in good hands. Tell him Eve recommended him!'

'I take it he's in real estate.'

'Oh ... no. He's a solicitor. Peter Nicholls is the estate agent ... but they are both very helpful.'

He thanked her and for a moment she saw a flicker of something in his expression and she immediately turned away, biting her lip. Her praise for Stanley Scayne had been a little too fulsome, perhaps, and James Ferber was obviously very perceptive.

After James and Toby had left, Dorothy was full of praise for the American and Eve missed them both. It was so long since she had enjoyed the company of a man and it brought home to her the sad fact that she might never enjoy such a relationship again.

Later, she went to bed a little sobered by the thought of a lonely future and dreamed that Harvey was standing outside the cottage gate, watching her without speaking. She called to him and he smiled but when she tried to go out to him, the front door appeared to be jammed and refused to open. Trapped inside, she wrestled with the door handle while her heart beat unnaturally fast. When she finally succeeded in getting out of the house, the street was empty. Harvey had vanished and she awoke in the middle of the night, deeply anxious and with tears in her eyes.

Thirteen

James and Toby never did move on to Hertfordshire. They rented a small town house in Exeter and discovered much in Exeter that pleased them. They exchanged visits with Eve and the girls and the weeks became months, summer came and went and 1919 gave way to 1920. The war was fading from people's minds and so was the epidemic – except for those whose lives had been irrevocably changed by them.

Without being aware of it, Eve was growing fond of James and sometimes thought that he was feeling the same way about her. But she could say nothing, not even to her mother, although she longed to confide in someone. Was it possible, she wondered, that she could love another man? Occasionally she caught something in his voice when he spoke to her or believed she saw more than affection in his glance – but maybe she was imagining it. For some people there was only one love. Louise might have been the only woman for James.

Eve glanced at the calendar one day and saw that it was almost Easter. Dorothy suggested an Easter egg hunt in the garden and the three children had a wonderful time searching out the small treasures that were hidden for them.

Only one thing was clouding Eve's pleasure. During the past year Stanley Scayne's health had slowly deteriorated and suddenly his heart condition became much more serious and the cause of great concern. The doctors agreed with each other that nothing could be done for him in hospital so he chose to be nursed at home by his mother. Eve and the girls made weekly visits to see him, and sent cards which Kate and Lucy had made for him.

Kate and Lucy were making reasonable progress at school. Although Kate was still fiery and quick to take offence, and was certainly not the brightest pupil in the small school, her teacher praised her as 'a hard worker'.

'Kate wants to be top of the class,' Miss Faraday told Eve. Her stern features relaxed into a smile. 'She never will be but she will never stop trying.'

Contrary to Kate's assessment of her younger sister, Lucy was not particularly bright either.

'Lucy tries to please but it doesn't worry

her when she gets her sums wrong,' Edith Anstey told Eve with a sorrowful expression. 'She's often careless and doesn't always pay attention, but it's difficult to be cross with her. She's a sweet, sunny child.'

There were only thirty-one children in the entire school and Eve had quickly learned to appreciate the benefit of the 'family' atmosphere where older brothers or sisters were reassuringly near to their younger siblings and teachers and parents lived in the same close community.

Eve, for her part, had been relieved to learn eventually that she was entitled to a small widow's pension.

'Better late than never!' was Dorothy's tart comment.

Dorothy was proud of the fact that she, too, was making a small, if irregular, contribution to the household finances by knitting for the wool shop in the village. It pleased her no end to know that a cardigan or jumper she had knitted was on sale in the window of the shop.

'Why don't you walk down to the shop and see for yourself?' Eve suggested one day. 'I'll come with you so that you can hold on to my arm.'

Dorothy's immediate reaction was to declare it 'out of the question' but she was urged on by Lucy.

'Your legs still work,' she pointed out, 'and you haven't got weak ankles.'

'If you fall down, we'll pick you up,' Kate offered.

'You can do it, Mother! I know you can. And Miss Barry will be delighted to meet you.'

Dorothy hesitated. Being confined to the cottage had so far meant that she missed out on many of the excursions which excited Eve and the girls.

'I'll try it,' she told them and was gratified by the delight of the others.

Supported by Eve and with Kate and Lucy hopping and jumping around her, she made cautious but satisfying progress along the cobbled street. Inside the shop she was met by the owner, a small pretty woman with greying hair and a shy smile.

'Mrs Collett, this is such a pleasure!' she cried. 'To meet such a skilled knitter. Your garments are quite perfect.'

Dorothy said, 'Oh really! You're too kind! I'm sure if you had the time you could...'

'Oh, no! That's the point.' Miss Barry leaned forward confidingly. 'I hardly like to confess that I hate knitting. I don't have the patience. The shop was left to me by my aunt and it brings me a nice little income but I never knit! But your work, people comment on it all the time. In fact an Exeter woman came in only yesterday and has asked if you would knit a bed-jacket for her mother. She's chosen the wool already and has the pattern. Shall I show you?'

Eve left the two of them discussing the order and took Kate and Lucy to the village shop to buy a few groceries and some stamps – and the inevitable decisions each girl had to make over the spending of a penny.

'Liquorice laces!' demanded Kate, eyeing the shelf full of glass bottles which contained the sweets. 'They last longer.'

'They do not! I'm having dolly mixtures ... No, a barley sugar stick,' Lucy decided.

The happy group walked home together. An innocent enough event, but from then on, Dorothy's lazy days were over. She was no longer allowed to consider herself an invalid and, although she sometimes grumbled, she was secretly happier for it.

The friendship between James and Eve had slowly changed to a deeper affection and from there to a reluctant but undeclared love. If Eve and James were honest, they each felt illogically guilty because of the partners they had lost. For her part, Eve felt wrong for allowing her memories of Harvey to fade. Though they were never forgotten.

One afternoon, in Dorothy's room, mother and daughter chatted and Eve tried to explain that becoming so fond of James felt like a betrayal. Dorothy was emphatic in her refusal to see this point of view.

'How can it possibly be a betrayal?' she demanded. 'Harvey himself wanted you to have another love in your life. He told you so in his last letter. He didn't want you to end your days a lonely, grieving widow. And James is a fine man, Eve. His wife – if she had loved him which we assume she did – would have wanted him to be happy also.'

Eve sighed. 'I know you're making sense, Mother, and I want to be persuaded but...'

Dorothy's eyes widened. 'Has he asked you to marry him? Is that what this sudden soul searching is all about?' She was knitting a pair of socks for Kate.

The girls were at school and James and Toby had gone for a walk. Eve had cried off, pretending to have a headache.

Now, a faint blush brought colour into Eve's face. 'Not exactly but ... I think he might. If he does ... I want to say "Yes" but...'

Dorothy put down her knitting. 'Perhaps you don't like him enough? Are you telling me you don't love him because that's not what I see, Eve. Whenever I see you together I think you would make a very happy couple.'

'I know we could but...'

'But you don't think you want to take on

Toby?'

'Mother!' Eve glared at her in frustration. 'You know that's not true! I adore Toby as much as I do the girls. And he is happy with Kate and Lucy and they treat him like a brother.'

'Then what is it?' cried Dorothy. 'James Ferber is obviously very fond of you or he wouldn't still be living in Exeter. You are very fond of him and the boy. It doesn't have to be a wild romance, you know, Eve. That is the way it is when you first fall in love. If that special feeling is lacking it doesn't mean you shouldn't wed him. Love has a habit of growing.' She sighed. 'You should talk to James. Bring up the subject in a roundabout way if necessary.' Seeing that her daughter hesitated, Dorothy frowned. 'Is there another reason? Out with it, Eve!'

Eve searched for the right words. 'I haven't asked James yet about the girls. I want to adopt them but would he? Suppose he doesn't. Then where are we? He may not want to lumber himself with a ready-made family. There's the expense, apart from anything else.'

'But if he'd stayed married they would probably have had more children. He did say once that Toby was a lonely child.'

'But we have to remember that he never met the Beattys. He knows nothing about the girls' family. He might have doubts. I don't want to force the girls on to him but I can't abandon them. I won't even think about it ... and I do love him ... If he loves me and is willing to adopt the girls, why doesn't he say so?'

Dorothy was silent. She knew that Eve had written formally to the South London Home for Orphaned Children several weeks ago.

Eve said, 'As you know, the orphanage hasn't seen fit to reply.'

'No doubt they're still rushed off their feet, overwhelmed by the aftermath of the epidemic. It takes time for a large institution like that to return to normal working after a major upset. It's called bureaucracy. You have to be patient, Eve.' She smiled. 'Or am I asking the impossible? You always were impatient. Do you remember your little garden plot? You were seven or eight. You planted some marigold seeds and expected them to bloom within the week! When they didn't, you lost interest entirely.'

Eve rolled her eyes. 'I am no longer eight years old, Mother, and I have not lost interest. I simply want an answer. What is the point of trying to discuss this with James if the orphanage is going to turn me down? No doubt they would prefer to place the girls with a husband and wife and there must be plenty of couples who have lost children.'

Dorothy picked up her knitting. 'Now I have to concentrate on the heel but think on this, dear. If you marry James you will be a couple and they are sure to consider you a suitable applicant. Stop anticipating the worst, Eve. Stop dithering and talk to James.'

Eve's reply was lost in the frantic knocking on the front door which reminded them of the time. School was over and Kate and Lucy were home.

Eve jumped to her feet. 'They'll be wanting their tea,' she said and for the moment at least, the thorny subject was pushed to the back of her mind as she hurried downstairs to let the girls in.

That night Eve lay in bed, staring unhappily at the ceiling and thinking about James Ferber. She knew she had not been entirely truthful when she talked to her mother. Dorothy had no idea that there was another reason why Eve hesitated to think positively of marriage with James.

The truth was that since the first day she had met Stanley Scayne, she had felt drawn to him. The scales, she knew, were tipped against her and she had never allowed him to know how she felt, always waiting for some sign that he felt the same way about her. At first there was the suspicion at the back of her mind that she might simply be reaching out to the first man who showed her a kindness – the first man, that is, after Harvey's death, when a woman is at a very vulnerable stage. Another problem was Stanley's age. He was six years younger than her and she had to admit also that he had never shown anything but a generous and friendly interest in her and the children. Lastly there was his determination to remain single.

Until the last few months she had never been convinced that Stanley's heart trouble was life-threatening and suspected that if he met the right woman he would marry if the woman in question was willing to share the possible risk of early widowhood.

Once or twice, before James appeared on her doorstep, Eve had made a very tentative move in his direction but each time it appeared to have gone unnoticed. They did exchange visits from time to time and his mother, who was in robust heath, was very good to Kate and Lucy, but Eve wondered if she had read too much into this.

Was it fair, she asked herself, to let James imagine that she had loved only him? Should she confess her earlier feelings for the young solicitor or would that hurt him unnecessarily? At one time she had thought about doing the unthinkable – confronting Stanley about her feelings – but had shied away at the last moment. She knew she would feel a complete fool if he rejected her. Now, it seems, she had fallen in love with James. What did that say about her, she wondered ruefully.

If only she dared talk to her mother but that was out of the question. This was a dilemma she would have to solve for herself.

Sadly, eight days later, the dilemma was resolved in the most final way when Stanley Scayne was rushed back into hospital.

'It's nothing,' his aunt insisted, when Eve managed to speak to her. 'He's had these problems before. They always deal with it.'

She didn't offer further details and Eve was reluctant to pry too far.

'How long will he be in the hospital?' she asked. 'Is he well enough for visitors?'

Mrs Bloom pursed her lips. 'I doubt if they would allow it. He really is very poorly and you're not family.'

'Well, if you visit him, perhaps you'd give him our best wishes.

'I will, dear. I'll tell him you were asking after him.'

There was no time, however, for Stanley's condition worsened dramatically and he became unconscious and died later that same day.

The funeral was held on the following Monday. Eve took the two girls to the service to say a last 'goodbye' to the man who had done so much to transform their lives. While the coffin was being lowered into the grave, rain fell relentlessly and the wind howled and the bedraggled guests were glad to return to Mrs Scayne's home where they would sit down to a warming casserole, and toast Stanley with a glass of sherry.

Eve struggled with her guilt. Stanley had known what was coming to him but had made light of it. After the meal, Mrs Scayne took Eve to one side. The loss of her son had brought about a great change in her. There was sorrow in her eyes and her voice was tremulous.

'I want to tell you something, my dear,' she said, 'about Stan. He was very fond of you, you know, but...'

'I was in...' Eve stopped herself. She must never say that she had been in love with him, she told herself, because it was not true. She had wanted to fall in love with him but, lacking any encouragement, had never allowed herself to do so. The spark between them had never become a flame.

'I liked and admired Stanley,' she amended shakily. 'I wish now that I had told him how I felt. I didn't understand how short his life would be. At times I hoped ...' Choked, she could not go on.

Mrs Scayne patted her arm. 'He knew

exactly how you felt, Eve. He told me that if he had been fit he would have asked you to marry him. You were the only woman he'd ever wanted but he was convinced he would die young like his father...' She took a deep breath and Eve could see that she was close to tears. 'And he was right. So young and he's gone from me! Jack, my husband, was only twenty-five when he collapsed and died. There was a post-mortem and they found he had an enlarged heart and a very weak muscle. It made him breathless at times because fluid collected in his lungs. But we never suspected anything was seriously wrong with Jack until he collapsed.'

'You wouldn't. No.' Eve recalled that Stanley had often appeared breathless.

'Poor Jack.' Mrs Scayne took out her handkerchief and dabbed at her eyes before she could go on. 'We never guessed he had a faulty heart. The coroner said he must have been born with it and we should be prepared for it to be passed on to the baby.'

Eve was shocked. 'Only twenty-five years old! How dreadful for you.'

A slight shrug was Mrs Scayne's only answer but then she lifted her head, in control once more. 'I was widowed two years after Stan was born and never remarried, and I think Stan grew up feeling that he could never inflict that sort of loneliness on another woman.'

'It must have been a struggle for you.'

'It was, but Jack's parents were very good to us and helped me. Stan was very close to his grandparents.' She turned to say goodbye to an elderly man who was hovering in the passage, on the point of leaving. 'Thank you so much for coming, Mr Plaistow. I appreciate it.' She forced a smile. 'My son thought very highly of you and enjoyed working for you.'

'And we valued Stanley,' the man said, 'and envied him his cheerful disposition. It's a tragedy that we have lost him at such a young age. I doubt we shall find another young man who showed such promise. You have my sympathy.'

She took him gently by the arm and walked with him to the door. From the window, Eve saw him clamber clumsily into a pony and trap and settle himself beside his young driver.

When Mrs Scayne came back she said, 'That was Albert Plaistow. A very wealthy man but won't give up his pony and trap. Loathes motor cars.'

'Like Peter Nicholls.'

'Not quite ... Mr Nicholls bought a motor car but ran it into a ditch on the first day. Wouldn't set foot in it again. Frightened he might kill himself!' She paused for a moment to collect her thoughts. 'Mr Plaistow is a good man. A church goer. Stan worked for him ever since he left school and they'd as good as promised him a partnership. Still, it was not to be. God in his wisdom...' She shook her head.

Eve said, 'You can be very proud of him.'

'I am, my dear.' She straightened her back, tidied her hair and swallowed hard. 'I surely am!'

Two weeks after Stanley Scaynes' funeral Kate sat at her desk in the classroom of Todleigh Junior School and hated Miss Farraday with a deadly passion. With a pencil, Kate was writing her lines in the Punishment Book. Her name was at the top of the page and beneath it was the same line repeated eleven times. There were nine more to be done.

I must not pinch Bernie
I must not pinch Bernie
I must not...

Miss Farraday moved slowly round the room, putting things away in various cupboards and tidying the books on the bookshelf. Her petticoats rustled and her new shoes squeaked a protest with every step. From time to time she glanced impatiently at Kate.

'Haven't you finished yet?' she asked sharply. She was a tall angular woman who had once been attractive, but an unhappy love affair had ensured a life in the teaching profession. Disappointment had embittered her but she was a good disciplinarian and it amused her to live up to her nickname of 'the dragon'.

Kate scowled. 'I can't write any more.'

'And why is that?'

Kate stabbed the pencil into the wooden desk top until it snapped. 'My pencil's broken.'

'Then find another one.'

Kate rose slowly and made an elaborate show of looking for the pencil jar. 'I've done eleven lines,' she grumbled. 'Why do I have to do twenty?'

'Because I said so. You were very unkind. You pinched Bernie's arm and made him cry. I don't like little girls who pinch.' She threw some dead flowers into the waste-paper basket and emptied the stale water into the sink.

'He told a lie,' Kate insisted. 'Bernie told a big lie. He said Lucy smells and she doesn't!'

'I've told you before to take no notice of Bernie. He's a silly boy, Kate. He only says things like that to make you angry. He does it to get you into trouble.' She reached for the blackboard rubber and began to clean the board, aware of Kate's baleful stare.

The classroom door creaked and they both turned to see Lucy peering into the room. She was bundled up in Dorothy's knitted gloves and scarf but there was a drip on the end of her nose and her cheeks were red from the wind.

Miss Farraday said, 'Get along home, Lucy. Kate is being very slow today.'

'She can't go home on her own,' Kate said. 'She has to walk with me and I haven't finished my lines and I can't find the pencils.'

Miss Farraday glanced at the clock on the wall. Nearly half past four and she was eager to be on her way. The trouble with lines, she reflected, is that they always punished the teacher. Outside, a cold wind blew dark cloud and she feared it would rain at any moment. Her feet ached and she wanted to get home and feed her cats.

The caretaker would be in soon to sweep up. With a loud sigh, she said, 'You can finish off at playtime tomorrow, Kate.' She held out her hand for the Punishment Book. As Kate sprang to her feet she said, 'Remember, Kate. No playtime tomorrow until you've finished the rest of your lines.' But Kate had abandoned the book and was already attempting to make her escape.

'I shall have to speak to your mother about your behaviour, Kate,' Miss Farraday told her. 'You had the cane this morning and now these lines!'

But her words fell on deaf ears as Kate dodged between the desks and the classroom door slammed behind her, long before Miss Farraday reached the end of her sentence. Too late she remembered that Kate's mother had died of flu and she regretted her careless words.

Outside a grinning Kate grabbed Lucy's hand and they rushed from the playground before the dragon could come after her.

'I hate her,' Kate confided. 'She's horrible.'

'I hate my teacher,' said Lucy. 'She's horrible too.'

'No you don't and no she isn't. You like her. She's nice.' They turned a corner, reaching the High Street, and Kate paused to look over someone's garden fence. 'Shall we take the biscuit lady some flowers?' she wondered aloud, eyeing some bedraggled golden rod that had somehow survived the winter.

Lucy hesitated, glancing round nervously. 'There's a lady looking out of the window,' she told Kate. 'She's watching you.'

It was the wrong thing to say. Kate at once snatched a stalk of the tall yellow flowers, broke it off and ran off down the road, laughing. With a gasp of panic, Lucy ran after her.

They walked in silence for a few moments then Kate said, 'We should call her Ma. The biscuit lady, I mean.'

'But she's not our ma.'

'And then Mrs Collett could be our granny.'

'But she's not.'

'I know that, silly! I said she *could* be. And Toby could be our brother – and don't tell me he isn't because I know he isn't. And Mr Ferber isn't our pa. You saw our ma and pa – when we went to see their grave. They were buried there. Remember?'

Lucy frowned. 'I didn't see them.'

'But that's where they are. Under the ground.'

A large brown dog trotted past, minding its own business and Kate tapped it lightly with the golden rod. It turned its head reproachfully but trotted on.

Lucy said, 'I wish we had a dog.'

'No good wishing.'

'Oh! She's looking over the gate for us!'

Alerted, Kate glanced up and saw Eve watching for them because they were late home. Having second thoughts about the flower she carried, she dropped it on the cobbles and walked on empty handed. She knew it was no good wishing for anything but it didn't stop her from trying.

Half an hour later James Ferber arrived with Toby and one look at his face told Eve that he was excited about something. While the three children played hide and seek in the garden and Dorothy enjoyed a brief nap upstairs, Eve and James sat companionably on opposite sides of the kitchen table as he told Eve his news.

'I've been offered a pathology job in Exeter,' he said, unable to keep a gleam of triumph from his eyes. 'I applied several weeks ago but said nothing in case I didn't get it.'

'But you did get it! Well done! Does that mean you are going to settle in this area and not explore anywhere else?'

He grinned. 'It means exactly that! I wasn't even sure that I'd be short-listed – I heard they had five applicants for the post – which is in the coroner's department. Which is connected to the hospital, of course, but separate.'

Eve was trying to decide exactly what this news meant – if anything – for her. Trying not to let her own excitement show, she asked, 'When did you know that you'd got the job?'

'Two days ago. I was called back for a

second interview and I must say they gave me quite a grilling. Because I'm American and my record isn't known to them. All they had was a letter of reference from my senior officer at Camp Devens although they said I was highly recommended. There was a representative on the Board who favoured a man from Sidmouth...' He frowned recalling the man's scarcely veiled disapproval.

'But they finally chose you! I'm so pleased, James.' Questions flitted through her mind. Did this mean James would stay in this part of England for a long time? And if so, for how long? Would he give up his rented accommodation and buy a house? And if so, would he live in it alone with his son? She admitted to herself that she had dreaded the moment when he and Toby would move away. With a start she realized that she was not listening to him and made an effort to concentrate on what he was telling her.

'There was a local man, which I thought gave him an edge, and an elderly man who was reputed to have a drink problem and...'

At that moment there was a wail from outside and the three children appeared. Lucy was crying and there was a thin trail of blood running from her left knee. Eve busied herself with a little first aid, glad to have a chance to gather her thoughts. Suppose this was the moment when James proposed. Was she ready with an answer? Had she given it enough thought.

'She fell over,' Kate explained. 'She's got weak ankles.'

'Weak ankles,' echoed Toby, nodding.

Lucy stopped crying. 'I *haven't*!'

Kate said, 'She should have kept the black boots.'

Eve washed the small graze, tied a token bandage round it and sent them out to finish their play.

Eve smiled at James. 'You don't have to pretend that all the others at the interview were hopeless,' she told him. 'You were given the job because you were more experienced than them. You were the best candidate.'

He shrugged modestly. 'I'm delighted because ... because I didn't want to move away from you and the girls. Toby would miss them ... and so would I and ... I'd miss you as well.'

Eve tried to think of something to say but no light phrases sprang to mind. Silently she waited, not wishing to assume too much and unwilling to commit herself.

He went on. 'There's something I've been wanting to ask you, Eve, but ... I know that Stanley Scayne meant a lot to you and I...'

'You knew?' The words came out before she could bite them back. She was mortified that her feelings had been so transparent.

He nodded and cupped his hands around his mug of tea.

'I want you to marry me but I decided not to ask you in case you turned me down but ... Is it the right time now, do you think? I know Harvey hasn't been dead long or poor Stanley...'

Eve's heart began to hammer within her chest as guilt mixed with hope. Her thoughts flew to Harvey and she wondered what he would think of her if she said 'Yes' to James. Would it feel like a betrayal or would he be glad for her? Probably he would be relieved to know that she would be able to start a new life with a man he had respected. And Louise? Hopefully she would want her husband to remarry and give Toby a loving mother.

'It seems a lifetime since Harvey died,' she said slowly. 'So much has happened.'

James drew a long breath, stared into his tea and gave her time to hide the shock he had given her. 'I think we'd make a rather fine family,' he went on. 'If you feel you could try to love me. I'm a patient man.'

Eve reached forward, took the mug from him and set it down on the table. Then she took his hands in hers. 'I want you to understand that there was never anything between me and Stanley. No understanding of any kind. Stanley was determined not to marry because he knew he might die young. I did feel a great affection for him but he was never more than a good friend. That was his choice.'

'I wouldn't like his memory to come between us. I wouldn't want *anything* to do that ... More than anything I want us to be together but I'll respect your feelings.'

Eve released his hands because her own were trembling. 'I wouldn't want you to forget Louise, and Toby must remember her. And I'll remember Harvey always but ...' She picked up his hands and kissed them. 'I'd be happy to marry you, James. I love Toby and the girls think the world of you both – and so do I. We could be happy, couldn't we?'

'We deserve it, I think.' He stood up and came round the table to draw her to her feet. 'We've all lost those we loved but we're not alone in that. The world has changed for millions of people – the influenza has blighted lives all over the world. We're survivors but we've all been through hell and back! I guess we're being offered a second chance and I think we should take it.'

He held out his arms and for a long moment they held each other close and kissed. Then Dorothy rang her bell. Eve sprang back guiltily. In the excitement of the moment she had completely forgotten her mother. She looked at James in alarm.

316

He laughed. 'I reckon the children will need a grandmother!' he told her. 'And I guess I need a second mother-in-law!'

Eve sighed shakily. 'I'll bring Mother downstairs and you fetch the children. I can't wait to see their faces when we tell them.'

Ten minutes later Dorothy was seated in the armchair with Toby on her lap, and the two girls were sitting on the floor, gazing up expectantly at Eve and James who sat close together on the sofa.

Suddenly nervous, Eve turned towards James. It had been decided between them that James would break the news.

He cleared his throat. 'We've got some news to share and we hope you'll all be very happy when you hear it.'

Kate said, 'We will,' and smiled at Lucy.

'Yes, we will,' Toby added.

James laughed. 'I haven't told you yet!' he protested.

'You're going to get married?' Kate said.

'Is that it?' Dorothy cried. 'Oh I do hope so!' She turned to Eve. 'You didn't tell me!' she said reproachfully.

Eve smiled. 'I didn't know myself until ten minutes ago. It's been rather sudden.'

Lucy whispered something to Kate.

Dorothy said, 'Well, now, Toby, you are

going to have a new mother. Isn't that splendid news?'

Toby glanced at Kate who nodded. Still not convinced, he slid quickly from Dorothy's lap and ran to his father. James lifted him on to his lap and gave him a reassuring hug.

Eve said, 'And we were wondering about you and Lucy.' She watched Kate's expression carefully. 'I'd like to adopt you, and so would James. What do you think? Would that be a good plan?'

To her surprise Kate was silent.

Dorothy filled the awkward gap. 'Then I could be the grandmother! That would be fun.'

James looked at Eve, puzzled by Kate's reaction.

'What is it, Kate?' Eve asked gently. 'We thought you'd like the idea.'

Lucy looked at her sister. 'Don't we like it, Kate?'

Kate took a deep breath. 'We want to stay here. We don't want to go back to ... to the orphanage.'

Eve held out her arms to the two sisters. 'I'm sorry. We haven't explained it very well, have we? Come here and I'll tell you how it will be.'

The two girls scrambled to their feet and moved cautiously into a bear hug from 'the biscuit lady'.

Eve explained as simply as she could that first she and James would be married – 'As soon as possible!' James told them. And then they would adopt Kate and Lucy.

Kate said, 'But where would we live?'

'Here, probably, but we might find a different house one day.'

'So we don't have to live in America?' Lucy asked. 'Miss Anstey says they have grizzly bears.'

James laughed. 'In some places there are grizzlies but America's a big place. We could all go to America for a holiday and you could see how you liked it. Toby has a grandmother over there and I know she would love to meet you.'

Kate turned to Toby. 'Then you would be our brother!' A grin suddenly lit up her face.

'Have a little think about it,' Eve suggested.

'We don't need to think, do we, Lucy?' said Kate, turning to her sister. 'We like the idea.'

Lucy nodded.

'I like the idea, don't I, Kate?' said Toby.

Eve glanced at James and then Dorothy and let out a sigh of relief. After a shaky start, it seemed the idea had met with everyone's approval.

Later that night as Eve lay in bed, she stared up at the ceiling with a broad smile on her face. She had just been in to check on the girls. Both Lucy and Kate were sleeping soundly, Sam's rattle clutched as usual in Lucy's hand.

It seemed that if you wished hard enough, good things could happen, Kate thought as she lay in the other room. Her eyes flickered sleepily. Perhaps, on the day they were adopted, she would wear Ma's best hat...